This is a work of fiction. Names, characters, places, and incidents either are the product of the author's imagination or are used fictitiously. Any resemblance to actual persons, living or dead, events, or locales is entirely coincidental.

Cover design by Julia Gerbach

ISBN 9798986125961 (paperback)

ISBN 9798986125909 (ebook)

www.katherinegrantromance.com

ALSO BY KATHERINE GRANT

The Countess Chronicles:

The Ideal Countess
New Year's Masquerade
The Duchess Wager
The Husband Plot

The Prestons:

The Baron Without Blame
The Viscount Without Virtue
The Governess Without Guilt
The Charmer Without a Cause

Northfield Hall Novellas

(an unordered series for the mood reader)
The Hellion of Drury Lane
It's In Her Kiss
Three Nights With Her Husband

Plus, a free short story, The Spinster, available exclusively at www.katherinegrantromance.com

The Governess Without Guilt

Katherine Grant

Chapter One

1814

THE SCHOOLROOM AT ROBIN Abbey offered two escape routes: the door to the corridor and the window to the courtyard.

Sophia Preston considered both options as she sat in the front of the room, waiting for her three pupils to finish scratching out French conjugations on their chalkboards. She didn't consider the door much of an option. It might lead her from the room, but she would still be trapped in the drafty old Abbey with no one but the well-meaning Cosgrove family and their household for company.

The window, on the other hand, sat two stories above the courtyard. If she survived the drop, she would surely break an ankle or wrist or perhaps something worse on the gravel beneath. An ominous prospect. One, she knew, a sane person wouldn't consider at all preferable to polite company with conventional people.

In the months since arriving at Robin Abbey, home to the Baron and Baroness Widlake and their six and a half children, Sophia had begun to entertain the idea that she was not completely sane. For this was a good position with kind employers who let her be herself. Perhaps it did not include dances in London and shopping on Bond Street, as she had envisioned when first imagining herself a governess, nor were there gentleman to flirt with, nor were her charges at all keen to heed her attempts to steer them towards independent thinking. Still, Sophia's account grew fat from Lord Widlake's bank draft. She lived free from the confines of her family and their rules at Northfield Hall. And she did it all as a governess, just as she had proclaimed often and loudly that she would.

She must be insane, else she would be happy, not contemplating an escape out the window.

In unison, her three charges–the Misses Danielle, Francesca, and Mary Cosgrove–raised their heads. Sophia heard it, too: the clatter of hoofbeats and carriage wheels coming down the drive.

"Is it him?" Miss Mary asked, spilling her chalk to the ground in her nine-year-old's excitement.

Miss Cosgrove–the thirteen-year-old, eldest sister who considered herself too urbane for excitement–condescended, "Who else would it be, when Father sent the coach to fetch him from the inn this very morning?"

"Oh, please, may we look?" This from Miss Francesca, the eleven-year-old, who clasped her hands together as if to pray as she presented the question to Sophia.

Sophia didn't know if all children were like this or only these three, but she had soon discovered that whatever learning happened in the schoolroom occurred by accident, in between battles over whose personality commanded the most power.

The skirmishes sapped more energy from her than the actual lessons did, and those already stole her enthusiasm for the day.

"Oh, please?" Miss Mary echoed.

The girls might wage their battles, but Sophia was determined to win the war. "Once you have finished your conjugations." She stared them down until they bent over their slates again.

Victory in hand, Sophia permitted herself a sojourn to the window. All morning, she had told herself she would not take too much interest in the new arrival. He was the accoucheur–or man-midwife, to those without French–there to deliver Lady Widlake's coming baby. New blood in Robin Abbey, perhaps, but Sophia knew better than to get her hopes up. He might be dull. Conservative. Unattractive. She could not plan for him to be her antidote any more than she could leap from the window.

That said, it did not hurt to get a glimpse of the man.

The schoolroom boasted an excellent view of Robin Abbey's central courtyard. In one sweeping glance, she could take in the sunlight spiking off the Abbey's white stone, the mud spattering the carriage though it had been repainted just two weeks ago, the shadow of movement as servants hustled through the cloisters to greet the new arrival.

Yet, in the schoolroom a good ten feet above the court-yard, Sophia's view of the man himself was limited. When the coach-and-four came to a stop before the Abbey's entrance, she could see Mr. Anderson's hat extend from the interior of the carriage: a modest stovepipe fashion with expensive beaver felt that glinted in the afternoon sun. From there, she observed the cloak billowing out from his shoulders.

She could not see what interested her most. The length of his legs as he stepped onto the drive. The bulk of the body wrapped beneath that gray wool cloak. The sparkle—or lack thereof—in his eyes.

She watched for these signs, anyway. Impatient to a fault, as her family liked to tease. Sophia leaned forward, her breath fogging the window, as if a few extra inches would reveal to her the inti-mate details of the doctor's physique.

He was not strictly a doctor, nor did she strictly have no idea what to expect of his appearance. The household had been preparing for his arrival for weeks, almost more than anticipating Lady Widlake's Great Event itself. Sophia knew already that he had studied in Edinburgh, that his glittering reputation stemmed from a successful delivery for the Countess of Gresham, and that he was an Anglo-Indian with skin as brown as his mother's.

None of this told Sophia what she most wanted to know. Did he stride with confidence, or match his shuffle to an obsequious hunch? Was he austere and solemn, as if always a breath away from delivering bad news, or did he cheer the room with learned wit?

When he looked at a woman, did he see merely her role in the world, or did he notice the flesh and blood beneath her gown, waiting to be stirred to ecstasy?

"Is it him after all?" asked Miss Mary. "Did he bring chocolate?"

Miss Cosgrove heaved out a deep sigh. "Don't be a child, Mary. What will our visitors think if you always demand chocolate of them?"

"Mr. Brewer brought chocolate last year for Jacob. And before that for the twins. Francesca told me. Didn't he?"

"Mr. Anderson isn't Mr. Brewer, is he? He has never met you, nor does he concern himself with your sweet tooth. You are being gauche."

"I am not!"

"Miss Preston?" Miss Francesca cried out, just as her two sisters' voices reached the high-pitched peal that guaranteed Sophia a headache for the rest of the day.

When envisioning herself a governess, Sophia had imagined she would be like Mama, who had loved teaching the children of Northfield Hall. She would have chuckled at this squabble and settled it with some humorous wisdom.

Now, Sophia didn't have the patience to emulate her mother. She found only the energy to intone, "If you have not finished your conjugations, then you should not be speaking."

The scrape of chalk against its board replaced the bickering. For now. But Sophia had been governess to the Misses Cosgrove for four months already. She knew better than to trust the peace.

Below, Mr. Anderson paused on the drive, head tilted up and away from her, as if to take in the whole of the Abbey in one glance. He wouldn't be able to do that, not from where he stood. It rose two stories–three, if one counted the bell tower punctuating its southwestern arm–and squared its stone wings around him, almost enclosing the courtyard on all four sides, save the drive from which he had entered. Even if he turned in a circle, he wouldn't be able to see where the new wing ended, jutting backwards as it did to accommodate the staterooms.

He looked upwards, all the same. Then the footmen–Frank and Jasper Gibson–joined the scene, claiming Mr. Anderson's bags from the coach with fluid efficiency. The accoucheur's attention returned to mortal beings. Sophia could see his head bob with the movement of speech, though she was too far away to glimpse the specifics of his face. He was shorter than Jasper, who sprouted up past six feet tall, but looked about the same height as Frank. A good height. Sophia liked a man whose eyes she could meet without craning her neck backwards.

"I have a question."

Sophia jumped: the whisper came from right beside her, yet she hadn't heard Miss Francesca cross the room. The girl held her chalkboard like some kind of innocent. She even held it up and pointed to the verb *convoiter* to carry on the charade of scholarship. But she gave herself away when she rose onto her tiptoes and darted her gaze at the window.

"Oh, very well." Sophia stepped aside. "Come see what Mr. Anderson looks like."

Miss Mary rushed to join them. For her part, Miss Cosgrove murmured about how unseemly it all was even as she sashayed up to press her palm against the window glass.

In the courtyard, Mr. Anderson held out a hand to Frank. At first, Sophia thought he was trying to take a valise. Then the footman accepted the hand, bowed, and slipped his palm into a pocket, and she understood the accoucheur had paid a tip.

Mr. Anderson offered a tip to the coachman, too. The coins caught the sunlight as they spilled from Mr. Anderson's black glove into the coachman's. Sophia wondered, if she were closer, whether she would see that the gloves were new, on display like his generosity for the benefit of his new employers. And his boots—did they gleam from a fresh shining, or did they carry the dust of travel?

"He doesn't look anything like Mr. Brewer," Miss Francesca breathed.

"Why should he?" Miss Cosgrove responded. "They share a profession, not a bloodline."

"I still hope he has chocolate for us," said Miss Mary.

Sophia wondered what Mr. Anderson would think, should he look up to discover the spies in the schoolroom window. Would he be flattered to be the center of attention? Grin and give a flirtatious smile to the young girls desperate for his distraction? Or would he be shy and turn away and stutter over his words when they all finally met?

She hoped for something in between. A man who was not unaware of his effect on others, who enjoyed giving a little pleasure here and there when all it cost him was a smile, but who did not abuse the power of his charm.

A man should always be more kind than he is proud, Mama used to say.

Sophia pushed the echo away. Mama's advice had suited Sophia when she was an audacious fifteen-year-old. She didn't like to guess at what her mother would say to her now, if she discovered Sophia as a diffident governess.

"May we go meet him?" Miss Mary asked. "I pressed a dandelion in my Bible to give him as a welcome gift."

"A dandelion? But that's a weed!" protested Miss Francesca.

Sophia placed a hand on both girls' shoulders to quiet them. "We must remain at our studies. You will meet him soon enough. I imagine we will all dine together tonight."

"Besides," Miss Cosgrove sneered, "it is not done for a young lady to present anyone but her family or her betrothed with a gift."

Sophia felt the weight of their eyes on her. Their previous governess had been more concerned with teaching them the minutiae of etiquette than with scholarship. Though Sophia took the opposite approach, Miss Cosgrove in the mighty wisdom of a thirteen-year-old considered anything not related to finding a husband a complete waste of time. She therefore found every lesson of Sophia's both suspect and wanting.

At first, Sophia had found it inspiring. A goal by which to measure her success at Robin Abbey. But now that four months had passed without so much as a begrudging concession from Miss Cosgrove, she found it exhausting.

Everything about governessing, in fact, was exhausting. Which was why she ignored the girls looking at her. Let them condemn her as incompetent or inappropriate or bookish. Sophia had only eight months left on her contract with the family, and then she would free herself for another adventure.

In the meantime, Mr. Anderson was here.

"You may present him with your flower, after the proper introductions have been made."

The valises were sorted, and the coachman was nudging the horses around the well to head out the courtyard to the stables. Shoulders forward, Mr. Anderson followed Frank and Jasper up the stone steps to the Abbey's entrance. Desperation propelled Sophia: she pressed her fingertips into the window glass as if that could freeze him in place. She needed him in sight so she could drink him in, measure him beyond his hat and height and coins, keep tasting an elixir of hope that he might be the distraction she yearned for.

As if he heard her silent plea, Mr. Anderson hesitated on the steps, just within view. He swept off his hat and tilted his face upwards, as if to catch the sun.

He was not the one who froze: Sophia did. Heart, soul, and quim.

Handsome. Even from a distance. She could see the line of his jaw, the slope of his nose, the expression in his brow. The glow of his brown skin.

She got only that glimpse. It lasted less than a second before he resumed his march into the Abbey.

It was enough. For the first time in weeks, Sophia's spirits lifted. With Mr. Anderson around, escape from Robin Abbey might no longer be necessary.

SHE DID NOT MEET him until that evening. The whole family was invited to supper–including all six Cosgrove children, even the three-year-old twins and baby Jacob–on account of the doctor's arrival. Sophia dressed in her dark blue silk gown, covered at the neck with a white fichu. For a lady, it bordered on drab and unattractive, but for a governess, it was elegant. It even managed to set off the advantage of her breasts–of which she was inordinately proud, as if through her own sheer will she had produced such large and pretty things–without being the slightest bit immodest. While the maid Polly dressed the children, Sophia heated her curling tongs and coaxed soft spirals out of her front tendrils, before setting off the stretch of her neck with dangling pearl earrings.

A regular governess ought not have such fine jewels. Sophia was no regular governess, though, and she had no qualms about showing it. She was in service for the adventure of independence, not to stuff herself into someone else's vision of how she should behave.

Wearing her audacious gowns and frivolous jewelry was one of the last ways she clung to this fantasy, anyway. Sophia had her independence from a husband and her family, yet after a year and a half as a governess, she was beginning to suspect employment was just as much of a trap.

Sophia's hopes returned to Mr. Anderson. She did not have a physical partner here at Robin Abbey. It was not wise to dally with the footmen, though she did find both Frank and Jasper beguiling in their own unique ways. Nor did she dare sneak off to the stables with a groom or seduce her way into the good graces of the gardener. Lord and Lady Widlake tolerated her various idiosyncrasies, but a governess must above all things keep to her own class of educated men in professions. And in the four months of Sophia's term at Robin Abbey in its quiet valley in Northamptonshire, she hadn't yet come across a man of her class of any age, much less one with whom she wanted to flirt.

Sophia descended to the formal drawing room with a knot of nerves fizzling in her stomach. Which was ridiculous. This was not her coming-out ball. She was not on the market for a suitor. For all she knew, Mr. Anderson was a stuck-up, pious pig of a man who would scorn her for looking him in the eye. She need not worry about him judging her.

The only question being asked that evening was whether the man-midwife charmed Sophia. He was the one whose palms and armpits should be sweating despite the October chill.

She entered the drawing room with her charges in tow. The three Misses Cosgrove all curtsied on cue, though nine-year-old Mary wobbled on her ankles. She recovered herself and shot a pixie look up towards Mr. Anderson, as if to discover whether the visitor found her charming.

He smiled with a distinct politeness. The kind of spread-lipped performance that did not quite reach the eye. Then he paired it with a bow, and said in a soft, gentle voice, "I am delighted to make your acquaintances."

Not quite obsequious, though neither was he a fountain of charm. When he rose from the bow, Sophia took stock of his physique: he was tall but not unusually so, slender, and boasted a face made to be painted with its arched nose and endless lips. He wore a fashionable black dinner jacket, tan trousers that hugged his thighs, and well-polished shoes. White gloves covered his hands, matching the simple cravat at his collar, which both set off to an advantage the brown of his skin.

Handsome, even at close inspection. Sophia felt almost delirious with delight. Her imagination spun away from her, conjuring an entire persona for Mr. Anderson that would satisfy her every need. Kindness. Humor. Obsessive intellect. Passion paired with reason.

She reined in the fantasy in that same instant. She did not want to project unrealistic expectations upon Mr. Anderson only to be disappointed when he didn't meet them. So long as he wasn't a man bridled by principles, she would be satisfied. For that was the one trait she couldn't abide: a person who lived by impossible rules and expected everyone around him to do so as well.

She had lived that way long enough growing up at Northfield Hall, and she couldn't stomach it any further.

Mr. Anderson's gaze moved to Sophia. His eyes, she discovered, were rather large for his face. Black in the low light, framed by long lashes, they made him look a little startled to behold her. Perhaps he truly was startled: before she even acknowledged him, his cheeks darkened with a blush.

"Our governess, Miss Preston," Lady Widlake introduced. She was slung across the sofa rather indecorously, her ankles raised on a pillow and her hands resting on her swollen stomach.

Sophia nodded rather than curtsy. Carefully–so as not to flag the attention of anyone except Mr. Anderson–she slid her lips into the slightest smile. "We have been looking forward to your arrival, Mr. Anderson. I hope your journey was not too arduous."

"Not at all." For a moment more, he stared at her. Then, blinking, he looked away. Turned away, more precisely, and planted himself on the opposite side of the room, taking up Lord Widlake in conversation about the property.

Perhaps he recognized her as a member of the radical family Preston. Perhaps he was offended that she did not drop to her knees in deference to his authority. Perhaps he was shy.

Whatever the reason, he offered not even a flicker of interest in her. Rather the opposite, in fact.

Sophia could allow her hopes to dampen at this. In fact, for a moment, they did, burning her confidence into a pile of ashes at her feet. Mr. Anderson could only be her savior if he found her at least half intoxicating as she found him. If he turned away from her like this each time she entered a room, Sophia might as well escape by the dark of the night.

But she had not forged her own path in life by giving up at first sign of failure. By the time she had finished her sherry—while supervising Miss Cosgrove as she recited a Shakespearean sonnet for her mother—Sophia shook off despair. Mr. Anderson required nothing more than a little seduction.

Luckily, Sophia smiled to herself, seduction was her second nature.

Chapter Two

B Y THE THIRD COURSE–DUCK soup–the anxiety began to loosen its grip around John's bowels. So far, everyone at Robin Abbey had proved polite, intelligent, and even kind. Lord Widlake asked interesting questions and, even more rare, listened to one's answers. Lady Widlake, despite confessing to discomfort from her condition, glittered with a sense of humor that permeated the conversation. Her mother, Mrs. Edwards, took the part of devil's advocate almost as if by rote, but the rest of the family seemed to anticipate it–almost relish it–so that John could smile past his discomfort at a mother-in-law disagreeing with her son-in-law on whether Napoleon should have been executed instead of exiled.

In all, this was not a worst-case scenario. The family was neither insulting nor insipid, so that John would not cower in the coming months of his position in their home. Nor were they mean; the food itself was rich, and there were seven courses in total planned for this informal meal. Too, John had noticed the hearths all generously supplied with coal, and a whole box of luxury beeswax candles furnished to his room that could last him four months, if necessary. He would be quite comfortable during his stay, and he would be in good company.

John had every reason to expect this appointment to go well. Which would lead to more appointments with even more significant families, so that before long, he would have a reputation to fund his own practice in London. He would buy a townhouse, retrieve his mother from her latest position, and establish a life for himself.

Therefore, he informed his body, he could relax.

"Do you disagree, Lord Widlake, that the government has a responsibility to care for each and every one of its citizens?" Mrs. Edwards asked, her spoon descending into the soup bowl so fiercely that broth splashed onto the white tablecloth. John, seated beside her, resisted the urge to proffer his napkin to clean the mess.

She was the type of woman one could read within a quarter hour of meeting her. This was not a middle-aged woman to be dismissed, not even with her barely-concealed middle-class accent. Of average height, average weight, and average visage, she made her mark upon the world with her personality rather than her looks. She adorned herself with opinions as other women did jewels, and it was clear she had long ago decided the bigger the opinion, the better. Already, she had opined to John about Britain's responsibility to India, the growing corruption of nabobs, and her feeling that the Hindu religion deserved more respect.

Which told him even more: she curated her opinions based on which ideas she suspected most impassioned her audience. In his case, a man clearly of Indian descent. Though, if she had paused to get to know him before spraying her thoughts at him, she would have learned that he far preferred to discuss any other topic in the world than the British presence in India.

At the moment, her son-in-law was the victim of her opinions. Lord Widlake replied, "I do not disagree, madam."

"Then how can you sponsor a candidate such as Mr. Fenton for the by-election, when he disagrees with Mr. Cobbett that we must return to coin currency?"

"Mama," Lady Widlake interjected in a voice so calm it could put a lamb to sleep, "you are growing shrill."

There were similarities between the mother and daughter, to be sure. Soft, round faces made prettier when they spoke. Wide shoulders and wide hips. And mannerisms so similar it almost seemed one mimicked the other. Yet where Mrs. Edwards came off as crude and jarring, Lady Widlake glided through the conversation as if she were an egret swooping down to the lake to catch a fish and then return to the sky. Her words were crisp, her manner gentle, her style impeccable. Between the coif of her hair, the perfect tailoring of her gown, and the elegance of her conversation, she seemed to float beyond the rest of them not as a real person but as a paragon of what a lady should be.

"Mr. Cobbett makes many claims, madam, and most of them with no more aim than to enrage the easily manipulated," Lord Widlake responded to his mother-in-law. "You would do well to give him less of your attention, a tactic of Mr. Fenton's which I happen to admire."

"Well, I like that!" Mrs. Edwards gave up the soup spoon altogether now. It clattered onto the saucer. A drop of her broth landed in John's.

He pushed his bowl away.

Mrs. Edwards hadn't finished yet. "And you, Miss Preston? What do you make of Lord Widlake's claim that Mr. Cobbett's readers are easily manipulated?"

John had succeeded in ignoring the governess up until that moment, even though she sat in clear view beside Lord Widlake on the opposite side of the table. But he couldn't manufacture a reason not to look at her when all other eyes turned to her.

He had encountered governesses before. The finest families had them in their households to teach their daughters how to embroider and keep the house and become attractive wives. But the governesses John had met before were always plain, often years older than him, and without any flame of life at all.

Miss Preston sparkled. With external beauty, yes, but also with something more. Some essence that made her eyes beam, her skin glow, her aura gleam, until John felt he had gone blind with desire. And that was only in the first instant of meeting her.

If his bowels clamped with anxiety at embedding himself within a new family, his skin broke into a sweat at being in the same room as Miss Preston.

Now, she smiled at Mrs. Edwards. Her whole face changed with the smile: not only did her lips curve, but the corners around her eyes crinkled, her eyebrows lifted, and her nose hooked downwards. An alchemical reaction that changed her from a lurking beauty to an active threat. "In my observation, the general population is as easy to manipulate as Mr. Cobbett's readers."

A biting remark for a governess to make. Then again, Mrs. Edwards's question had been pointedly directed at her. John wondered if Miss Preston bore any relation to the notorious Lord Preston, who was both a radical leader in the House of Lords and a known ally of Mr. Cobbett.

Miss Preston's eyes swung his way. Dark irises framed by darker brows. More contact than he had expected to bear from her. "What do you think, Mr. Anderson?"

John swallowed. He glanced at Lord Widlake, then Lady Widlake, in hopes they might save him. Yet neither seemed to sense anything abnormal about the conversation. Which made John's stomach tighten even more. Perhaps there wasn't anything abnormal. Perhaps it was him. Perhaps his anxiety was heightening a common question into a great dramatic test simply because an intimidating woman on his left and an impossibly attractive woman opposite were staring at him, waiting for his opinion.

Good conversation was more important than the right opinion, after all. As long as he maintained his reputation as a fashionable guest, he could do himself no harm.

"I cannot agree with you entirely, Miss Preston," he said with more gusto than he felt. "In my experience, it is merely the general population of men who are easily manipulated, while the women pull the strings."

Miss Preston leaned back, allowing the footman to step forward and remove her soup. When she looked up at John once more, her teeth had plunged into her lower lip. Even from where he sat, he could feel the tease behind the gesture. "I suppose an accoucheur like you would know best."

John felt his anxiety transform into something newer. Hotter. Familiar enough for him to recognize as dangerous. Desire.

That was best extinguished before it ruined him altogether.

H E AVOIDED MISS PRESTON for the rest of that evening and even managed to forget about her by the following morning. After a breakfast in his room, he set to reorganizing his quarters. His hasty unpacking the afternoon before had left the room too haphazard and sparse for his taste. He was not a monk: he was supposed to be one of the finest accoucheurs in the country, and his chambers had damn well better reflect that.

Lady Widlake had installed him in one of the guest chambers along the northeastern wing of the Abbey. Two casement windows, a four-posted bed with a velvet canopy to keep him warm at night, a full hearth, and space for a desk in addition to a table and two chairs. John had originally lined his medical books along the back edge of the desk, but in the morning, that looked as if he were crowding the desktop to prevent himself from doing any work. He moved them to the thick stone windowsills, which had the additional advantage of showing off their gilded pages. His medical bag–brown leather with a nickel clasp–he placed on top of the chest of drawers provided to store his clothes, with his spare forceps displayed before it. Then he hid his silver and shoe polish, sewing kit, and stack of unpaid bills in the bottom drawer.

Better. It was better. Anyone poking their head in would be confident that he was, in fact, a surgeon. More important, that he was a gentleman. One who could afford the silk breeches and new boots he currently wore.

For an accoucheur, appearances were everything.

There remained only one thing to store: the letter from his cousin Garrett. He had tucked it in the pocket of his travelling cloak when he received it at the previous family's home, and there it remained.

He supposed he should reread it before tucking it away. Except the mere memory of it enraged him to the point that his throat swelled and his fingers curled into fists.

Your Mrs. Ghosh retired two weeks ago and may now be found on Neptune Street in Lambeth in service of a Captain Attree.

And that had been in the postscript, after Garrett dribbled on and on about his new marriage. As if John's mother wasn't even a relation of Garrett's. As if her safety and well-being should not have been the very first thing included in the letter.

As if John himself would care even less about *his Mrs. Ghosh* than Garrett did.

He couldn't read the letter now. The day stretched ahead, one in which he needed to serve the Cosgrove family with impeccable manners and discernment. Garrett's insult-cum-correspondence would have to wait for some night when John could lock his door and deal with his outrage properly.

John didn't like to leave any task unfinished, though, so he removed the letter from his cloak and tucked it in the desk drawer to await a reply.

And then he took the dreaded crotchet hook from his medical bag and put it on display atop the chest of drawers.

A reminder to the household and himself alike that no man exerted complete control over fate.

He nearly jumped out of his skin at the knock on his door. He drew in a breath, then exhaled, willing all discontent to go with it. Checking everything was in its place, he answered the door.

It was Miss Preston. Brown hair braided underneath a lace cap. Dark green wool gown with a gauzy fichu tucked protectively into her bodice. Brown eyes, darker than her hair, sizing him up, just as they had the previous night at dinner.

"Mr. Anderson, I do hope I am not interrupting."

"Not at all." He stepped into the corridor and pulled the bedroom door shut. They were two unmarried people of the same class in plain view, should any servants pass by. It would not do to spark gossip.

Miss Preston did not back away, however. She let him approach, so that his movement brought him close enough to smell her perfume. Something fruity and sweet. Something expensive, he suspected, and that surprised him. He did not think governesses were paid enough to afford quality perfume.

"Are you feeling ill?"

She blinked. Then narrowed her eyes. "Do I not look well?"

He had said the wrong thing. He had presumed, since most people knocked on his door for medical advice. Now he had offended her. John rushed to say, "Oh no, I didn't mean to imply that. You look well. Quite well. A good flush to your cheeks. Vigor to your movements. Gleam in your hair. The picture of health, I should think."

"And the bloom of my youth? Is that still present, or have I lost it?"

John sucked in a breath. Which equated to sucking in the scent of her. They shouldn't be standing so close. He shouldn't be saying these things at all. "Quite. Miss Preston, how may I help you?"

"You may allow the Misses Cosgrove to join you in attending their mother one of these mornings. I should like them to learn about the natural science of childbearing."

Having said it, she clasped her hands behind her back, watching him with those bright eyes, expectation written across her face.

John couldn't help noticing that the posture thrust her breasts upwards, closer to him. Not on purpose, he was sure. But he was a man. He had noticed them last night, first thing, and he couldn't stop himself from glancing down now. From feeling that physical prick of interest that came with the suggestion of large, pert, soft tits. Only inches away from his face.

Ungentlemanly thoughts. He banished them.

"The young ladies are interested in natural science?"

"Of course. In particular, the natural science involved in giving life. It is, after all, most likely a challenge they will each have to face." Miss Preston curved her lips into a smile that was not quite innocent. "Do you not agree, Mr. Anderson?"

"If they are so blessed, of course."

"Then when may we attend you and Lady Widlake?"

John would have said yes. Except the way she expected the answer, as if she were his better, chafed at him. They were of equal positions in this household. Close to genteel, yet employed by Lord and Lady Widlake for specific services. Miss Preston demanding John teach her pupils was the equivalent of him requesting that she catch the baby upon its birth.

She should at least phrase it as a question.

"If I determine Lady Widlake is of sound condition, ma'am," he replied instead. And then, turning on his heel, he marched down the hall as if he had a very important appointment.

Appearances, after all, were everything.

CHAPTER THREE

B Y VIRTUE OF SETTLING in, John delayed honoring Miss Preston's request for three days. That first morning, he engaged Lady Widlake in a long interview to examine both her physical and spiritual state. The latter was worse than the former, since she had managed to convince herself she would not emerge alive from this childbed. "I almost died four years ago, Mr. Anderson, and the infant didn't survive. I have the premonition that a birth will be the death of me."

That she had since then successfully delivered three children—twins, no less, and another healthy boy—made no difference to her presentiment. Therefore, John spent the second and third mornings in ornate rituals that had nothing to do with her body and everything to do with making her feel cared for. He ordered her room refashioned with only cotton cloth, had the paintings replaced with drawings by her daughters, and prescribed her half hour walks with her husband or mother twice a day.

By the fourth morning, he had to admit that Miss Preston's idea was a good one. For Lady Widlake to see her cheerful children would remind her of all the hope involved in giving birth, even as he evaluated her to prepare for the next great event. So, reluctant as he was to cede power to Miss Preston, he invited the governess and the Misses Cosgrove to join him after breakfast in Lady Widlake's sitting room.

Lady Widlake greeted them as if they had arrived at a London drawing room. Her maid, Shaw, set out silver trays of tea and cakes. The lady stretched on her settee with a ring of embroidery in her hands, wearing a finer silk morning gown than John had so far seen.

As she was not supposed to be eating tea cakes—she needed to even out her humors if she was to manage her bowel movements—John eased that plate away from her while claiming the empty chair beside her. The young ladies arrived just behind him, entering in a line that ended with Miss Preston, and one by one, they curtsied to their mother before pressing delicate kisses to her cheek. Well, the elder two managed delicate kisses. The youngest left a pink imprint on the lady's face.

For sisters, they did not look much alike. Oh, they shared their father's broad forehead, their mother's narrow nose, and a general ease in their comportment. But beyond that, they were each distinct. Danielle, the eldest, was dark-haired, dark-eyed, and dark-tempered. Francesca, the eleven-year-old, was pale, her hair mere wisps clouding her scalp, her skin clinging to her bones. And then there was

Mary, who still spoke with a rasping lisp at age nine. She was all curls, dimples, and japes.

Miss Preston was the last to enter his view, executing a short curtsy to her mistress before taking the seat across the circle from John's. She wore a simple day gown of deep and dusty green, with a white underdress that that climbed all the way up her neck to ruffle against her chin. Her cap that day was an opaque cotton, with carefully curled tendrils of brown hair escaping to frame her cheeks.

She did not look at him at all. Which suited him perfectly, as he didn't want to be looking at her.

The Misses Cosgrove settled upon their mother's settee. The eldest sat at her mother's feet, the youngest beside her, while Lady Widlake wrapped an arm around Francesca, who was looking rather pale and listless that morning.

"Now, Mr. Anderson, you may proceed," declared Lady Widlake.

He cleared this throat. He conducted examinations like this each morning with his patients, yet he wasn't sure how to do so in such a way as to instruct young girls on the facts of life. He decided a little context was in order. "Now, you must understand first that your young brother or sister is growing here, inside your mother's..."

But it was indelicate to mention the body part in her presence, even though it was the organ that brought them all together in the room that morning. John hurried past it. "Your mother's body provides the nutrients it needs to survive until it is strong enough to exist on its own. The question is, how well are the baby and your mother getting along, and how may we make them more comfortable?"

He couldn't help but glance at Miss Preston. Her eyes were on him now, a dark gaze that collided against his thoughts.

He had to clear his throat again. "Your mother is already on a lowering diet to improve her digestion and reduce the heat in her body. To begin my examination today, I will check her heartbeat."

John noticed his fingers and palms were slick with sweat as he positioned himself beside Lady Widlake. He wasn't accustomed to being observed at all, much less by children, much less by a woman who set him on edge. He cleared his throat again. "I must press my ear close to hear it." And, with nothing left but to do it, John put his head against Lady Widlake's chest.

The heartbeat was loud and clear, as it had been every morning that week. Her breath remained sour, his biggest concern.

"I check for the child's heartbeat, as well," he narrated as he moved his ear to Lady Widlake's belly.

"The baby has a heartbeat?" Mary asked from her mother's feet, eyes wide.

"Yes, after a certain point." John listened to it from a few angles, pleased that it sounded strong.

Mary's curiosity, apparently, had only just been piqued. "Do I have a heartbeat?"

"Of course you do," her sister Danielle snapped impatiently. "You have a heart, haven't you?"

From behind her teacup, Miss Preston said, "Perhaps Mr. Anderson will show you how to listen to the baby's heartbeat." And her eyes connected with his.

She did not mean the glance sexually. John was sure of that. She was a governess. Her reputation was everything. If she was so forward as to flirt with the accoucheur, she could lose her position and all hopes of a future one.

And yet. Even in that one glance, her teeth sank into her bottom lip, as if his discussion of the heartbeat drove a stake of desire inside her. And she had such kissable lips. Pink. Plump. Curved. Her cheeks, too, looked soft and generous. Her whole body, in fact, was contoured and plump. The kind of body a man could explore. Enjoy with his hands. Worship with his lips.

This was ludicrous, how wildly he was losing control of his own thoughts. John turned away. "Yes, I think you will find it quite simple."

Miss Cosgrove went first. John helped her find the best spot to hear the baby's heartbeat. He thought at first that she would maintain her stony stoicism even through this exercise, but then delight broke a smile across her face. "I can hear it!"

She yielded to Miss Francesca next, who more eagerly listened first to the baby's heart and then to her mother's. By the time it was Miss Mary's turn, she was worked into a lather of excitement. She pressed her ear to the baby, to her mother, to each of her sisters. When her mother told her to stop, she cried, "But I haven't checked Miss Preston's heartbeat yet!"

It was a wail to start a tantrum. Loud, shrill, and accompanied by the red threat of tears in her eyes. One could hear the mucus rising at the back of her throat, a promise of what would come next if she didn't get her way.

Lady Widlake soothed, "Miss Preston's heart is healthy, just like mine and Danielle's and Francesca's, pet. No need to worry."

"But what if it isn't?"

"Do be quiet, Mary," pleaded Miss Francesca.

"But what if Miss Preston's heart is broken?"

"You would hardly know how to tell," Miss Danielle said, exasperated.

Miss Preston locked her eyes on John again. His own heart–traitorous thing that it was–drummed a little off-kilter when she said, "Mr. Anderson, you had better check my heartbeat so that Miss Mary needn't worry."

He knelt before her. It was the easiest way to bring his ear within range of her heart. That it also lined his eyes to her breasts couldn't be helped. He could make out the structure of her corset and, in particular, the artificial lift it gave her bosom. This, he told himself, he needed to note in order to place his ear in the correct position.

John had pressed his ear to a woman's chest to listen to her heart a thousand times before. Never had it felt intimate. Never had it felt suggestive. Never had he memorized the exact feel of her curves beneath his cheek or the scent of her pear perfume or the racing rhythm of her heart.

But then again, he had never before encountered Miss Preston.

He pulled away. He turned to Lady Widlake, who didn't watch them with any curiosity at all. He bowed to Miss Mary. "A perfect heartbeat, I am pleased to report."

The girl clapped her hands together in delight. "Oh, I'm so glad to hear it, Miss Preston."

"As am I. Thank you for the examination, Mr. Anderson." Oh, but her voice was low and delicious. John didn't dare look at her again. He turned the conversation to leeching. He thought it the best method to distract everyone–himself, most of all–from the heat thickening between him and Miss Preston.

He wasn't afraid of a little flirtation, but only when it remained that. Already–from just a few interactions–John's body sparked towards Miss Preston in ways he had never experienced before.

John didn't think he could handle a flirtation with Miss Preston, not if this was how his body reacted in an innocent encounter. Better to hold himself at a distance than discover what would happen if he returned her smile.

Chapter Four

M R. ANDERSON WAS AVOIDING Sophia. Already, he had been at Robin Abbey for over a week, and Sophia had barely seen him at common meals, much less run into him in the corridors. If she was going to seduce him before Lady Widlake gave birth, she was going to need to find more excuses to cross his path.

It was for that reason—and not any real urge to go shopping—that Sophia agreed to join the family on their trip into Boughampton. They went every month or so, and as soon as they returned, Mary started begging to go again. When she was finally answered that yes, in fact, they would be going into Boughampton that very week, her excitement spilled into shrieks and hops and gushing.

Her enthusiasm was almost enough to send Sophia running back to Northfield Hall, tail between her legs, in search of any fate that didn't include children.

They woke earlier than usual to prepare for the journey, well before the sun rose at half seven. Sophia dressed in her fine Berkshire linen, trimmed with embroidered suns and moons, a wool spencer, and–in deference to the autumn chill–a flannel under-skirt. She added silver earrings, a warm hat, and her freshly shined boots to complete the outfit. More turned out than the average governess, to be sure, but Sophia wasn't concerned with the average governess. She felt pretty, which was all that mattered.

Already, she could envision a day full of excuses to flirt with Mr. Anderson. Sitting next to him in the carriage, perhaps. Walking side by side down High Street. Asking for his opinion on the purchase of a book, or pen, or–if she dared–a new perfume.

When she reported to the courtyard with her sack breakfast, however, she discovered her fate was to ride squished onto the bench in the wagon between Nurse and the lady's maid Shaw, while Mr. Anderson rode in the box beside the coachman of the family carriage. Over the chatter of the servants and the rattle of the vehicle over the dirt road, Sophia periodically heard Mr. Anderson's voice responding in its smooth and steady manner. Once, she heard him laugh, a loose outburst that scattered like birds into the sky.

They arrived at Boughampton as the parish church tolled half past nine. It was a beautiful autumn day, with the smell of apples and fallen leaves in the air. The kind of day everyone else cooed over, while Sophia reached for her handkerchief to prepare for allergies. Add to that the dust of the road, and by the time the wagon settled in the yard of the town inn, she could hold back no longer. Without even disembarking, she let out a great Preston sneeze.

She caught it in her handkerchief. No mucus dripped, no volley of eruptions followed. Still, all eyes turned to her. Shaw lurched away, as if the drama of Sophia's sneeze were contagious.

She knew she shouldn't be embarrassed by a simple bodily function. Yet she couldn't help it, not when everyone stared as if she had revealed a face full of bilious pox. It was enough to make her wish her siblings were there to joke off the moment. Even Papa would have eased the situation, with an extra handkerchief and a fond word for violent sneezes.

Mr. Anderson approached, a hand outstretched to assist her from the wagon. "Are you quite well, Miss Preston?"

"Quite." Especially if the outcome of the sneeze was Mr. Anderson pressing his spare hand to her waist as she hopped from the wagon bed to the ground. "Nothing more than allergies. Thank you."

He retracted his arms quickly enough, folding them behind himself with a polite smile. Still, Sophia had enough time to feel the strength of his fingers and the steadiness of his grip. She could almost rewrite the past minutes as a scheme she had planned to force Mr. Anderson to look her way again.

She angled a small, not-quite-innocent smile at him before they were forced to part.

Lady Widlake led Sophia, Mrs. Edwards, and the girls to the modiste while Nurse managed the little boys. Mrs. Edwards dominated the conversation, soliloquizing on the Corn Bill. "Really, this is the sort of thing on which you should be educating the girls," she said to Sophia by way of tying up the conversation as they entered the shop. "You a Preston, too."

As if springing from the loins of Lord and Lady Preston destined Sophia to be rabid about all political topics. Mrs. Edwards loved to imagine this of Sophia, and to assume that Sophia had deep opinions on all of the other lady's pet topics by virtue of her birth. When in reality, Sophia knew no more about the Corn Bill than every layperson, which was that the powers-that-be wanted to fix the price of bread too high for the common man to afford.

Unlike the rest of her family, that was more than Sophia cared to know about any political matter.

Unfortunately, Mrs. Edwards had not finished her diatribe after all. Sinking onto a stool provided by the shop for companions, she continued, "Why Lord Widlake did not take the opportunity to condemn their lordships for yet again placing their own interests above the common Englishman's, I cannot imagine. He squanders every opportunity he has to lead on these debates and instead follows along like a puppy dog. Do you not agree, Miss Preston?"

Sophia forced herself to inhale before responding. She was not uncomfortable amidst philosophical debate–a Preston hardly could be, when Mama and Papa had ended each day quizzing the children on political theory at supper–but she had discovered quickly that Mrs. Edwards cared only to have her own opinions repeated back to her. Sophia preferred to avoid the conversation entirely. She reached for the politest parry: "I'm sure I don't know."

"Don't you want any new dresses, Mother?" Lady Widlake interjected, her voice as soft as if she were trying to coax one of her children out of a tantrum. She was a kind woman who, at heart, preferred things to go easily and disliked addressing conflicts head-on. Sophia considered that a boon for her own employment, since Lady Widlake was reluctant to bring up any complaints she might have about how Sophia was educating the young ladies, but otherwise she did wish the woman would grow a backbone.

Then again, Sophia mused, perhaps the problem was that the lady's backbone had disappeared in the midst of serving her husband with seven pregnancies in fourteen years.

"No, no, you enjoy the shopping, child. Now, Miss Preston, I cannot stomach that kind of response when it is just between us women. You won't offend any fragile male egos with an opinion here. So tell me honestly: do you not think Lord Widlake is missing the opportunity to lead the Whig party on a campaign against paper currency, as he missed an opportunity with the Corn Bill this past session?"

"That is a leading question, ma'am, and I make it a habit never to answer a leading question," Sophia rebutted. The trouble was that Sophia knew if she were any other governess, Mrs. Edwards wouldn't plague her so. It was only because Sophia happened to be the child of Lord Preston—a greater hero to Mrs. Edwards than King Arthur himself—that she pressed. The woman couldn't see that Sophia's chief goal in taking up the mantle of governess was to remove herself from Papa's shadow. "Now, if you'll excuse me, I must help Miss Francesca."

It was more of that for the rest of the morning. Enough for Sophia's jaw to ache from clamping her teeth together. If it wasn't Mrs. Edwards with an overblown opinion, it was one of the girls losing control of her emotions, or Lady Widlake trying too hard to preserve peace.

Sophia hadn't expected that governessing would enmesh her so in a family not her own. In her first position, she had lived at her Aunt Charlotte's home, descending to the Wallace townhouse each day for lessons and to squire the seventeen-year-old Miss Wallace to tame events in drawing rooms and salons. She had known her life would be quieter in the Cosgrove household, but she hadn't prepared herself to spend every waking moment of every day in the company of the family.

She wasn't entirely sure she could withstand another eight months, no matter how generous Lord and Lady Widlake were with her.

The sun was high in the sky when at last Sophia found an excuse to peel away. Lady Widlake wanted to take her daughters to call on the vicar's wife. Sophia pleaded the excuse of seeing to personal errands. Then she set out to see if Mr. Anderson had shaken himself free of Lord Widlake.

She did not have to look far. He was in the chemist's shop, deep in discussion with a potbellied man behind the counter. Mr. Anderson stood with his chin bent, hands clasped behind his back, as he examined something on display. From this angle, Sophia noted that his shoulders drooped inwards, as if waiting for someone to roll them back into their sockets. Her palms itched to do the job.

She shook herself. It was one thing to lust after a man. It was another to stare longingly through a window with fantasies that had nothing to do with carnal pleasure.

Sophia moved on to the butcher's, which neighbored the chemist's shop, and pretended to examine the loins on display. She waited no more than a minute before Mr. Anderson exited the shop. He betrayed no surprise upon finding her. Indeed, he tipped his hat. "Purchasing meat, Miss Preston?"

"I cannot help but admire a good loin when I see one." Sophia suppressed a smirk as she fell into step with him. "Where is your next destination? I have a feeling it is the same as mine."

"I am going to the stationer's."

"Why, what a coincidence."

They fell into step together, but Mr. Anderson neither chuckled at her flirtation nor did he supply any conversation of his own.

Sophia would have to do all the work, then. "Where did you study medicine?"

"Edinburgh."

"A city I have not yet visited." She had vivid pictures in her head, however, since so many of her set traveled there. Dark skies, narrow streets, gray stone of old castles, and such cold that one didn't thaw until the summertime. Yet despite the permanent frost, everyone spoke of endless dinner parties, thriving conversation, burgeoning science experiments and literature that left one's heart singing for more.

It was a candidate for her retirement, though it was rather far from her family at Northfield Hall.

"Do you hope to travel?" Mr. Anderson asked.

"Certainly. How am I to be satisfied with where I am living if I do not first sample other places? I would not declare veal my favorite meat without tasting beef, duck, and pigeon to rule them out."

"I did not know it was in the purview of governesses to select their homes, beyond choosing to accept placement with a given family."

Sophia studied him, for he delivered this so evenly she could not quite tell whether he meant it as censure. Citing how one was supposed to behave, after all, was one of those verbal gates society used to keep a person penned into their tiny cage of expectations.

Sophia had always been interested in breaking down those gates.

"I am heartbroken you have not yet noticed, Mr. Anderson: I am no ordinary governess."

She threw down declarations such as this regularly, almost always to entertain herself with how the other person would react. Her father, for example, would smile a little bigger, the perennial sadness lifting a little from his eyes. Ellen, her elder sister, had the opposite reaction and usually picked a fight with whatever position Sophia declared. Their brothers were less predictable, sometimes agreeing with Sophia and sometimes taking Ellen's side.

With Mr. Anderson, Sophia had no sense of whether he would pick up on her intended self-deprecation, or if he would hear her words as some sort of gross self-exaggeration. And—most unusual—instead of feeling the thrill of expectation as she waited for his reaction, she wished she could snatch back her words.

For she did not want to see distaste color this man's face.

He raised an eyebrow. His eyebrows were such remarkable slashes across his face that this would have been dramatic, no matter the emotion behind it. But to Sophia's relief, his lips quirked, too. And he looked at her the same way he had in Lady Widlake's sitting room: as if she were a scientific marvel, one that he wanted to dissect and study until he understood her completely.

Well, he was welcome to strip her clothes and examine her every nook and cranny, if that was what his study required.

"Are you an ordinary accoucheur?" she prodded, delighting again in provocation now that she knew he liked it.

He turned his chin away from her. "I try very hard to be."

"Well." Not quite the answer she had been hoping for. They had reached Chapple's Stationery Shop. If Sophia didn't make her offer clear now, she wasn't sure she would get another chance. "I could teach you to be extraordinary, if you wanted."

Mr. Anderson looked about them, as if to seek out eavesdroppers from the quiet High Street. "You play with matches, Miss Preston, and could start a fire."

"I am the mistress of fire, Mr. Anderson, and I can light your path, if you desire." Sophia knew very well how this looked. A young, unmarried governess propositioning a respectable surgeon; she could be turned out for her words. Too, she stood before him a plump woman too professional for marriage, wearing a dress too staid to be seductive, offering him nothing but risk. If she were not right in her gambit, Mr. Anderson would turn away from her in horror–and might even go straight to Lord Widlake in disgust.

But Sophia liked gambling too much to do it clumsily.

Mr. Anderson wet his lips with his tongue. He had an elegant mouth, almost regal in how slender and straight it was–until he did something like that. Then it felt like a secret whispered hotly against Sophia's skin. "And if I did desire? What would happen then?"

Triumph was pale compared to the surge of wet need sprouting between Sophia's legs. She curled her fingers into fists to keep from throwing them on his person that very instant. In fact, she drew herself into as cool of a posture as she could muster, so that anyone on the street might see a governess advising the surgeon on how best to fix the button on his overcoat.

Not a woman in heat, impatient beyond imagination to get the man before her naked and between her legs.

"Then you would meet me at midnight in the bell tower."

Mr. Anderson held her gaze for just a second too long. Then, he opened the stationer's door and entered the shop, as if she hadn't said a thing.

Sophia followed him in, breathless.

"Ah, Miss Preston! I wondered if I would be honored by everyone from Robin Abbey today." This from Mrs. Chapple, the shopkeeper's wife. A stout woman in some later decade than Sophia's, she ran the shop while her husband famously never seemed to appear. "Lord

Widlake himself was in this morning, and you missed the rest just now on their way to the vicar's."

"Shame." Sophia hoped her cheeks were not red from her exchange with Mr. Anderson. She hoped the desperation of her quim didn't leach into her voice.

Mrs. Chapple's eyes drifted to Mr. Anderson. "You must be the man-midwife I've heard so much of."

As he conversed with Mrs. Chapple, Sophia examined the bulletins posted beside the door. Most were handwritten, as there was no print shop within ten miles of Boughampton, but a few stood out with bold, inked messages. A notice of a public assembly; an announcement torn from a newspaper regarding the East India Company; and a handbill proclaiming, "LORD WIDLAKE HAS FORSAKEN HIS DUTY."

She pulled down this last one. On the flip side, tiny print explained the author's view: Lord Widlake had abstained in the vote on Corn Bills rather than strike them down, he had voted to spend more on more war with America, and he was doing nothing about paper currency even though the war with France had now ended.

"I have some mail for you, too, Miss Preston," Mrs. Chapple reported. "I held it back from Lord Widlake, expecting you might come in here."

Sophia folded the handbill in two and tucked it into her pocket so that Mrs. Chapple wouldn't see she had removed it. Not that she cared about protecting Lord Widlake one way or another. She simply believed inflammatory messages such as this one did more harm than good.

With a smile, she joined Mr. Anderson at the counter at the back of the shop and accepted the envelope Mrs. Chapple offered. In a glance, she could tell it was from her sister Ellen, and from its thickness, she could guess it contained a fair share of family news. "Nothing but good tidings, I hope," Mrs. Chapple said, letting the sentence trail off as if hoping Sophia would fill it with details. *Oh, yes, good news that my father has once again enraged the Tories, or I expect it is another story of Benjamin falling in love with a woman who will never return his feelings.*

Sophia hid the letter away with the handbill, for contemplation some other time. She had come to the stationer's with a different—more hopeful—purpose. Though it heated her cheeks to ask for it beside Mr. Anderson, she saw it through: "I'll have the usual, too, if it is available."

Her *usual* was not stationery at all, and it was hardly a regular purchase, as she had only been in town once before this. It was code for a package Mrs. Chapple offered women of discretion. A box that appeared to contain pens and flowery stationery, which in fact included fresh pessaries and the necessary potions to prevent conception.

Sophia hadn't made much use of the last box she had purchased, but she hoped to be in need of it very soon, and she preferred fresh materials to a sponge and elixirs that had been gathering dust for months.

Mr. Anderson eyed the box as Mrs. Chapple handed it over. Embarrassment—which she refused to acknowledge—rushed Sophia's explanation: "I must confess to a predilection for anything with pink flowers."

"I have yet to meet anyone who is not moved by the beauty of a pink flower," he responded solemnly. For his part, he had a stack of letter paper, wax for his seals, and a bottle of ink. Sophia waited for him to pay before she completed her own exchange with Mrs. Chapple.

"All these pound notes are too much for me to keep track of," the shopkeeper muttered, tucking their banknotes beneath the counter. "I miss the days of coins and gold, and I don't mind saying so even if you do take it back to Lord Widlake."

"I cannot think he would hold it against you that you have an opinion on a matter that touches everyone's life," Sophia replied. "Otherwise, I daresay he would have sent Mrs. Edwards away years ago."

"That is the truth if I ever heard it."

The woman geared up for another blast of small talk, so Sophia turned for the door. "It was lovely to see you, Mrs. Chapple, but I am afraid I must be on my way or Lady Widlake will find me remiss in my duty."

Mr. Anderson followed her onto High Street. "I am not sure if I will sleep well tonight, Miss Preston. I often don't after a day of excitement."

"A walk around the Abbey might help." Sophia dared herself not to smile. "I always find the bell tower peaceful at midnight."

He tipped his hat, as if to acknowledge her advice, then took the direction opposite from hers. In the last moment, he looked back, though, and quirked his lips into a small, quiet smirk.

"I shall consider it."

And Sophia knew what his answer would be.

CHAPTER FIVE

J OHN CONSIDERED NOT GOING. Of course he considered it. He was a man of reason. Red-blooded with lust like any other sexual creature, but not so craven as to put physical wants before rational needs.

And going to that bell tower was not rational. If anyone saw him or her, if anyone heard them, if anyone even twigged to the possibility of the accoucheur meeting the governess in the dark of midnight, then his reputation would never recover. He might not be dismissed on the spot—as Miss Preston surely would be—but any recommendation of his services would be more circumspect, caution inciting suspicious pauses in his former clients' referrals. What husband would entrust his wife's body to an accoucheur with a reputation for seducing innocent women?

A wiser man would not go to the tower. One who cared for his budding career would not go. One who had an eye on saving enough money to establish his own practice would not go.

John went to the tower.

After all, Robin Abbey was a quiet house. Lord and Lady Widlake managed it with a calm, open-minded attitude, accommodating Mrs. Edwards's outbursts of opinions and Miss Preston's undimmable shimmer. The servants so far hadn't obviously rifled through his things or asked pointed questions. And it was midnight. Everyone else was asleep.

He took with him his taper candle, just as if he were wandering the Abbey to find a midnight cup of tea. He still wore his full suit, including the white cravat tied *à la Maratte* to match Lord Widlake's style. The bell tower stood at the very end of the Abbey's southwestern wing, practically the polar opposite of John's chamber. Walking along the cloisters gave him the excuse–if someone encountered him–that he wanted fresh air before sleep.

No one did encounter him. Not even the moon; the whole night was black as a closed coffin. Except for the dim wavering light of his taper. Quiet, too, without the chirp of summertime insects. It was no wonder the monks had chosen this site for their solitude all those centuries ago. On a night like this, one could feel completely alone.

John shook off his thoughts. He was on the verge of frightening himself, even though he knew better than to believe in ghosts.

The door to the bell tower was heavier than the rest of the doors John had encountered at the Abbey. He had to set his taper on the ground, brace both his legs, and pull with all his might before it swung open. Bending to retrieve his taper, he glanced around, thinking he might wait there for Miss Preston, since he doubted she would be able to manage it on her own.

But, unless he snuffed the candle, that would expose him to anyone with a view of the courtyard who might look out their window. John ducked inside the bell tower, instead, and waited by the door.

From somewhere far away in the Abbey, a clock chimed the hour. The dead of night. The start of the new day.

It was not a large tower. The entrance featured a slit of a window and the start of a narrow stone staircase. As John took in his surroundings, he became aware of another sound: footsteps on the stairs.

Panic seized him. An immediate cold sweat that drenched his palms and armpits and back. A cramp that clenched his bowels in a vise. A stupidity that had him snuffing the taper before the interloper discovered him.

It was by the interloper's candlelight, then, that John watched them descend the final twist of the stairs. Boot, stocking, and skirt, in that order.

Amazing, how quickly the fear flooding his body could be replaced by anticipation.

Miss Preston had not changed since supper. She wore the same simple evening gown, whose color he couldn't now discern nor remember. Despite the chill of the night, she wore no cloak. And as she joined him on the level floor, John realized she had made one adjustment to her outfit: the fichu that always wrapped around her neck and across her bosom was gone, plunging her neckline into a square almost down to the very tips of her breasts.

"Who did you think I was?" Miss Preston chided by way of greet-ing. "Lord Widlake, here to catch you in the act?"

John swallowed. Lifted his gaze in time to watch her lean in and, touching her wick to his, relight his taper.

"A fair concern, don't you think? If we are caught…"

She placed a palm on his sleeve. Muffled through her glove and his layers of clothes, the touch still radiated across his body. Bringing his attention back from windmilling hypotheticals to the here and now.

To the woman who smelled of pears, whose eyes glowed with mischief, whose lips begged to be kissed.

"We won't be caught," she promised.

John envied her that confidence. And then he decided to emulate it. Today, he decided, was the day he faced his fears head on. He had at last sent a reply to Garrett, and for the first time, he hadn't minced his words with his cousin. He had been polite, grateful, but firm: his mother deserved better treatment than Garrett's last postscript. What a thrill it had been to hand the letter to Mrs. Chapple, to know that even now it was in a sack headed for London, that within two mornings it would land on the silver correspondence tray at Gracechurch Street.

He had posted that letter, and now he was following Miss Preston up the bellfry stairs. John resolved to quit second-guessing himself.

The bell tower rose a story higher than the rest of the Abbey. Miss Preston led him all the way up to its top floor, which wrapped around a giant gaping hole where once the bell would have hung. Taking his candle, Miss Preston settled both lights in the southwestern corner, out of view of the slit windows. A blanket and cushions waited on the floor.

He swallowed. It was one thing to imagine what might happen in this encounter. It was another to see her preparations laid out, as matter-of-fact as if she had been planning for an educational picnic with her pupils.

John hoped he didn't fail her.

"Have you done this before, then?"

He didn't know why he asked it, nor why it came out as a rasp from his throat. Miss Preston's eyes gleamed in the candlelight.

"Depends on what you mean by 'this.' Taken a lover? Yes. Taken a lover here in the bellfry? No." She stepped close again, her gloved hands skimming across his shoulders. "Taken a man as fine as yourself? No, I don't think I have."

She was tall for a woman, rising almost to meet his eyes without lifting her chin. He wasn't used to that. He caught her waist as an experiment, drawing her against him. Underneath the gown and smallclothes was soft, generous, warm flesh. John's mind leapt forward, imagining her naked in the candlelight. His blood heated, until he wouldn't have been surprised to see steam rising from his veins.

He reeled back the vision, lest he overwhelm himself already.

Miss Preston, leaning into him, wrapped her hands behind his neck. The hems of her gloves tickled against his bare skin. "And you, Mr. Anderson? Have you ever done this before?"

John wondered what kind of answer she wanted. That he was not a virgin, he assumed she had already concluded. That he was not repeating the sins of his father, he could assure her. He had no past wife, betrothed, or even sweetheart to confess to. Only a few flirtations, a handful of dalliances, all of which had been discreet, kind, and a trifle awkward.

That he had never been so painfully attracted to a woman in his life as he was in this moment to her, he could not imagine confessing.

Miss Preston could not want to know any of that. He lifted a hand from her waist to clear a falling tendril of hair from her forehead as he answered. "Not with anyone as extraordinary as you."

She smiled, her teeth catching up her lower lip as if to hide her pleasure. John kissed her then. It felt right that he should be the one to do it, even though she had been doing all the seducing up until that point. He wanted her to know he was not some wide-eyed youth following her leading strings. He was a man with desires, and since she was offering up her desires, the least he could do was be honest about wanting them.

She did not taste like pears. He had not expected her to, of course, and yet it was a little surprising. She tasted far more human than that. Her lips were so plump that he could hardly tell where they began and where they ended. Not that he cared. For the kiss suffused his body with a light, heady nothingness, pushing out all observation, all thought, all anxiety. He did not need to match sensation to logic, desire to reason. To exist was enough. To feel her mouth part, to taste her tongue, to glide from one moment into the next without any measure of time. It was all enough.

Her hands roamed his body. He liked that, especially at first, when her gloved palms slid down his arms and then across his chest. He imagined her measuring him, evaluating him, imagining what his torso looked like without the nuisance of clothes. It made him feel attractive. Desirable. He moved his own hands, cupping his fingers around her jaw as the kiss deepened and teasing her with the other palm. Her torso was so luscious, so generous with curves. He made a topographical study of her back. That, paired with the kiss—which had grown more intense, more urgent, with harsh breaths heating each other's cheeks—flooded his senses. Almost, but not quite, to the point of overwhelming him.

Then Miss Preston's hand plunged down. Her palm curved around the spot where his cock strained into his trousers. And she began to rub.

John pulled away. Pushed her away, more like it. He watched her stumble backwards, toward the corner with the candles and the blanket, and hated himself. For he had been enjoying the kiss, hadn't he? And he was a man, wasn't he? And he had known very well what she implied when she invited him to meet him at midnight with a blanket and pillows laid out, hadn't he?

"I'm sorry." How he had wanted this time to be different. Miss Preston flinted his body to a fire with a mere glance. John had hoped that would be enough to evict every trace of doubt from his body. But if he had only been honest with himself, he would have known this would happen, as it always did, and saved them both the embarrassment. "I am very much enjoying your company. It's only that I don't like to progress too quickly in these matters. If you see what I mean. I only enjoy it if I..."

He didn't really know the answer here, so it was hard to explain. His body required him to have some further knowledge of a woman than simply "she is attractive" and "she wants you." Yet it wasn't quite that he needed to get to know her personally, nor was it that he needed six months of grappling each other to progress towards the full act. It was some obtuse equation that even he didn't know.

Miss Preston waited for him to finish his sentence with her fingers curved across her lips. She did not yet look horrified. Still, there was a caution in the way she held her torso straight, her eyes almost but not quite meeting his.

"The more familiar we are with each other, Miss Preston, the more I will be able to offer you fleshly delights."

Her hand dropped, revealing her lower lip caught up in a smile again. "Is that it?"

John had given this speech to a few women. It had taken him some time to realize what was the matter with him when he simply stopped enjoying an experience after it crossed some invisible line. For the past five years, though, he had understood this about himself. Sometimes, he had the opportunity to explain it to his lover before they did anything more than share a meal. More often, he forgot about it, wrapped up in the optimism of desire, until she tried to wrestle him into a position for intercourse.

Most often, his speech resulted in tears. Occasionally angry words. Always hurt feelings.

No one had ever smiled at him, until now.

"I thought you were going to elucidate some depraved necessity. You would need me tied up against the wall, or arse up in the air, or dressed like the Prince Regent."

She threw out the options with such delight that John teased her, "And if I had confessed to those desires?"

Miss Preston let loose her lower lip. "I'm willing to try anything once or twice."

He didn't want any of the fantasies she had described. Yet her willingness—her eagerness—shot desire straight through his body.

If only he were a different man, whose heart didn't always stand in his way.

T HE MAN WAS CLEARLY uneasy. Despite the fact that he'd been burning her with as intense a kiss as she could remember. His hair stood all on end from where she had dragged her fingers across his scalp. His nose and ears glowed red from all the blood she had stirred beneath his skin. His cock pressed against his trousers, a clear profile of a long, thick, eager member even in the shadows of the candle.

And yet his arms had crossed his body. He had thrust her away, as if she were a poison. He watched her now with wide, dark eyes. His expression was universal, one she had seen on children, on puppies, on horses: fear.

Sophia didn't quite know what he feared she could do to him. And she supposed someone motivated by self-interest alone would conclude that nothing of interest would happen that evening and retreat to her room, no matter that the accoucheur was so uncomfortable. But that would be a short-sighted, selfish person. Sophia indulged herself in being selfish, but she prided herself on being a strategic thinker.

If she could make Mr. Anderson comfortable with her, then by the time the infant was delivered and he off to his next household, she could coax several satisfying fucks from him.

Besides, Sophia liked the man. She hated to see him cave in on himself, arms tense, as if he waited for a cutting remark.

She turned to the makeshift bed in the corner and, with a few quick moves, rearranged it into a sofa. Sinking onto one of the cushions, crossing her ankles beneath her, she patted the other for Mr. Anderson. "We might as well start getting to know each other, mightn't we?"

He did not immediately follow her instruction. "You are not offended?"

"Why should I be offended?" In that first moment, when he had shoved her from his arms, ugly fears had reared. Had he found her grotesque? Too much stomach and not enough breast? Bad breath, bad kissing, bad manners? Had this all been a set up to teach her a lesson for being a whore?

But that had been a flash. Not even a full clock's tick. The world did not revolve around Sophia–as much as she would have liked it to–and she understood before she finished her gasp that Mr. Anderson's reaction was about something to do with him.

She did regret grabbing his cock without permission. Most men, in her experience, liked that kind of wanton behavior, but she should have proceeded with caution, considering how little she knew about this particular man.

Mr. Anderson still stood before her, more a flickering apparition in the meager light than a full silhouette. "Perhaps you are accustomed to being desired with no qualifications."

Sophia had never taken a lover who wanted to become better acquainted with her on an intellectual level. She preferred instant chemistry, the kind that required nothing more than a few physical encounters to be sated. She wouldn't call that unqualified desire, however. "I appreciate a man who discerns between grape juice and wine. Why should I not appreciate a man who has similar discernment in other areas?"

Finally, the man smiled. His was not a perfect grin. It had the strange effect of making his otherwise slender face look square and fat. One would not want to be frozen for eternity with that expression on his lips. Still, it was endearing. It almost made him look like an innocent youth.

He sat on the cushion beside her. Their shoulders brushed against each other, yet he made no move to add distance, which Sophia took as another positive sign. She tucked the blanket across their laps for warmth.

"Now, what would you like to know about me, Mr. Anderson?"

It took him only a half-breath to summon the question. "Is it true you are a relation to Lord Preston, Baron Ashforth?"

Whenever someone asked her–and they always did–Sophia toyed with the idea of lying. *No, and I have never heard of such a man. Is he notable for some reason?* Or, *Yes, I am of the branch of the family that shuns Lord Preston and his insanity.* Not because she was ashamed of her family, precisely. She loved them, each and every one. It was just that being a part of the Preston brood came with so many expectations, none of which she met. Avoiding foreign imports. Fighting rabidly for Whig policies. Sacrificing for the good of the common man. Life would be simpler if Sophia could pretend she hadn't any idea who her radical family members were.

So far, she had been unable to get herself to lie. "He is my father."

This triggered the next question, which always followed her confession. "And he has placed you as a governess?"

Again, a logical question. She could not blame anyone–and particularly not Mr. Anderson, with whom she was trying to curry favor–for asking. Governesses were supposed to be women down on their luck. Fine daughters of fine families who had no money left for a dowry nor independent income.

Whereas her father was a radical leader in the House of Lords. Her sister Ellen was married to a viscount who stood to inherit one of the country's great fortunes. Her family's estate, Northfield Hall, produced well-known linens, honey, and woodwork, and they famously shared all profits with everyone who lived and worked on the property. This, the general public assumed, meant that the Preston family was extremely wealthy.

In reality, it meant the family itself had very little money left, since her father insisted on giving it all away to the less fortunate.

Still, Sophia could have married a wealthy gentleman, if she had so chosen. In radical circles, her father's political cachet and her titled upbringing more than made up for a paltry dowry.

"My father has nothing to do with my placement as a governess," Sophia answered Mr. Anderson. "Really, he has had no control over me since I reached my majority. I am a product of my parents' experiments, you see. Raise a girl to believe everyone deserves the same opportunities, and she will believe it of herself, too."

"Do you consider governessing an opportunity, then?" The skepticism dripped from his words, no matter how he tried to school his face into a polite expression.

This, Sophia remembered, was why she always avoided getting to know a person. They asked the very questions one did not want to answer. What was she supposed to say? *I have discovered it does not suit, but I cannot for the life of me think of what I will do next.* "An opportunity for independent income, certainly. Why, should I consider chaining myself to some husband to be more of an opportunity? When all that means is I must bear his children and beg for money at his whim?"

"You do not want to marry? Ever?"

Sophia had been asked this many times, but never by a man with whom she had recently been tangling tongues. The men she engaged with played their own games, one which required them to avoid the "m" word at all costs. After all, if they mentioned marriage, then she might trap them in one, since they had already taken pleasure in her flesh.

She didn't know if Mr. Anderson was brave, naïve, or stupid for daring to ask her that question now. All she would have to do was let out the loudest scream of her life, and the household would come running to discover her compromised by the accoucheur. By sunset, they would be married by special license.

There was a part of her—a large, tempting part of her—that wanted to tease him. To widen her eyes, bat her lashes, and accept him on his proposal of marriage. Just to see his reaction. It would serve him right, for asking such a question.

"No, I do not." And as punishment for making such personal inquiries, she added, "The only thing worse than being married would be bearing children. You see, I am a selfish creature, and I am determined to remain so."

She expected shock. Horror. Perhaps even injury. After all, he was an accoucheur. She rejected his entire livelihood with such a declaration.

However, when Sophia slid her gaze over to the man beside her, she only saw curiosity in his eyes.

That would not do at all. It was time she took control of this conversation before he darted her with any further questions. "Now tell me about yourself, Mr. Anderson. What compelled you to dedicate your life to parting ladies' legs and pulling out their babies?"

He did not react to her offensive phrasing. "My father set me up to attend medical school before he died. One of the first tutors I had there, Mr. Pool, was an accoucheur. He took me under his wing, and from there, I suppose, it was predestined."

He said it so reasonably, without any of the defensiveness Sophia had felt when answering for her life. She pushed, "It is not because you are absurdly fascinated by the vagina?"

For a brief moment, he was shocked. She could tell from the way his eyes widened and his body stiffened. But her victory didn't last long. He actually smiled again. "I am absurdly fascinated by the vagina, in other contexts."

And then he looked at her in that way of his. The one that telegraphed exactly what he meant. She was instantly wet, thinking of that gaze directed on her vagina, that fascination pinned on how he could bring her to orgasm.

It was enough to heat her through again, despite the chill of the night.

"If that is true, then I suppose it is worth suffering through a few more personal questions so you can show me what you find so fascinating."

He kissed her on the lips. Nothing intense or longing, yet neither was it a peck. The kiss of a lover, acknowledging the other but asking for nothing more. When he pulled away, her lips still tingled.

"I find you absurdly fascinating, Miss Preston."

"Of course you do. I am extraordinary." The response was automatic. Sophia was glad for it, for her unthinking glibness, because she couldn't quite think at the moment. No man had ever called her fascinating and satisfied himself with only a kiss. She was used to compliments functioning to build the moment, the way kisses led to a climax.

She didn't know how to interpret a compliment that led nowhere.

"Are you the first surgeon in your family?" It wasn't what she actually wondered. If she paused to ponder the man beside her, her thoughts swirled in unaskable questions: had he always looked at people so intensely? What part of her did he find most extraordinary, and why did it appeal to him? If they fucked, would he cradle her afterwards or disappear?

"I am." He answered her spoken query. "My cousins are barristers, and my father was a solicitor for the East India Company."

"You have no brothers or sisters?"

Mr. Anderson paused. She watched his mouth form around words then hold them back.

Sophia wasn't surprised the question required a complex answer. It was common knowledge–information that Lady Widlake had offered up before he even arrived, in the same breath as saying he studied in Edinburgh–that his mother had been a native of Calcutta. Sophia knew what that implied: more likely than not, she had been a mere mistress, a dalliance for Mr. Anderson while a fragile wife remained behind in England.

It was the latter part of his response, then, that stunned her: "I had three siblings from my father's marriage, but they died with my father and his wife in a sweep of scarlet fever. That was fifteen years ago."

"I'm sorry to hear it." Sophia hated stories of people dying of illness. Give her a freak accident, a bolt of lightning, a battlefield death, even a disappearance at sea. Illness reminded her too much of losing Mama, whose wasting disease stretched across Sophia's adolescence. "You must have felt very young and alone to be without both your parents."

"My mother is alive." Mr. Anderson frowned. Sophia realized she had not received many of those from him before. She didn't like it: the knitting of his brows made her stomach curl with guilt. "She lived with me in my uncle's household. She began as the cook and then became housekeeper."

"Your father did not raise you himself?"

"No, he thought I would benefit more from having my cousins as an example."

They both knew that wasn't the real reason. Not with the senior Mr. Anderson keeping a wife and children in his own home. Poor Mr. Anderson had been brought to England only to be cast out.

"Bugger that, and bugger your father, too. You deserved a better lot in life."

The words were ones she had learned at Northfield Hall from people in similar circumstances to Mr. Anderson. If they'd had drinks, Sophia would have said it as a toast and washed it down with a healthy amount of alcohol.

But Mr. Anderson did not respond in the usual way. Instead, he jolted to his feet. "May he rest in peace. My father did the best he could by me, and I won't have you disrespecting him so."

"I mean no disrespect," she lied. "I only mean that your father was clearly the kind of man who considered the world his oyster simply because he was English. Or because he had the money for it. I'm a selfish person, but even I wouldn't bring my mistress to a different continent and set her up in my brother's household while returning to my respectable wife. You and your mother both deserved better."

"You know nothing about my family," Mr. Anderson hissed.

Sophia gulped back her argument. It wasn't up to her to force him to see his father in the light of reality. She tried to think of what might calm him down. "I apologize. It strikes me as unfair, that's all. And I wish I could do something to make life fairer for you."

He ran a hand through that silky hair. He was too far into the shadows for her to see his expression, but she could feel him avoiding her eyes when he responded, "Life is unfair. There is no use being angry at someone who has more luck than you. There is only making the most of what you've been allotted."

It was a sentiment diametrically opposed to the philosophy of her family, who had faith that humanity could improve itself to provide an equal life for everyone. Under different circumstances, Sophia would have embraced Mr. Anderson's ideal as much more realistic and clear-sighted. But to hear him say it with such conviction, when she felt in her bones that he deserved better, lit inside her a deep, dark fire of rage.

And then, somewhere below them, a door opened with a slow scrape against stone floor.

Sophia blew out the candles. She crept to the edge of the belfry, to the great empty space where the bell used to hang. From there, she could see nothing but shadows across the floor beneath them.

But there could easily be a person on the ground floor.

Mr. Anderson knelt beside her. Into her ear, making almost no noise, he whispered, "What do we do?"

"If someone is down there, we shall have to wait them out." There was no other solution, really. The bellfry's windows were mere arrow slits, and even if they allowed a human form through them—which they would not—neither she nor Mr. Anderson could survive the drop onto the Abbey's roof. They had to wait for the exit to clear.

"How do we determine if someone is down there?" Mr. Anderson asked.

Really, did he expect her to do everything?

But before Sophia could flash her frustration at him, the question answered itself for them. The stairwell connecting the first story to the ground floor lit with an orange glow.

Someone was there, and they had brought enough candles to illuminate a wide swath of the tower.

"That's how," she replied to Mr. Anderson, as if she had planned this all along. Then she pulled him away from the edge and back onto their makeshift seating. "We have to hope they don't come up here."

"Hope?" For the first time, his voice rose above the hush of a death murmur.

"Well, what do you suggest?" She far preferred to be annoyed with him, who demanded that she have the answer for everything, than with herself, who had gotten them into this situation. Her plan had been simple. How was she to have known someone else would be using the bell tower for midnight activities?

New sounds drifted up from below. Muffled, mechanical ones. Sophia could not quite make them out, but they were repeated thuds and bangs. This mysterious midnight activity was not carnal.

That was not a relief. A carnal interlude would have lasted no longer than a half hour. Whatever this person was doing, Sophia could only hope it would conclude before sunrise.

The bellfry was far too cold, damp, and dark for her to stay there until sunrise, with or without Mr. Anderson's company.

She couldn't see his face, not with their candles snuffed. That annoyed her, too. None of this was his fault—none of it was even his idea—yet she felt an overwhelming, all-consuming anger at him. If only he hadn't tempted her. If only he hadn't refused her. If only they had fucked and left the bell tower before any of this nonsense began. If only he hadn't allowed the universe to conspire against them.

Sophia bit down on her lip—hard—to keep from saying any of this aloud.

"We could try to scare them away," he suggested. "Pretend to be the ghosts of monks haunting this bell tower for crimes of the past."

"Nuns," she corrected, while trying to picture how they might haunt the tower without giving themselves away.

"Nuns?"

"The Abbey belonged to an order of Cistercian nuns. Cloistered from the world. They took vows of silence, too, and communicated to each other by signing." Sophia thought of the nuns often, particularly when the wind howled against her bedroom window, and always with a shudder at the prospect of so forsaking oneself. "What shall we do, wrap ourselves in the blanket and descend in silence as if we are about to pray the sinner into Hell?"

"Our intruder may not care as much for historical accuracy as you do."

The mechanical sounds paused, and she and Mr. Anderson froze. When, after a minute or so, the noises continued, he let out a shaky exhale. "I shall go down. I will say I could not sleep, took a walk about the Abbey, and fell asleep while praying at the top of the bell tower. If it's a servant, I will ask them to help me with some task, so that you can escape without notice. If it is a family member, I will…I'm not sure what, but I will come up with some reason to get them out of the tower long enough for you to run off."

As a plan, it left much to be desired. However, it was better than shivering through the night, hoping that whoever was there left sooner rather than later.

Sophia gathered up the pillows and blanket and moved to crouch near the stairs while Mr. Anderson descended. He thundered each step, letting the heels of his boots clip loudly against the stone. When he was halfway to the first story, the machine sounds ceased. The light vanished, and a different, louder thud echoed through the tower.

The sound, Sophia suspected, of a door closing.

Apparently, their interloper did not want to get caught any more than they did.

"Damn," Mr. Anderson stage-acted. "Now how shall I see where I am going?"

She listened to his footsteps descending the last of the stairs and then crossing the floor. The door opened once more. The way it scraped against the stone floor each time it did, Sophia was surprised the whole household hadn't yet been awakened.

"Where did that fellow go?" Mr. Anderson asked, in the same pitch to wake the dead. "How strange! He as good as disappeared!"

Sophia didn't need any further hints. Seizing her bundle of blanket and pillows, she scampered down the stairs, one hand on the frigid stone wall to keep herself from falling. Mr. Anderson stood in the courtyard, looking about as if in search of their friend. Sophia slipped behind him. "I'm off, then," she whispered, as quietly as he had done before. She wasn't even sure he heard her, for he didn't react, only turned his head in the opposite direction.

"Must have been a ghost," he announced as she snuck into the shadows of the cloisters. "Never trouble a nun, I always say."

Sophia heard him shut the bell tower door after that. She didn't look to see his next course of action. Their evening was over, their communication sealed off like the bell tower behind them.

It wasn't until she was in the safety of her room, the key turned in the lock, that Sophia could admit to herself that she hoped he would give her another chance. And that she feared, with a deep, sickening feeling in her gut, that–thanks to how she offended him with her Preston ideals–he wouldn't.

CHAPTER SIX

R EGRET SEIZED JOHN THE next morning. In daylight–cloudy
though it might be–he saw clearly a hundred things he had
done wrong the night before, beginning with risking his career and
ending with speaking so viciously to Miss Preston.

John didn't like to see that part of himself. He hated that it
had come out in the company of a person so undeserving as Miss
Preston. And all in the name of defending his father.

John had long ago stopped losing sleep over the question of
whether to forgive his father. There were days when John didn't
believe his father worthy of defense. Days when he felt abandoned
and ignored due to the very fact that he had not been allowed to live
in his father's household. His father had engaged with Amma–even
told her he would marry her–when all along a wife had awaited him
in London. A story as old as time, and one whose villain was clear as
day.

Then there were days when he saw the story for what it was: his
father had made poor choices, perhaps, but he had tried to make

things right anyhow. Given that John and Amma were not legal family, his father had done his best to provide them a comfortable living and a prosperous future.

No matter what the truth was, John still couldn't stomach anyone but himself or Amma blackening his father's name.

Yet all Miss Preston had done was express sympathy. That he didn't want or need it was neither here nor there. He had been one breath away from calling her character into question, so desperate was he to defend his father.

He hoped she would give him a chance to apologize.

John did not see Miss Preston for most of the day. He looked for her as he went about his duties. Every time he turned a corner, he expected to run into her. Or he heard a laugh, and he thought it was hers, only to discover it was the maid Polly's.

John didn't know what he would say, when they next encountered each other with the eyes and ears of the household on them. He only knew that even more than he regretted his behavior the night before, he yearned to steal a glimpse of her smile. Yet he didn't see her: not by coincidence in the corridors and not by schedule at the family supper. And by the time the sun set, John had revolved back to regretting the risks he had taken.

The less he saw of Miss Preston, the better.

He stopped in after supper to check on Lady Widlake, who had been in bed all day with a backache. He noted with alarm that she had now developed a fever and chills. John sat with her for an hour or so, placing cool towels on her forehead, ankles, and hands. Then he administered her an elixir of milk, bark, and honey.

Mrs. Edwards hovered the whole time, opining on everything from the towels provided by the maid to his treatment methods, insisting he should be offering opium instead.

"It is too risky at this late stage," John explained at last.

"Pooh. I took opium throughout my pregnancy and it did neither me nor Agatha any harm."

Lord Widlake, who sat in a chair in the far corner of the room, harrumphed at this.

John reined in his own irritation. As overbearing as the woman could be, she was, after all, a mother worried about her daughter and a grandmother concerned for her unborn grandchild. As his mentor Mr. Pool said, compassion must rule over expediency. "We must not compare the fact of the pregnancy but also the circumstances. You were a young bride when you delivered Lady Widlake, were you not? And she was your first child?"

He was confident in this knowledge because Mrs. Edwards herself had thrown it out over the last few weeks, as if to stake her expertise in the ground. Now, she nodded, her eyes narrowing as she sensed her words turning against her.

"Lady Widlake is in more advanced years, you see, and this is her seventh time in this condition. We must treat her more delicately, for her body is growing tired."

For the briefest moment, John thought he might actually have gotten through to her. Then her hands flew into the air. "Oh yes, you say that now, but once the babe is delivered you'll warn his lordship off for six weeks, then let him have at her again. Meanwhile, you deny her opium when she is ill, because it is natural for a woman to suffer. She aches, Mr. Anderson, and you think a mixture of milk and bark will cure her?"

"I am more concerned with the fever, ma'am."

"I do not *have at* Lady Widlake," her son-in-law said, rising from his corner. "We are blessed with health and children. Do not make this into one of your pet topics."

Perhaps roused by the unusual anger threading her husband's tone, Lady Widlake stirred from the sleep to which she had only just succumbed. "Whatever is the matter?"

Mrs. Edwards flew to her side, elbowing John out of the way to clasp her daughter's hand. "Tell Mr. Anderson that you need opium."

Lord Widlake advanced to the bed, too. So far, John had found him to be a mild-mannered man, one whose personality was as understated as the brown hair thinning across his scalp. Now, however, there was steel in his words. "Are you so obsessed with being right that you refuse to heed the advice of those who know better than you?"

Lady Widlake looked from her mother to her husband. Her eyes shone a bit with the fever, which was precisely why John wanted her to rest, but in matters of the family, he knew his role was to wait for them to resolve the matter themselves.

"I have no need to prove that I am right," Mrs. Edwards answered Lord Widlake. "I know that I am. I am her mother. I know what my child needs, and she needs her husband to stop using her body for endless gestation. Perhaps, my lord, it is you who is trying to prove something by getting your wife with child at every chance."

"Mother –"

But Lord Widlake did not allow his wife to interject. "Leave this room, madam, and do not let me see you again until I am no longer tempted to eject you from my home altogether."

Mrs. Edwards was red with fury, and even her hair quivered atop her head. Her mouth opened–as if even now, she would find some other vicious words to throw out–but she shut it again. In a great huff, she left the room.

The row remained in the air. Lord Widlake glowered at his wife. She swallowed. For his part, John tried to not even breathe, so that they would not remember him until they had calmed down.

"She is overexcited from the trip to town." Lady Widlake's apology came out thin as a reed. "She did not mean it."

"She is vulgar and common and belligerent."

"I cannot help that she is my mother."

John's response would have been different. Had someone insulted his mother, he would have struck back, no matter how much power that person might have over him. He knew this because he had done it a hundred times, earning himself whippings and scorn and even ejection from an Edinburgh assembly dance. Even though

Mrs. Edwards *was* vulgar and common and belligerent, Lord Widlake had no right to wield those insults against her.

The clock in the hall chimed eleven.

Lord Widlake drew in a great breath of air. On his exhale, he mustered up a smile for his wife. "You are the miracle that escaped her influence. My sweet, kind, pleasant Agatha." Bending, he kissed first the back of her hand, then her palm, and finally her forehead. "Get some rest."

He turned for the door, startling a little when he discovered John still there.

"See to her, Mr. Anderson."

Lady Widlake closed her eyes when her husband left the room. "I apologize for the ugliness. Tempers are high this close to the Great Event, as I'm sure you know."

"Do not think on it. Now, are you in great pain?"

She shook her head. "I want some sleep and for these chills to go away."

"Then I remain opposed to opium." John gave her another portion of his elixir. "If you wake in the night, you may take one more portion. Hopefully, you sleep through until morning, though."

Lady Widlake settled back into her pillows. No sooner had she shut her eyes, however, than came a knock on the door. "Let them in," she murmured, though John would have turned away whoever it was. He decided to remain at her side, calling, "Enter," as sternly as he could to indicate his displeasure at the patient being disturbed.

It was neither Mrs. Edwards returned to interfere nor Lord Widlake with another bout of temper nor even a meddling maid. Miss Preston herself stepped through the door, with young Miss Francesca in tow. The girl looked hollow and wan in her white flannel nightdress.

"I am sorry to disturb you, Lady Widlake, but Miss Francesca has some sort of rash on her neck. I thought Mr. Anderson might take a look."

"A rash?" Lady Widlake sat up, then pressed her palm to her forehead in regret of the movement. "Oh, Francesca."

For a moment, when Miss Preston first crossed that threshold, John's body leapt with excitement, remembering that kiss from the night before. But Miss Preston did not give him one of her weighted smiles. In fact, even when invoking his services, she barely spared him a look.

John shifted his attention to the girl. He had been briefed on Miss Francesca Cosgrove almost as soon as he arrived at Robin Abbey. Born three weeks earlier than expected, she had been sickly her entire life–and poor Lady Widlake had conniptions each time the daughter showed signs of illness. Now, he hurried to say, "Ah, I'm sure it is from exposure to something in the village yesterday. I shall take a look, and I daresay it will be gone by morning."

"Oh, do, Mr. Anderson." Lady Widlake fell back onto her pillows again. "You must do everything Mr. Anderson says, Francesca, and I shall be that proud of you."

John herded Misses Preston and Francesca to his room for inspection. Only a small fire burned in his hearth, so he paused to assemble a collection of candles at his desk to create a spot of light by which to see the girl's rash. He felt his fingers moving slowly and stupidly under the observation of Miss Preston; it took him three tries to light the taper.

He settled his attention on the young lady. "Let us see what the trouble is, then. Are you in any pain?"

"No, sir." The rash stretched in red splotches from just below her left ear all the way down to her shoulder.

"Did you try on very many sample dresses yesterday?" He tested the rash to discover it was scaly but not hot to the touch.

"Yes, sir."

"And have you had a bath since?"

"No, sir."

"I daresay your skin is irritated by that. I shall treat this with a poultice overnight, and then we shall examine it again in the morning." Turning to Miss Preston, John tried not to notice that she wore a silk robe tied over a nightgown. "Could you request that the kitchen send up oil, vinegar, and spirits of wine?"

He saw the glimmer of resistance across her face, a certain tightening of her lips and crossing of her eyes that suggested she might object to being ordered about. She was, after all, the daughter of a baron, and he a mere surgeon of dubious background.

Or perhaps she was still piqued at him for how he had spoken to her the night before.

Miss Preston did not throw his order back in his face, however. She ducked into the hall, then returned after a few moments to say, "It appears everyone has gone to bed. I shall fetch what you need myself," before disappearing to the kitchen.

"Why are some people ill and others not?" Miss Francesca asked as they waited.

She watched him with wide, solemn eyes. John rather felt she would imprint whatever words he found on her memory and recite them for the rest of her life. It was the kind of attention he was unaccustomed to receiving, and which made him long to be invisible. "A very good question, Miss Francesca, but I am afraid no one has found a definitive answer yet."

Her head tilted as she considered this. "I should like to be a physician when I am grown. Are there any lady surgeons?"

"Not yet." And John couldn't imagine a world in which anyone would submit to the expertise of a woman, no matter how educated she might be. A child didn't need to know that, however. Particularly not a child like Miss Francesca, whose wealth and prestige allowed her to live in a castle of dreams for a while longer.

It almost made him remember how he had so longed to be a true doctor—one who studied for years at Oxford and spoke three Classical languages and danced around with the prestige of being a Learned Man—even after his father informed him that a bastard could never be admitted into those ranks.

Miss Preston returned then with the requested ingredients. John arranged them beside the candles on his desk. "Let me show you how to make this poultice, Miss Francesca, so you will be that much ahead of your peers when you apprentice for medicine."

It was a simple recipe. He mixed equal parts oil, vinegar, and spirits of wine. Then he soaked clean strips of cotton cloth in the solution. "You may use any kind of cotton you have at hand. For you, however, the daughter of Baron Widlake, we use the finest muslin." John wrapped the plaster around her neck like collar rings, until the girl resembled a mummy. "There. Now, go to sleep with a towel beneath your head so your pillow does not get too wet, and you shall be better by morning."

Miss Preston had been watching them this whole time, of course. John had done his best not to notice. It was rather easy to quiet his anxiety when he had a task at hand so rote as plastering up a rash. Now, however, he remembered her. Smelled her, even, for she had stepped close enough that notes of her pear perfume drifted above the base aroma of oil and vinegar. "Will you see Miss Francesca back to her bed, Miss Preston?" he asked, not knowing if it was a request or a query.

She began her reply looking at the girl. "Of course, and I know Miss Francesca will sleep well having been under your care." Then the governess raised her gaze, her dark eyes sweeping across his face. He fancied a hint of color rushed her cheeks as she said, "If you are available, I will return, for I fear I also have a condition that needs treatment."

He rasped out, "I am at your disposal."

She did not mean a personal encounter, John told himself. She likely had some terrible rash herself, or perhaps a cold, or cramps from her menses.

Or it was personal: perhaps Miss Preston wanted to upbraid him for speaking to her so rudely the night before.

John owed her an apology, not for the content of his words but for the manner in which he had vaulted them at her. He had stood up on behalf of Amma to Garrett in his letter; he could do the same on behalf of his father without getting brutish in the face of Miss Preston.

Even if she was wearing nothing but a nightgown and wrapper.

In the full light of his hearth, John had been treated to a complete view of her nightclothes. Or rather, he had been treated to a complete view of what her nightclothes revealed that her day gowns didn't. Ungoverned curves being top of mind.

John wasn't sure he was ready for her ungoverned curves. But neither did he want her to return in more clothes, and even less did he want her to not return at all. So he would need to get ready for her ungoverned curves, even if the thought of what she might expect of him stabbed anxiety through his internal organs.

She returned just as the hall clock chimed midnight. She had lost her nightcap, so that her hair in its plait roped down her shoulder, ending just above her right breast. John's mouth went dry.

"I'm sorry to keep you awake even longer. Everyone else has long since gone to bed." Miss Preston sauntered over to his desk. She trailed a bare finger along its edge. John waited. His mind had gone blank from the way her hips swayed. "I'm afraid I, too, have developed a rash. Would you take a look at it?"

His stomach flipped. It was not a ploy for private conversation or anything else, then. She really did seek medical advice.

"Certainly. Where does it trouble you?"

She untied the silk robe. Her nightgown was white and covered in frilly lace. She unhooked the ivory buttons from the top of her collarbone and moved down. One button at a time, until she reached the last one, just beneath her bust. She parted the gown to reveal her chest and breasts, stopping shy of her nipples. "It is all across here."

He had to swallow in order to deliver saliva into his mouth. He had to order his feet to take the step forward, and then the next. He locked his hands behind his back so that they did not leap into action for which he was not yet ready.

Her skin was pale, at least compared to his, enough that he could see ribbons of blue veins crisscrossing her chest. Her breasts were as plump as the rest of her, rising generously even without the help of her corset. The right breast pointed directly at him, the nipple peaked beneath her gown like the bulls-eye of an arrow target. The left breast rolled a little to the side, as if playing coy. Its nipple, he discovered, was lower than the one on the right. An intriguing juxtaposition. One he wanted to observe forever. Explore in all its possible iterations. Jiggle in his own hands and lick with his own lips.

"I do not see a rash," John managed to say.

"Don't you?" Her palms cupped her breasts exactly as he wished to do. "I feel it all over. A terrible burning. Perhaps my skin is hot to the touch?"

The door stood open at an angle to the hallway. If a maid or Mrs. Edwards or Lord Widlake passed by, they would have a clear view of Miss Preston offering herself to him.

She caught his nervous glance at the corridor. "You are the only surgeon in the house, and everyone has gone to bed. Rather than rouse a maid to play chaperone, we are leaving the door open. There is nothing improper about this situation."

Her thumbs circled her nipples–still hidden beneath the very edge of her nightgown–as she said this.

John knew he wanted to say something to her. Something he'd been meaning to say all day. Only, for the life of him, he couldn't remember what it was.

"Please, Mr. Anderson. I cannot sleep while I burn from this rash."

And so John did it with the door open. He touched her neck first with just the fingertips of his right hand. She let out a little gasp–something he felt, more than heard, in the puff of air that reached his cheek. Her skin was smooth. Supple. A texture one wished to touch forever. Warm, too, especially considering the chill in the air. He allowed his left hand to replace her palm against her right breast. It was sumptuous enough to spill out of his grasp. His right hand moved of its own accord, feeling the soft layer of plumpness above her rib cage, luxuriating in her skin, before drifting to that flirtatious left tit. Then he had both breasts in hand. Miss Preston's teeth sank into her lower lip. She lifted her chin, perhaps asking for a kiss.

That would be too much. John didn't know why. Didn't know how he knew. But he knew as he stood with her pliant tits spilling out of his palms that to add a kiss to the mix would overwhelm him.

"I know of a remedy to this type of ailment." He didn't mean to whisper, but that was all the volume he could muster at the moment.

Her irises had mixed with her pupils in the candlelight, so he saw nothing but dark pools in response.

"It requires manual stimulation." John caught her nipples in a gentle pinch. Her breath tripped again. "Would you like to try that treatment?"

"Yes. Whatever you recommend, doctor." How her voice had lowered, turning into a rasp. John wondered how close she was to being overwhelmed, too.

He glanced once more at the door. The corridor was silent and dark, a black void compared to the bright candles behind Miss Preston.

She was the one who wanted this risk. And she was the one with the most to lose. So John positioned her against the edge of the desk in full view of any passerby. He lifted her gown above her knees without care to whether anyone might see. He trailed his fingers across the insides of her thighs in a completely unprofessional manner without closing the door.

By the time he reached her quim, she had already let out a moan. "You must be quiet as you receive this treatment," he rebuked. She was wet, her desire drenching her labia and clitoris even before he started exploring. He measured the length of her labia from the hood of her peak to the valley of her vagina. He circled her opening, then slid his way back up to her clitoris. How he wanted to see her. To take in the full glory of this woman's luscious and complex organ. To taste it for himself.

But he knew that would overwhelm him, too. This was as far as he could go. He could manage this and no more, as long as he focused on her experience. As long as he felt her wetness and did not notice his cock throbbing against the pressure of his pants. As long as he listened to her breaths growing faster and shallower and did not notice his own pressing closer against his chest. As long as he imagined the heat flooding her body and did not mind the desire mounting in his own.

She was a woman who knew her own pleasure. "Go faster now," she directed, "and put your fingers inside me sometimes." John did as she asked, sailing his fingers along her length before plunging one, then two, and then three inside her vagina. She was so hot there, her muscles already clenching, and he knew that meant she was getting closer to an orgasm. He stretched his thumb up to tickle her clitoris as he encouraged, "Clasp my fingers with your walls. Again. And again." Her vagina was strong, gripping him there so that even had he wanted to pull away, he was not sure he could have. He increased his speed against her clitoris, then, at the last moment, used his spare left hand to claim her right tit again in a tight, hard grasp.

She came with abandon. A great spasm through her body; he caught her in the cradle of his elbow so that her flailing head and arms didn't knock over any candles. She let out a sob of pleasure. To muffle it, he pressed his wet hand against her mouth. Miss Preston opened her lips and sucked his fingers with her tongue.

That was too much. Too intimate, and too close to pleasure, and John couldn't handle the anxiety that spilled over him. It was as if, instead of spending his seed as his body was meant to do, he covered his internal system with bitter adrenaline that left him jittery and nervous. And ashamed.

He did not want to use women the way his father had.

"Do you have a similar rash?" Miss Preston asked, grabbing at him. "I should love to return the favor."

He stepped back, so that even if someone looked in the door, they would not see him. "No, thank you. This has been enough."

She had been understanding before. Perhaps she would be again. Except John had a feeling it was different now. That she had allowed him inside her and therefore he should allow her the same level of access to his body. But he couldn't do it. He wouldn't do it. Even if that meant she wanted nothing more to do with him.

He lifted her silk robe from where it had spilled to the floor. "Perhaps I shall see you at breakfast."

I T TOOK SOPHIA A moment to catch up. Her body thrummed with pleasure. She hadn't been finger fucked in too long–and never so thoroughly as this. Usually, her partner touched her for mere moments, a few teasing plunges to test her readiness before taking her with his cock. To be isolated by Mr. Anderson's fingers, to not even be kissed as he brought her to a deep and endless climax, left her reeling. In the best way possible.

Even as she took the robe from him, Sophia felt only the luxurious texture of the silk against her bare hands. It was his words that finally hooked her spirit back into her body. And his tone: distant, closed off, as if spoken to a patient and not the woman he had just brought to supreme pleasure.

"We still don't know much about each other, do we?" She felt him shuttering into himself like a house preparing for winter.

He crossed the room to the hearth, knelt, and added more coal to the fire.

Early in her carnal experiences–not her first time, but a few lovers on–Sophia had found herself the plaything of a second son of a marquess. He was handsome enough, witty, and had a lock of hair that always fell across his eyes, a combination that seeped into Sophia's fantasies. At first, they had met on mutual terms, sneaking into retiring rooms and gardens and carriages for quick trysts. But after they had pleasured each other three or four times, the dynamic had changed. Even now, Sophia couldn't quite say why. She only knew that her lover had started calling her terrible names as he thrust inside her. He had glared at her when she flirted. And when she told him she no longer wanted to meet him, he had grabbed her jaw to force a kiss.

Sophia remembered how chilling it was to be intimate with someone yet feel so irreparably removed from them. And that was what she feared Mr. Anderson suffered just now.

She buttoned her gown so that every inch of skin below her neck was covered and tied the robe just as tightly. He did not want her touch, nor her flirtations. Perhaps he didn't want her company. Whatever he needed, she would respect.

It was the least she owed him, after he had delivered her such a spectacular episode.

"In fact, you are quite a mystery, Mr. Anderson. Even at mealtimes, you manage to spark a conversation among the rest of us without giving your own opinions. And that is a feat when Mrs. Edwards runs loose."

He turned his chin enough for Sophia to see the smile pushing across his lips. "Mrs. Edwards only cares to hear her own opinions parroted back to her."

"True." She sat in the wooden chair waiting to the side of his desk. The length of the room spilled between them, and his back remained facing her. Still, Sophia didn't think he wanted her to leave yet. "Come on, then. Tell me something about yourself."

Mr. Anderson rotated in full. He leaned against the mantle, regarding her, arms crossed and one ankle stretched ahead of the other. "What should you like to know?"

The truth was that he was a blank slate. Sophia knew the way his nose contoured down his face, yet she had no idea where he had been raised or whether he liked his occupation or what he dreamed of. What he found funny. What he abhorred. Whether he liked sweets. Whether he had an opinion on her family. Whether he stood for anything or believed in any power greater than himself.

And in a way, she didn't want to know. Because she liked him the way he was. And she didn't want to find out that he scorned the aristocracy he served or that he had a bastard child in Edinburgh or that he eschewed tobacco for all the same reasons as her father. She didn't want to discover reasons not to like him.

"I owe you an apology," Mr. Anderson said into her silence. "I lost my temper with you last night. I'm not proud of it."

"I apologize, too. I did not mean to insult your family. I assumed you resented your father. Most people I know bear anger towards their parents."

As soon as she said it, Sophia wanted to bite back the words. They were almost an invitation to ask her about Papa. And she hated talking about Papa. No one ever understood how she could love him with her whole heart and still not worship the ground he walked on.

Mr. Anderson resisted the temptation. "My father's life was dictated by circumstance, as mine is. As anyone's is. I don't feel any resentment towards him for making mistakes."

"And your mother? Does she resent him?"

"My mother..." Mr. Anderson let out a sigh heavy with an emotion Sophia didn't understand. "She doesn't resent anyone. She is the happiest person I know. Always smiling. Always forgiving."

Sophia circled her fingers around the candlestick beside her. "At the risk of provoking you again, you say that in a way that makes it sound like you think she should resent someone."

He sank onto the carpet, folding into himself. "My cousin married recently. A month ago, perhaps. He wrote to tell me of the news and that his wife has replaced my mother with a new housekeeper. A 'more appropriate' housekeeper, he said. And now my mother has taken a position in a stranger's household."

Sophia waited. Not because it was the right thing to do but because she didn't know what to say.

"I don't know this Captain Attree. My cousin's home has been her home for thirty years. And he just...turned her out."

His words came out flat. As if he didn't have emotions about it. Except, of course, even Sophia could tell he carried great, overwhelming feelings about it.

"She sounds very resilient. I'm sure she is making the most of the new position."

"I am her son. She shouldn't have to make the most of anything." When Mr. Anderson looked up, Sophia discovered all his emotion swirled in his eyes. Anger. Guilt. Fear.

She didn't want to know so much about him. She looked away.

"In any case, she must be very proud of you. A surgeon. More than a surgeon. Accoucheur to the fashionable set." Sophia had witnessed weeks of endless discussion between Lord and Lady Widlake as they agonized over which accoucheur to hire when they discovered that Mr. Brewer was already engaged. Mr. Anderson had been selected as much for his sterling reputation as for his expertise in delivering live infants. "How glad your mother must be to know you are so successful."

"I suppose so."

"Are you proud of yourself?"

He frowned, as if the question itself were a puzzle. "I suppose so. Proud, if not satisfied."

"Well, I know a trick or two to satisfy you." The flirt came naturally. Sophia couldn't have stopped herself from saying it even if she had wanted to.

Mr. Anderson didn't smile. He watched her from the carpet. "And are you proud of yourself, Miss Preston?"

This boast came without thought, too: "Of course."

And she was proud of herself, in a way. Proud of creating choices for herself. Proud of refusing Aunt Charlotte's prods towards marriage and Papa's guidance towards virtuous sacrifices. Proud of finding herself governessing instead.

Even if she hated the life she had found for herself. Even if she was too scared to look more than a year into the future because she didn't know what she could do next.

Sophia was proud of herself for not giving into anyone else's expectations. And she was too proud to admit to the rest of it. So she summoned a smirk and said, "Proud and, at the moment, very satisfied."

At last, he smiled. His narrow face turned into boyish, square delight. "Of course. You are an extraordinary woman, after all."

She noticed for the first time that his jaw had grown dark with the shadow of a beard. They hadn't kissed, and so she hadn't gotten to rub her own cheek against that stubble and feel its tickle all the way to her core.

She wondered if he looked more like his father's family or his mother's. And whether his mother missed her homeland. And how often he visited his cousins.

But those were too many questions. Sophia didn't want to wonder so much about him.

Mr. Anderson ran his fingers through the fringe at the edge of the rug. "Do you think Lord and Lady Widlake love each other?"

A strange question. Sophia had never much considered it. "I suppose so."

"I can never quite tell. I observe intimate moments that no one else ever sees, and yet, I can never tell whether my patient loves her husband or vice versa." He glanced up, his eyes connecting with hers in a way that felt too close.

Sophia made it a habit not to worry about the people around her. Lord and Lady Widlake had no complaints about her services as a governess, and that was all she needed to know about them. For the exercise, however, she tried to remember their interactions. Tried to think if they modeled love, or just an example of living in the shadow of the same person for a decade.

"Did your parents love each other?" Mr. Anderson asked.

"Yes." She assumed everyone knew the story, since it was the kind of established gossip that had circulated London for decades. "They married even after my grandfather forbade it on account of my father being too radical."

"And it never faded?"

Sophia hadn't ever questioned her parents' relationship. They cherished each other in small ways, they confessed their love for each other more often than any child needed to hear, and when her mother had died six years ago, Papa nearly buried himself with her. "Not even with death," she answered Mr. Anderson.

"Then you would know what love looks like."

If her parents were the model—or even her sister Ellen with her husband Max—then love was obnoxious, visible, and constant. It was stolen glances and arms wrapped around shoulders and never making a decision without consulting the other. It was making other people feel outside and alone.

It was losing oneself entirely in the identity of another, and never recovering.

"Why does it matter to you whether Lord and Lady Widlake love each other? Love is not half as valuable much as poets make it sound, I should think."

Mr. Anderson blinked. "I would have expected you of all people to value love over other reasons for marrying."

"Love and marriage go hand in hand as stupid inventions that we need not carry into the modern age. They are false philosophies tying two people together for a lifetime. I told you last night I have no plan to get married, so why should I want to fall in love, either?"

Sophia surprised herself by how vehemently her opinion came out. Her voice rose, so that should anyone be walking in the dark corridor they would almost have no choice but to peek in to see what the ruckus was about. There was no reason for her passion; these were neither new views to her nor ones she felt were particularly interesting.

It was the way Mr. Anderson looked at her. It was the fact of him asking her questions instead of kissing her into oblivion like any other lover would do.

She rose. "I have tarried here too long. I should retire to my room before someone discovers us."

Mr. Anderson scrambled to his feet, too. "I did not mean to offend you, Miss Preston. If I have..."

"You haven't." Unsettled her, yes. Provoked her, perhaps. Sophia didn't need an apology from him so much as she needed to escape that room before he forced some other admission from her. "I am overtired. I shall see you in the morning."

He caught her hand just before she reached the door. His palm was smooth, dry, and warm. Sophia waited, thinking he would say something. But he only held her for that moment, almost briefer than a breath. Then he let her go.

CHAPTER SEVEN

ON THE SATURDAY AFTER their trip to Boughampton, Lord Widlake summoned John to his study. John had just finished with his morning examination of Lady Widlake, and when the footman delivered the message, his stomach flipped. Lord Widlake had found John's services wanting. Or he had a complaint about John's behavior in the household. Then, as John descended the stairs towards Lord Widlake's study in the northeast corner of the Abbey, he discovered Miss Preston going in the same direction.

It had been three days since their last midnight meeting. John kept waiting for Miss Preston's signal, which did not come. Perhaps because she was disappointed that he still wasn't comfortable beyond mild fondling. Perhaps because she was angry at having had to share so much of her life. Perhaps because she had decided he wasn't worth the risk of discovery.

She looked beautiful that day in a soft blue muslin and amber earrings, but then, John supposed, he always thought her beautiful.

"You've had a summons, too?" There was no trace of anxiety in her question. In fact, she asked it rather as if to query whether he had been invited on the same picnic.

His heart descended. For if they were summoned to Lord Widlake's study together, that could mean only one thing:

They had been discovered.

Jasper, the pimpled footman, opened the door and introduced them to their host. John took a deep breath, memorizing its sweetness, the faint tinge of tobacco, in this last gasp as a respectable, employed accoucheur. When he left this room, he knew, his reputation would be in tatters.

The study conformed to a fashion magazine's design, even though it had been stuffed into a room that had once served as a private chapel. Bookcases with glass doors stored ledgers, a collection of Bibles, and other leather-bound volumes with gold lettering proclaiming their titles. A giant imported desk occupied most of the room, under which a gleaming silk Persian carpet lay unfurled. A stuffed fox hung above the fireplace.

The effect cowed John suitably. He had done wrong, he had known it even as he brought Miss Preston's dripping quim to climax, and now he must own to God and country that he was a failed, miserable man.

A man, Heaven help him, just like his father.

Then he noticed the other people in the study. Stooping to the right of Lord Widlake's desk was a slip of a man whose suit hung from his limbs and whose moustache drooped all the way past the edge of his chin. Meanwhile, Mrs. Edwards–surprisingly silent–sat in the other chair.

"I apologize for the interruption to your duties," Lord Widlake said by way of preamble from behind his desk. "May I introduce Mr. Ord, agent of the Bank of England. He has come to me with a most grievous matter that we must address."

He nodded at Mr. Ord, who wet his lips with a long tongue before speaking. "Mrs. Chapple discovered that she was paid in false banknotes this week. I am tasked with finding the person who did this. Unfortunately, the trail has led me here, though it pains me to darken the doorstep of our esteemed Baron Widlake with unpleasant business."

The lord nodded, as if accepting this as his due. "I have given leave to Mr. Ord to examine your purses. If you could please bring them here so we may all determine that no one at Robin Abbey utters bad banknotes."

"Begging your pardon, my lord," Mr. Ord said with another lick of his lips, "but if they bring their purses here, they have an opportunity to eliminate the bad notes first. I'm afraid I must examine everything before it is touched by its owner."

John's reaction to all this was not appropriate. He should have been outraged to be suspected of a crime. He felt only relief. A great, flooding rush that lightened his body. He almost smiled; discovering this, he clamped his teeth on the insides of his cheeks. He wanted to look at Miss Preston, to see if she felt the same, but he didn't dare, not when it might ignite him into giddiness.

"This is the problem with paper currency, I always say," Mrs. Edwards trilled. "It does nothing but erode the value of money until anyone can pass their own printing off as currency. If you do not see it now, Lord Widlake, I despair that you ever will see that we must return to coins."

"Thank you." Lord Widlake left no room for argument in his tone, and for once, Mrs. Edwards heeded him. "Mr. Anderson, we shall begin with you, if that is agreeable."

There was no way to disagree, of course. John led the way, and to his surprise, the whole group followed, not just Mr. Ord. Miss Preston managed to look completely at ease, swanning down the corridor while to John each step felt more and more like a death march.

John was not the culprit. He had nothing to worry about. And yet, now that he had determined this was not about his exploits with Miss Preston, his palms began to sweat again. His lungs could not draw in a full breath. He opened the door to his room convinced that it would not be as he had left it. Someone would have snuck in and papered it with false banknotes. Or perhaps he actually was the culprit. Perhaps someone had passed him the false notes, only John hadn't noticed and had instead used them all throughout town, and now he would pay the price for a crime he hadn't even been aware of committing.

The Bank of England pursued fraudsters without remorse in order to ensure that all of Britain quaked in fear at the sight of a bad note. Everyone in the country knew the price of counterfeiting: death by hanging.

Although John had heard that if one confessed and cooperated with the Bank, the authorities would show mercy by reducing the sentence to transportation.

Neither was a punishment John wanted to experience. Holding his breath—as if that would prevent a calamity from unfolding—he invited the group into his room.

The room was as he had left it, except a maid had cleared the used coal from the hearth. John went to the armoire, regretting the rebellious stab that had compelled him to leave the crotchet hook on display. He heard himself clear his throat as he bent to the lowest drawer and removed the leather satchel he used as a purse. He sounded like a nervous goat predicting its own slaughter. But everyone else was silent, even Mrs. Edwards, and their eyes were all on him, as if they knew this moment to be solemn, his last before being condemned a criminal.

John handed Mr. Ord the purse. He didn't even remember what he had left in there, whether he still had any banknotes. He didn't want to know. The deed done, he sagged against the armoire. He wanted to look at Miss Preston. He wanted to see her dark eyes and her pearly teeth sinking into that lower lip. But he didn't have the energy to hide his feelings for her at the moment. If he looked at her, even if they found him innocent of counterfeiting, they would discover his crime with the governess.

Mr. Ord laid out the contents of the purse across John's desk. An extra pair of gloves. A handkerchief. Five folded banknotes of various denominations. They unfurled onto a drop of yellow candlewax, which John had let stand on the desktop as a souvenir from examining Miss Preston. Seeing it now, his cheeks flamed. Evidence of his sin, only the rest of them would assume he was guilty of falsifying the money, not of fornication.

Mr. Ord held each note up to the window, where the sun strained to get through a thick layer of clouds. He turned it this way and that. He peered at it, cranking his moustache up as he wrinkled his nose. When he was through with all five notes, he turned back to the room and shrugged. "These appear to be genuine."

"As I expected," Lord Widlake was quick to say, clamping a hand on John's shoulder.

They went next to Miss Preston's room. It was on the opposite side of the courtyard from John's, sandwiched between the nursery and the servants' quarters. Apparently she kept it locked; she withdrew a brass key from a mysterious skirt pocket and, smiling, warned, "Do not blame the maids for my mess. I was not expecting company today."

Indeed, the room looked as if a five-year-old had stormed in and thrown everything out of place. John had imagined Miss Preston in an austere, modest bedchamber. Aside from the size of it, he had gotten it completely wrong. Her bed—a slim mattress made to fit exactly one body—boasted a red silk coverlet. Strewn across the mantle, desk, and windowsill were boxes of various sizes, some made of wood, others encrusted with jewels, still another made of enamel. One stood open to reveal a stack of letters. Littered between the boxes were jars and glass bottles holding liquids and ointments and creams. A silver-backed hairbrush teetered across two of these lids, while a jade-framed hand mirror rested face-up on her bed pillow. The armoire stood open, linens spilling out of it onto the floor. Miss Preston rummaged through this first, then moved on to a pool of petticoats at the foot of her bed, before finally finding her reticule wedged between her mattress and the wall.

He recognized it, for it was velvet and beaded and belonged in a London ballroom rather than a market town. She handed it to Mr. Ord with another of her mischievous smiles. "There you have it."

Moving to the window, Ord cleared away a few boxes and jars to create a place to examine her reticule. Lord Widlake said suddenly, "Miss Preston is the daughter of Baron Ashforth, you know."

The man's moustache and eyebrows raised in unison. "Baron Ashforth?"

If there were one baron every Englishman had heard of, it was Sophia's father. Legends surrounded Lord Preston. He had turned his entailed estate into a self-sufficient farm where each laborer earned a share of the profits. He banned imports from the slave and colonial trades from entering his property. He campaigned with great passion for sweeping reforms that would, he promised, make Britain a paradise for every man and woman inhabiting the realm. Depending on which way one bent in political opinions, he was either a savior or a traitor inciting a rebellion on the scale of the French Revolution.

Lord Widlake answered for Miss Preston. "Yes, and of course, her sister is married to Viscount Berwick."

John saw the way she stiffened at these claims. They felt superfluous, assuming she was not the culprit. And John couldn't see how she would be. He had stood next to her as she paid for her items. She hadn't been at all nervous, at least not as far as he could detect. Besides, what would she gain from passing false banknotes?

Mr. Ord returned his attention to the reticule. First, he pulled out a necklace of glass beads. Next came a letter, thick and franked with a member of Parliament's seal. Then he revealed a crumpled handbill, which he smoothed out and revealed to the room:

LORD WIDLAKE HAS FORSAKEN HIS DUTY

"That's not mine." Miss Preston's cheeks splotched with red. "What I mean to say is, I took it down so others wouldn't read it."

Their host crossed his arms.

Mr. Ord at last reached money. It came out haphazardly, first one bill, then two folded together, then another clump that had been wadded up into a ball. He stroked them each flat against the windowsill before examining them one by one in the daylight.

John couldn't see much of the bills from where he stood by the doorway. It felt too intimate, anyhow, to be standing in Miss Preston's bedroom watching a stranger manhandle her personal items. He trained his gaze on the floor and waited for Mr. Ord's proclamation that these, too, were true banknotes.

Except when Mr. Ord spoke, he said, "I'm afraid these are bad notes, my lord."

John looked up at Miss Preston so quickly that his neck seized in pain. Red filled her cheeks, spread down her neck, and spilled onto her collarbone. She turned to Lord Widlake. "This is a mistake. I do not know anything about bad banknotes."

For his part, Lord Widlake shifted from one foot to the other. "You are quite sure, Mr. Ord?"

Even as the man made a show of examining the banknotes again, Miss Preston said, "If they are false, I was not aware. You cannot think I am printing false money. I'm quite busy with the children, after all, and where would I do it, besides? And why?"

Her voice had lost its usual rich timbre, coming out more of a squeak than anything else. Instinctively, John wanted to move to her side and wrap an arm around her. Or perhaps he would huddle her into a carriage and hurry away to somewhere that no one could harm her.

He forced himself to remain still, even as Lord Widlake replied to Miss Preston, "A political statement, perhaps, on behalf of your father to embarrass me into introducing a bill against paper currency."

She scoffed. A highly inappropriate response to being accused of such action by one's employer. She threw her arms open as if to encompass the whole room. "What else must I do to prove that I am not a puppet of my father? I am clothed entirely in cotton and silk. My belongings are all imported. I smoke tobacco in an ivory pipe. Even the ink with which I write my letters is mixed with indigo!"

John heard a hint of pride in her voice. She valued herself for stepping so far out of the bounds her parents had drawn around her life.

It was possible, he supposed, that she would extend that rebelliousness to criminal behavior. Yet he couldn't quite believe that she cared either way about paper currency. If she were going to do something criminal, it would be bold and daring, like riding through the streets naked or having a child out of wedlock just because she could.

"That does beg the question, dear, of how you afford these luxuries." Mrs. Edwards could not quite keep the smirk from her lips. "I am sure that, generous as he is, Lord Widlake does not pay you enough to keep these expensive habits. Perhaps you ran out of money and decided to make your own."

"I am not so irresponsible as to spend my money as fast as that, madam." Miss Preston picked up the silver hairbrush. "This was my mother's." Now she held up an enamel box. "This was a gift from my Aunt Charlotte. You may know her as the Countess of Pemberly." She waved at the row of gowns hanging in her armoire. "These have been collected over the years from my coming-out, my days in town, and my own savings. Does that satisfy you, or should you like an accounting of every item I own?"

"Do not get hysterical, dear."

Mr. Ord asked, "Miss Preston, how did you come by these banknotes?"

"The usual way. I got them from my bank. The Bank of England, in fact, the last time I was in London."

"Yet where the Bank of England notes are signed by a clerk, these notes are signed payable by *The People of Northfield Hall*. Your family's estate is known as Northfield Hall, is it not?"

Up until now, Miss Preston had been cheerful and then indignant. With this last piece of information, she grew still. Her voice came out as barely a whisper. "Yes, it is."

"Mr. Ord, this must be investigated thoroughly before we take any hasty actions," Lord Widlake said. "Permit me to write to Lord Preston for his insight into the matter. In the meantime, I give you my word that Miss Preston will remain here under supervision and will not utter any further false notes into the market."

What he forestalled, of course, was the arrest of Miss Preston. An arrest that would splash across every newspaper in England. And, whether she was convicted or not, might shake the Parliamentary agenda irrevocably.

"I will allow it for the interim," Mr. Ord said with another moustache twitch. "However, I must return the stolen goods to Mrs. Chapple. If you would show me what you purchased, Miss Preston?"

She hesitated. Long enough for everyone to notice. "Miss Preston?" Lord Widlake prodded.

John remembered the box she had purchased, even before she removed it from its place in the cupboard beneath her desktop. A pink plush cover with a white button clasping the lid in place, the size suggesting a stationery kit. John noticed that her hands trembled as she passed it to Mr. Ord.

The other man must have noticed, too. "Did you use any of it since purchasing it?"

"No." She answered quickly. He opened the lid anyway to examine the contents.

Even from where John stood, they were clearly not stationery. Mr. Ord recoiled, as if confronted with an animal carcass. His gaze, which up until now had been respectful if guarded, turned into a glare. "This is one of those contraceptive devices."

Lord Widlake's gasp was sharp and clear. "Miss Preston, what is the meaning of this?"

Gone was her bluster. Gone was the anger turning her skin red. Miss Preston stood like a bare branch in the wind, all her protective leaves blown off.

John couldn't hurry her into a carriage. He couldn't whisk her away to Rome or Calcutta or somewhere else where they could live free. But he wasn't an accoucheur for nothing.

"If I may," he said, stepping forward, "I can determine what we have on our hands here."

At Lord Widlake's nod, Mr. Ord let John take the box. There was no doubt that this was a contraceptive kit: there was the cotton pessary–a wad of cloth tied with a string–and the potions of myrrh, honey, coriander, and bindweed to soak it in before inserting it in the vagina. He had wondered what Miss Preston meant to do about contraception in the event of their intercourse, and now he had to push away an image of her wearing this in the bellfry.

He poked his finger at the pessary and made a show of unstopping the bottle, smelling, then even tasting a drop of it. Finally, he nodded at Mr. Ord with a conjured smile. "Common mistake. This isn't contraception. It is a midwives' concoction to stave off menstrual cramps. Ineffective but harmless enough, and one you see in this part of the country. You see, you soak this sponge in the potion at the full moon, then draw it across the woman's stomach. Once her bleeding starts, you mix a tablespoon of that in and –"

Poor Mr. Ord was too delicate to hear the rest of it. He held up his hand to stop John, then retrieved the box. "I'll return it to Mrs. Chapple and be done with it."

John did not smile. He looked at Miss Preston's head–just the top of her hair–to get a sense of whether she would faint or not. When Lord Widlake said, "Thank you for your discretion in this matter, Mr. Ord," John followed him back into the corridor. He didn't even object when Lord Widlake closed the door and locked it, leaving Miss Preston imprisoned in her mess of a room.

But he knew he had only saved her for a moment. And he determined to do whatever he could to save her completely.

CHAPTER EIGHT

FOR A FEW MOMENTS, Sophia could do nothing but stand there. She heard the key turn in the lock. She listened to the footsteps hurrying away. She felt the pounding of her heart against the confines of her chest. And yet, for those first few moments, she could do nothing.

Then her fury returned. Hot, restless, frenetic fury. Those were not her banknotes. She knew that without a doubt. When Mr. Ord had brandished them like some kind of hunting prize, Sophia had only had to look twice to see they were on common printing paper, not the thin gauzy paper the Bank of England used. She would swear she had never so much as held them, else she would have noticed immediately they were not like the other notes swimming about her reticule.

Whoever the counterfeiter was, they had very little skill in their art.

Sophia seized her pillow and tore at either end, as if rending it in two would dissipate the helplessness rising in her chest. It didn't rip at all, which made her feel worse.

Someone had placed those notes in her purse. More than that, they had implicated her family so that she would be the one to fall under suspicion.

It did not take a genius to put two and two together. Mrs. Edwards was the one who had been crowing for weeks about the demerits of paper currency. Mrs. Edwards was also the one who thought the Prestons walked on water. And Mrs. Edwards was the one to whom Sophia could never quite manage to be polite.

She banged on the door with both fists. "I must explain!" She hit again with the meaty sides of her hands, making the old oak door quake in its hinges.

No one came. Not after she counted to thirty, and still not after she counted to one hundred.

At least they hadn't arrested her right then and there. If Mama were alive to see this, that would be the first thing she said. *"Well, Sophia, you see what you are afforded compared to the common man. Why, if this had been poor Mrs. Chow, she would be in the gaol awaiting the assizes quicker than you could snap your fingers."*

Sometimes, Sophia found it comforting to imagine Mama following her around and proffering commentary on the daily things in life.

This was not one of those moments.

For even though Sophia was not in gaol, she was locked in a tiny room. The whole household would have heard by now. Soon, word would escape Robin Abbey, and then it would make it to London, and then Sophia would be forever known as the criminal Preston.

If she emerged free from this situation, then her options for forging a path without the help of a father or husband would be much more limited. She might not even have a path with a husband, anymore. She might be at the mercy of her family for the rest of her days.

And if she didn't emerge free, then she would hang at the gallows.

Wilted against the door, Sophia shut her eyes. If only it were so easy to press out the world. To erase everyone else and every other concern so that all that existed was herself and her body. And maybe Mr. Anderson.

If he wasn't completely repulsed by a woman with nothing but a criminal accusation and a box of contraceptive pessaries to her name.

There was no point waiting for someone to open the door for her. Sophia knew she was innocent, and she knew who had done it, too.

Her writing table was, unfortunately, a mess. Sophia cleared a little space for her blotter, then pulled out her correspondence kit. Out tumbled letters from Nate and Benny and Ellen. She hadn't read the latest yet, and she still hadn't responded to the ones that had arrived two months ago. There were too many unasked questions and too little that she wanted to share of her life. Sophia let them land in a jumble on the floor.

Then she got to work. Sophia would rather not ask for help from anyone. But in this particular instance, she knew what she needed to do.

She had to beg her family for help.

BY SUPPERTIME, SOPHIA'S DETERMINATION had hardened around her soul like a steel casing. When her mind tried darting out into a future where she was arrested, it clamped down, smashing out the imagination before she could conjure a dungeon or straw pallet. She had a plan, it would work, and there was no need to worry about anything going wrong.

The first part of her plan went wrong when Lady Widlake herself arrived alongside Sophia's supper. Sophia had hoped to bribe the maid into handling the three letters she had written, but now Polly deposited the tray on top of Sophia's blotter and backed out of the room, while Lady Widlake lowered herself onto Sophia's mattress. "Well, Miss Preston, this is quite the bind."

Lady Widlake's palms rested on either side of her belly. Her hair had recently been coiffed by her maid, Sophia could see, for the pins were in precise position. Lady Widlake was otherwise afflicted with soft, springy hair that escaped Shaw's designs, and by the end of supper, her face would again be framed by wayward tendrils. For now, however, she was composed and imposing, staring imperiously at Sophia even from her half-lying position on the mattress.

Sophia ducked her chin. "I am beside myself. I know I am innocent of any wrongdoing, yet still I apologize for this tremendous interruption to your household, my lady."

"I cannot imagine what anyone is thinking, holding you responsible for those notes. I cannot understand a law where using such money is a crime. However, my husband assures me I do not need to understand it in order to respect it."

It was not often that Lady Widlake resembled her mother in any expression or manner. Yet in that pause, Sophia felt as if she were speaking to Mrs. Edwards, and she knew the pause was not to be filled by her own response. It was there for effect, to make her feel her own impotence as a listener. Had it been Mrs. Edwards, Sophia would have barreled through.

For Lady Widlake, she bit her lip to keep from speaking.

"Lord Widlake has decided you will remain in this room until the matter can be cleared up. That leaves my daughters without anyone to mind them. Nurse attempted to this afternoon, which resulted in the twins getting into more mischief than one would have thought possible in the span of mere hours, not to mention the neglect of poor baby Jacob. I haven't the energy to spend the whole day with them. For tomorrow, I have arranged for Mr. Anderson to see to their lessons, which triggered such a look of terror in the poor man. Anyhow, you see that I am in crisis over this."

This time, Lady Widlake looked at Sophia with a raised eyebrow, as if demanding a response. "What of Mrs. Edwards, my lady?"

Lady Widlake grimaced. "My mother is not suitable company for young ladies. She herself knows this, which is why she sent me away to school when I was their age. She is a much better companion for a married woman who needs advice on how to manage a household."

Sophia didn't see that the woman was much good for that, either. Especially since she suspected it was Mrs. Edwards behind this crime.

"What I am trying to express, Miss Preston, is my ardent wish that this matter be cleared up immediately. If you are guilty, confess so that I may hire a new governess. If you are not, then how did those banknotes end up in your purse?"

"I cannot confess, for I am without guilt, ma'am." But Sophia could not tell Lady Widlake her suspicions. Not without some modicum of proof. Guilty or not–annoying, frustrating, maddening or not–Mrs. Edwards was Lady Widlake's mother.

She decided instead to attempt what she had hoped to do with Polly. Reaching into the top drawer of her desk, she took out two of the three envelopes: one for her father and another for her sister, Ellen. "I have written to my family for assistance. Perhaps they will be able to help us find a solution. Would you post these for me?"

Lady Widlake had to heave herself forward in order to accept the letters. She inspected their addresses before saying, "I suppose this is all we can do for the moment."

Sophia wondered if perhaps she should bring Lady Widlake further into her confidence. Perhaps Mrs. Edwards wasn't the person involved at all. Perhaps this all returned to the mysterious sounds in the bell tower. If she mentioned that theory, then Lady Widlake could be the one to discover the truth of the matter.

Except to mention the intruder was to confess to her own presence in the bell tower. The culprit could simply question how Sophia knew about it in the first place, and it would become a question of whom the household would believe.

"You are not eating," Lady Widlake said, her voice a little gentler now.

Sophia looked at the tray. It had not seemed polite to eat while Lady Widlake expressed her displeasure. The plate of food featured three sausages, cauliflower ragout, and sliced potatoes. There was also a small bowl of broth soup, a glass of wine, and a cup of water.

Her mouth watered at the sight of it, let alone the smell. But she forced herself to turn away from it. And, in a weak voice, to say, "No, my stomach aches too terribly for me to even think of food."

Lady Widlake did not immediately jump to Sophia's bait. "You are upset from today's events."

"Perhaps. Though these pains began last night. Oh, but do not worry about me, my dear lady. I am sure I will be fine after a bit of rest."

"What kind of pains?"

Sophia brought her palm up to the top of her stomach. "Rather like stabs just beneath my ribcage. It was every now and then last night, but now it feels like it is almost every minute. Perhaps some chamomile tisane would help."

And then she winced for effect, as if currently afflicted with a pain.

At last, Lady Widlake reacted as Sophia hoped. "I shall ring for Mr. Anderson."

"Oh, I hate to trouble him." Sophia slumped against the chair as if she was growing too tired to even hold herself up.

Lady Widlake struggled onto her feet, lumbered to the corridor, and flagged down a servant to fetch Mr. Anderson. Sophia took advantage of the moment to slip her third letter from the drawer into her palm. A good thing, too, for when Lady Widlake turned back, she directed, "You may lie down, Miss Preston. I shall take your seat."

It was funny how dire straits brought out new sides of people, Sophia observed as she followed directions. In the months of her service at Robin Abbey so far, Lady Widlake had hardly issued a single order. She had been soft-spoken, gentle, deferential even in dealing with those in her employ. Only now, stretched to the ends of her patience, did she resemble a baroness.

Mr. Anderson did not take long to present himself, looking pristine as always in his black dinner jacket. Sophia felt the usual wave of desire at his appearance. Her fingers touched each other, remembering how it had felt to stroke his silky hair. She had hardly spoken to him since storming out of his room the other night, and now Sophia couldn't remember why that argument had felt large enough to stop her from inviting him on another nightly adventure.

But this was not about her carnal desires. Sophia closed her eyes, the better to look sickly, and curved both palms around her stomach.

Lady Widlake summarized Sophia's complaints. There was a drip of accusation when she said, "abdominal pains," and Sophia wondered if in fact the lady suspected her of something far worse than a stomachache. Perhaps she had heard of the contraceptive box. Perhaps she had not believed Mr. Anderson's lie about it.

What Sophia would give to be hiding a pregnancy instead of being accused of a crime she had not committed.

Mr. Anderson knelt by the bedside. He maintained a respectful distance even as his fingers probed her stomach, his gaze on his actions and not on her. But Sophia could see the dark stubble whispering its way up his neck.

His eyes met hers. "Could you describe your pains, Miss Preston?"

Sophia wondered what he thought of her. There was no hint of emotion in his gaze, so she could not tell. Did he believe her guilty of counterfeiting? Had he already condemned her? Could he tell her stomachache was a lie? Did he count that as the latest in a large string of counterfeit actions?

"They are like knives. Just here." She moved her hands to show him. And–just as she hoped–he lowered his palms over hers. She twisted her palm to deposit the letter into his grasp.

Mr. Anderson's breath hitched. His gaze flicked sideways, towards Lady Widlake. But he didn't turn his head. He kept up his examination and–in a movement so smooth that Sophia almost didn't see–he tucked the letter into his pocket.

He probed her stomach for a few more moments, massaging her entire abdomen with expert fingers, before proclaiming the pains to be a symptom anxiety. "A supper of clear broth, chamomile tea when you are thirsty, and plenty of rest."

"It is not a long-term condition?" Lady Widlake asked as she gripped his forearm to rise.

"Nothing to worry about. I'm sure it would have passed earlier if not for the disruption today." Leading Lady Widlake to the door, Mr. Anderson turned back, his hand patting the pocket with her note. He smiled at Sophia–a delightful, kind smile upon which she could get drunk. "I shall see if I have my special stomach potion in my kit. If I do, I'll fix it up and bring it to you with your tea."

And she knew she would see him in the silence of the night.

CHAPTER NINE

JOHN HAD STOPPED NOTICING his headache hours ago. He had stopped noticing most things about his body, in fact. No hunger. No sweats. No nervous sparks from his spine to his fingertips. Ever since Miss Preston had been locked in her room, he didn't have the luxury of experiencing his body. He was purely in his head, navigating the difference between the panic inside and the calm he must project to everyone else. That left no room for anything but action.

Lady Widlake had called him to Miss Preston just before the family supper. John had time enough to read Miss Preston's note before he was required in the dining room:

To the esteemed Mr. Anderson:

I am guilty of many things, but not this. After much thought, I suspect I know the true culprit. I must beg your assistance in this urgent matter.

Yours,

Miss P.

He waited until Lady Widlake was asleep to descend to the kitchen for the charade of mixing a stomach potion. She had been agitated all afternoon and as a result was overheated and exhausted by the time the family finished their supper. For his part, Lord Widlake locked himself in his study. John was glad the man at least seemed troubled by the accusation against Miss Preston, but he thought he accepted too easily that she might be at fault.

Mrs. Edwards, then, was the family member whom John most wanted to fool with his stomach elixir. At supper, she had been uncharacteristically quiet, but John had felt her eyes on him more than usual. Especially after Lady Widlake had called him up to attend to Miss Preston. As he slipped outside to the kitchen–which occupied a squat stone building fifteen yards from the Abbey–he caught sight of Mrs. Edwards in the drawing room window, a black silhouette watching him.

He took his time mixing the potion. It was a real cure taught him by a midwife in Edinburgh, best used for nausea or stomach cramps. John didn't believe there to be any scientific merit behind it, but he offered it up when his patients were uncomfortable and demanded some sort of solution. For his purposes tonight, it also required quite a show to create. First he boiled water and sugar in the same pot to make a simple syrup. Then, he had to mash rhubarb, yellow rosin, and rosebuds into a fine powder. For this, he used his personal boxwood mortar and pestle, a gift from Amma upon the completion of his studies. Next, he mixed the powder into the syrup. This he let cool for a half hour until it was a warm paste. Finally, John collected it in one of his thick glass medicine bottles. He helped the maid Beula clean the kitchen, too, since she had stayed up later than usual due to his mess.

As his last step, he took the potion to Miss Preston.

Mrs. Edwards, he noted, was no longer watching for him from the drawing room window. In fact, the entire ground floor of the Abbey was silent and dark. His taper flickered out as he reached the main staircase, and he had to tuck the medicine bottle under his arm so he could extend a hand to the banister to guide himself up.

Creeping through the dark corridor of bedchambers, it occurred to John that just one night ago, he would have been nearly crippled with anxiety. Even with the excuse of a medicinal mission, he would have been smelling the sweat at his armpits and fighting down nausea. For he knew as well as Miss Preston did there was nothing wrong with her. He was on his way to assist a woman whom he, in the eyes of propriety, had no business visiting.

Tonight, he felt nothing. Except determination. And he didn't know if it was a good thing or bad to be so cut off from his body.

Candlelight glowed from behind her door, a beacon guiding the last portion of his journey once he turned the corner into the southern arm of the Abbey. John kept his outstretched hand on the stone walls to stay steady. He knocked, softly so as not to wake Nurse or the children in the nearby rooms, before turning the key and opening the door.

Miss Preston sat with her legs crossed on the slender mattress. She had changed into her nightgown, the same one John had already explored more than he should. Her hair spilled from a nightcap onto her shoulder in a slim braid. Only one candle burned, across the room from her on the desk, which depicted her features to be even more plump and generous than in daylight.

This must be the worst day of her life. Yet John couldn't help feeling a sharp, deep spark of desire at the mere sight of her.

"How fares your stomach?" He locked the door behind him. If anyone asked why, he would say he feared her escaping.

"It still complains."

She said it so innocently that John wondered if he had gotten it wrong. Perhaps she truly was ill, in addition to desiring his help with the question of the banknotes. He held out the glass bottle. "Take three spoonsful of this every night until you no longer feel any symptoms."

Miss Preston took the bottle but set it aside without following his instructions. "Did you receive my note?"

For the first time, John noticed the sheen of anxiety across her eyes. He tucked his hands–loose, useless–into his pockets. "I did. I am at your disposal."

She tucked her hands underneath her ankles. It was a disarmingly childish posture, shrinking her from seductress to a young woman without a clue as to what to do next. John felt that urge again to wrap her in his arms and trundle her away.

He sat at the very foot of her bed.

"It is our midnight visitor in the bell tower, do you see?" Miss Preston was saying. "The sounds we heard must have been a printing press. You must have interrupted them printing false notes that night. Then, somehow, they got word that Mr. Ord was coming today, and they put fraudulent notes in my purse so that I would be accused."

John didn't disbelieve her theory. But he did see a few weaknesses to her logic. "How did they know where to find your purse? Even you had to look for it."

"Well, that makes it easier, doesn't it? I haven't the faintest idea whether they moved it or not because I don't remember where I put it in the first place."

She did have a point. John pushed, "How would they know that Mr. Ord was paying us a visit? As far as I know, he did not send word ahead of time."

Miss Preston had that look, the one John had seen when he asked her too many personal questions. He wondered how she would react now that she could not storm out of the room. "Perhaps they cooperate with someone in town who sent a messenger ahead of Mr. Ord."

John supposed it was possible–in a very unlikely scenario–that a rider could have arrived at the Abbey, delivered a secret message to someone in the household, and disappeared, all without anyone's notice. "Whoever it is would need a key to your room, wouldn't they? You unlocked it this morning."

"I have no doubt Mrs. Edwards made herself a copy of every key when she first arrived to Robin Abbey."

This Miss Preston pronounced with fire, her eyes flashing and teeth gnashing.

"You think Mrs. Edwards is the counterfeiter?"

"Who else constantly decries paper money? Who else is always needling Lord Widlake to do something? Who else would sign the notes from *The People of Northfield Hall*? Unless she expected to be caught, she would only invoke my family's home as an homage to it, and there is no one in this neighborhood who reveres my father more than Mrs. Edwards."

She did make a fair point. John tried to picture Mrs. Edwards sneaking around the house, printing banknotes, hiding them, distributing them. As much as the older woman spouted political theory, he couldn't quite imagine her working a printing press.

He could not imagine it of anyone in the household, though. Not the grooms nor the maids nor Lord Widlake.

"Unless the counterfeiter is not at Robin Abbey at all." John spoke his thoughts aloud, and he liked the sound of them. "Perhaps you were handed those banknotes as change for something else you purchased in town, and that is how you ended up using them."

"They were a different paper. I'm quite sure I would have noticed if I had tried to use one of those bills."

Except he had been flirting with her in the shop. Or she had been flirting with him. Either way, John remembered the stationer's in a vague fog of desire. Perhaps Miss Preston had been similarly afflicted.

She ran her fingers across the hem of her nightgown, which was folded like a tent across her legs and underneath her ankles. "You do believe me, don't you, Mr. Anderson?"

His name sounded different on her lips than on anyone else's. John felt each syllable as it formed in her mouth, as she tongued it forward, as she offered it to the world on soft breaths of air.

Of course he believed her. But John suspected he would lie to her, if only to hear her say his name once more.

"It takes an enormous effort to counterfeit banknotes. I should think if you were to enter the business of fraud, you would limit yourself to shaving coins rather than go to all that trouble."

She laughed. John wasn't sure he had earned a laugh from her before. It was surprisingly mannish, deep in her throat and punctuated with a snort. Then Miss Preston sobered. She gathered her knees up to her chest. "Still, you must think I have reaped this punishment for all the trouble I sow."

"What trouble? Flirting with a surgeon?" John allowed himself a good, long leer at her breasts. They were rather hidden behind flounces at the moment, but he knew how easy it was to unbutton those ruffles and free her large, splendid tits for play. "How is your rash, by the way?"

"There is still a tingle, occasionally. When you are near."

"Perhaps it requires another examination."

She still clutched her knees to her chest. "I am sorry for how I ran out the last time. I am not sure what overcame me."

John had seen it twice now, that flash of anger that propelled her from a room. He wondered if the trouble was that she could not identify anger or that she could not control the anger when it sprouted. "It is quite all right. You are as uncomfortable with personal intimacy as I am with physical intimacy. A perfect pair are we."

"I am not uncomfortable with personal intimacy. I have four siblings. I have been forced into personal intimacy my entire life."

The trouble was that John found her just as attractive–if not more–when her shoulders hunched defensively and her eyes sparked with indignation. He wanted to kiss her. He wanted to grab her wrists and pin her down and rub his lips across her entire body until she was limp with a different kind of passion.

A stupid idea. John straightened his jacket to banish it from his mind.

"I'm sorry. I did it again." Miss Preston pressed her face into her knees. "You are so kind to me, and in thanks I am a wretch to you."

"That is the hazard of being a surgeon, I am afraid. More often than not, our patients spit in our faces rather than thank us for the help."

"That's terrible." She raised her face just enough that John could see her forehead and dark eyes. The candle flame reflected off her irises. He waited, thinking she would say something else. For the longest moment, there was nothing but silence in the room. Silence, and a gust of wind whipping against the small glass window.

Then, Miss Preston lifted her head a bit more. She balanced her chin on the point of her left knee. And she asked, "Do you feel you know me well enough for another kiss?"

He should excuse himself from the room. It had been a long day, and she no doubt needed rest. He needed rest, if he was to see to his duties and somehow discover who had been operating the printing press at night.

But the answer to her question was yes. A resounding yes to the kiss. A definite yes to unleashing her tits once more. A possible yes to something more. John didn't need to answer for that more yet. All he needed to do was kiss her. Which was what he wanted to do.

And so he did.

⚓

S OPHIA DIDN'T MIND NOT knowing where this encounter would lead. For the first time all day, her mind had stopped spinning. It clung to this one thing: Mr. Anderson kissing her.

Though it was only a kiss of the lips, he somehow did it with his whole body. His hands cupped her head, his thumbs tracing along her jaw. His elbows leaned on the pillow behind her, framing her against the bed, and his chest landed on hers. The buttons of his jacket teased as they pressed into her breasts. His right knee stood between her legs, and the deeper the kiss grew, the closer his thigh crept to her quim.

Sophia couldn't decide what she liked most about being kissed by Mr. Anderson. Was it the way the rest of the world evaporated, her entire existence reduced to where her skin ended and his began? Or was it because her whole body turned to fire, an alchemy no other activity could achieve? Or did she love it so because she knew for that moment, however long it lasted, she was the sole object of his attention?

She never answered the question because she always got distracted by the kiss itself. Like now, with Mr. Anderson shifting. His weight on his legs, he trailed his right hand down her neck to the buttons of her nightgown. He fumbled, for he still kissed her with his tongue. Each prod drove Sophia wilder. She dug her own fingers into his back, wishing him free of his jacket and shirt so that she might feel his bare skin. When he finally unbuttoned her bodice, he claimed her left breast first in his palm, then in his mouth. He had already nearly brought her to orgasm from mere suckling when he paused, asking, "Is this all right?"

"Yes." Then, afraid that he needed more encouragement, she added, "You deserve it for helping me, after all."

The wrong thing to say, apparently. He released her breast from both hand and mouth. "I am not asking for anything in exchange for my help. I am helping you because I believe you and I think it is the right thing to do."

Sophia curled her ankles around his leg. "And I am not kissing you because you are helping me. I didn't mean it like that. The two are independent of each other. Though it could be fun to pretend, couldn't it?"

Not that she needed more passion for this encounter. She could already feel herself slick with desire between her legs, and her breasts begged for his touch, and she wanted to mash her face against his endlessly until the lines between their physical beings disappeared. Still, the added fantasy of him demanding this of her, of her offering it up in desperation, nearly made her hips buck against his thigh in excitement.

"Fun?" Mr. Anderson frowned. He released his other hand from behind her head.

"Never mind. I don't mean anything." Sophia forced her lewd thoughts away. She focused on his eyebrows, so thick and long that they reached almost to his side-whiskers. She had made him uncomfortable, and now she needed to make it right so that his brow would smooth and his lips would return to hers. Her instinct was to pull him into a kiss. Except she knew that would freeze him further. She reached for a conversation piece, something that would make him feel close to her. "I like a fantasy every now and then. Don't you?"

Mr. Anderson leaned back so that now he hardly touched her at all. Still, his eyebrows unclenched. Slightly. "What do you mean by fantasy?"

"Oh, you know. Like with the rash. Turning an everyday encounter into something sexual." Sophia cast around for another example. "Or, I like to pretend that the Abbey is still cloistered, and that I am a nun. I took a vow of chastity. I am forbidden to speak. Except I cannot help myself from being overpowered by desire for you."

Her body burned at saying it aloud. At this point, Mr. Anderson need only touch her once–anywhere that her skin was bare–and she would probably jerk into orgasm.

He didn't touch her. But he did look at her, a certain glow to his eyes that Sophia hoped wasn't a mere candlelight effect. "What would you do, then? If you were a nun and you couldn't speak?"

"Well." She had imagined this a hundred ways since her first night in the Abbey. It was her favorite fantasy for seeing to her own body before sleep. She had never quite expected to share this fantasy with anyone.

Sophia rose. If she were a nun, forbidden to speak, the surest way to communicate to the surgeon that she wanted him was with her body. Standing before Mr. Anderson–just far enough away that he couldn't touch her–Sophia unrolled her stockings. Then she pulled off her nightgown. The room was cold, since she didn't have a fireplace, and goosepimples poked her skin.

It was worth it for the look on Mr. Anderson's face. If kissing made her his sole object of attention, this expression–eyes wide, lips parted, hands curled–proved to her she was the sole object of his desire. Sophia cupped her breasts as she knew he wished to do. She trailed her palms around the curves of her waist. On the pretense of folding the stockings and nightgown onto her chair, Sophia turned and bent, presenting him her backside.

She had never yet met a lover who could resist the sight of her great big bottom.

When she turned back, Mr. Anderson almost looked in pain. Except his lips had twitched upwards, into the smallest of smiles.

Oh, how she wanted to mount him right now, this very minute, and ride him so hard that the bed clattered against the wall and the whole household awoke.

"If I were a nun, I would kiss you as if I had never kissed anyone before." Leaning in, she fluttered her lips against his mouth.

He remained frozen, his breath coming in desperate pants.

"And then, if you were amenable, I would..." Sophia couldn't think how to phrase it in a way that would not alarm him. She let her hands do the talking and curled her fingers around the buttons holding up his trousers. "Are you amenable? This nun would like to show you her desire."

Mr. Anderson hesitated. For a terrible moment, Sophia feared he was going to refuse on principle. Then she would have to sort out how she felt about him having principles and following them.

He didn't refuse. He nodded. Cleared his throat. And articulated, "I am amenable."

Sophia undid the six buttons of his trousers. He wore small-clothes underneath. She slid the whole kit down his waist, which was what she had always wanted to do anyway. Now she had him bare: his knees, his thighs, his hips, his buttocks, and most importantly, the stiff and throbbing cock rising between his legs.

She did not know if he worried about the look of it. She always feared how a partner would react to her quim, so she was careful to react appropriately to the cocks that came her way. "Oh, it makes me wet just to see it."

That was the truth. She imagined it filling her all the way to the cap of her canal, pounding her with thrusts that mixed pleasure with pain. It was both long and thick, already slick from his own excitement. Sophia wiped her hand between her own legs, then slid her fist around it. Mr. Anderson gasped, loud enough that Sophia hushed him. "Don't wake Nurse across the hall. Are you sure you are ready for this?"

He nodded. And grabbed the pillow to muffle himself as Sophia took him inside her mouth.

She loved to do this. She loved the feel of his legs against her breasts. His thighs telegraphed his desperation as she tasted him with her tongue from the tip to the base of his cock, and her nipples responded in kind, catching at the hairs on his legs for stimulation. She loved, too, to discover exactly what a new partner liked in this act. She tested swirls, licks, teeth. She listened for his inhales, she felt his cock grow impossibly harder in her own mouth, she felt his thighs stiffen as she brought him closer and closer to completion.

Mr. Anderson lasted a long time. Long enough for her to discover he liked touching her as she did it, his spare hand reaching for her hair, her shoulder, whatever he could grab. At one point, he even curled over her, his palm hooking onto a roll around her waist as she sucked him deeper inside her mouth. The pillow was lost by then, and he whispered, "You are a wicked nun," into her ear. Which was almost enough to send Sophia into her own paroxysm.

When he came, he lifted her by the jaw so that he spilled into the air. The mess landed half on his stomach and half on her quilt. Sophia plucked a handkerchief from the supply in her desk and wiped it all up as best she could. Then she joined Mr. Anderson where he lay stretched across the mattress.

"Does the nun receive no pleasure for herself in this fantasy?" he asked, though his eyes were still closed from the joy of an orgasm.

"Nuns receive pleasure in denying themselves pleasure." Which was true to Sophia's fantasy. But not to her reality. She brought her fingers to her quim. "I do require some release, though."

Rolling onto his side so that his whole body touched hers, Mr. Anderson slid his palm up her thigh until his fingers sat just beyond her wet curls. "You work the clitoris. I shall take the vagina."

At her nod, he plunged inside her. First with one finger, then two, and finally three. Sophia worked her peak, meanwhile, in the indescribable pattern of rubs and flicks and slides that she never was quite able to communicate to a partner. Never had she done manual stimulation in sync with a man before. It was heady, dizzying, bewildering, fulfilling. His finger thrusts were rough and urgent. It felt like fucking. It felt like being pounded. Only at the same time, she teased her most sensitive point into a whirling vortex of pleasure, so that she was liquid and solid all at the same time, limp and turgid, unspooling and pinned into place, until she erupted into a new plane of time and space that was pure carnal joy.

Sophia realized afterward, as she returned to herself, that Mr. Anderson had covered her face with the pillow to muffle her cries.

He did not stay much longer. After all, they had a charade to maintain. He pulled up his smallclothes and trousers in silence. Sophia didn't bother with her nightgown; she wanted to remain in this puddle of pleasure for a while longer. Still, Mr. Anderson turned and pulled the quilt up to her shoulders. He pressed a chaste kiss to her forehead.

"You are suffering a chronic stomachache, Miss Preston, not to mention that rash. You must get plenty of rest. I shall return tomorrow evening for another examination."

"Yes, doctor." As he closed the door, it occurred to Sophia that although they had not done the full act, she felt just as satisfied–if not more–as if they had.

An interesting thought to distract her before she must return to bleak reality.

Chapter Ten

J OHN DIDN'T REGRET IT until he woke in the cold chill of morning. His sleep had been deep, complete, dreamless except for a vague sense of flying as a bird in warm dry air. Then he opened his eyes and discovered it was well past eight, the fire in his hearth was out, and he had gone to sleep in only his smallclothes, so drunk had he been on Miss Preston's body.

He raced from the bed to his armoire. That alone was enough exposure to shock his skin with cold. The Abbey's stone walls were beautiful, historic, and solid, but warm they were not. Nor did his window keep out the worst of the autumn wind, which delighted to find open air after getting caught in the forests surrounding the estate. He piled on clothes, hardly caring about the order, until at last his feet were wrapped in wool stockings, his legs stuffed in trousers, his torso embalmed in shirt and vest and coat.

If only there were some sort of outfit to keep the chill of remorse from freezing the organs of his soul.

It wasn't that he regretted the act itself. In the moment, it had been perfect. Teetering towards overwhelming in the wonderful, delicious way that exploded into orgasm. Even when he pulled her away and spurted into the air like some kind of wanton child, the moment had felt right and natural. And working her into a lather next–never had John felt so powerful.

What changed in the morning was that John realized he still knew so little about Miss Preston. He had allowed her to play him like a fiddle while even now, he did not know why she refused to marry. Or why she distanced herself so ferociously from her family. Or why she would not even share the most basic facts of her life without descending into a tantrum.

Last night, he had tricked himself into thinking those facts didn't matter. What mattered, he had thought, was that she needed his help. She had been soft and vulnerable and holding onto herself like a child in need of a hug. John had allowed himself to get swept up. To believe that desperation equaled some sort of soul bond between them.

He knew well enough that a bond borne out of vulnerability could just as easily be broken when the other person felt safe again. Leaving him holding the fragmented chain, alone and cold.

John didn't want to fall for Miss Preston only to discover that she had never intended an attachment at all. That was too shameful. Too embarrassing.

Too heartbreaking.

The regret chilling his skin felt like a reminder from his body of what happened when he gave his trust too easily. When he mistook Garrett for a cousin, and not a man who happened to share his blood.

Dressed, he hurried downstairs. He had promised Lady Widlake to help with the young ladies in the absence of a governess, yet here he was, showing up later than any prior morning. He found them in the drawing room. Miss Cosgrove practiced the harpsichord while her sisters held hands and danced sedately about the carpet. Lady Widlake stretched on the settee, a wet towel across her forehead.

John wished he had time for a coffee. Some toast wouldn't be out of order, either. However, he had pledged himself to this new duty, and he would see it through. "I apologize for my tardiness."

Lady Widlake peeked out from beneath her towel long enough to exclaim, "Thank goodness you are here, Mr. Anderson."

Miss Francesca danced up to him. "My rash is still gone. See?"

He had been checking on it every morning since applying the paste. She was still all skin-and-bones, pasty, and rather hollow-eyed for a healthy girl, but at least the rash seemed to have been banished.

"Do not go showing gentlemen your rashes without them asking first," Lady Widlake scolded from her seat.

"I am glad you are feeling better. Now, would the young ladies like to assist me in examining their mother?"

Miss Francesca's answer was an enthusiastic yes. Miss Mary nodded with a little more caution. As for Miss Cosgrove, she continued plodding through Haydn, pretending she hadn't even heard the question.

John decided to ring for a maid to bring him coffee after all.

The day disappeared quickly. First, he tended to Lady Widlake with Miss Francesca acting as nurse. His patient suffered from sores in the mouth, a headache, a backache, and constipation, all of which John was sure were made worse by the stress around a felonious governess. He ordered her to bed for the day on a strict diet of clear broth, hot tea, and nothing else.

Then he corralled the young ladies into a semblance of a school day. In his life, John had been in many positions. Kitchen helper, pupil, troublemaker, surgeon, midwife, mender, cleaner, lover, wage earner, even employer. Never had he been in the position to mind children. It was, he discovered, a thankless task.

The twins Harvey and Herbert, sensing the disruption in the household, were at their worst, breaking free of Nurse to race around the house, raid the schoolroom, and throw anything from wadded paper to heavy books at their sisters. Poor Nurse hobbled after them, at one point grabbing them each by their braces and hauling them backwards, but her victories lasted no longer than three quarters of an hour before the little monsters returned for more mischief.

Throughout this chaos, John managed to teach the girls a few basic cures for cuts, had them each read and analyze a Donne poem, and set them to an hour of embroidery. For this last task, he had no clear idea of what they might accomplish, and he suspected Miss

Cosgrove led her sisters in a merry ring around him, but really, he didn't care so long as no outside observer found him wanting.

And there were outside observers. Shaw, Lady Widlake's maid, was assigned to sit in the room as chaperone, though she seemed happy enough for an opportunity to close her eyes. Nurse put in a word of advice each time she popped in to retrieve one of her charges; John didn't see how she expected him to heed her when she couldn't even keep three-year-old boys locked in a room. Lord Widlake popped in around nuncheon, on his return from a morning ride about the estate, and quizzed the girls on their activities.

By the end of the day, John's every limb ached from the effort of putting his best foot forward. He retired to his room for a quiet supper. What he most wanted was to climb into his bed and never leave it again. But he had promised Miss Preston he would help discover who was behind the counterfeit banknotes.

Then the maid Polly arrived with his supper tray—and a letter.

As soon as he saw it, he knew it was from Garrett. His cousin's handwriting—always a little heavy on the ink, smudging letters even on an envelope—obliterated John's appetite.

It was Garrett's reply to John's letter. How confident John had felt after posting it. How proud he was of himself for expressing his dismay at Garrett's treatment of Amma.

John didn't feel any confidence as he opened the letter. And his split pea soup and boiled veal went uneaten as he read:

To my cousin John:

I trust this letter finds you in good health. Your last arrived in time for my daily dinner with Mrs. Anderson, and we read it together, as we are wont to do now that she has graced my house with her incomparable person. It was with shock and shame that I read my own cousin's words to me.

Your Mrs. Ghosh was made welcome first in my father's household and then mine for more years than any good person may consider an obligation. My family extended generosity in money, shelter, and spirit to both her and you out of love for my departed uncle. When Mrs. Anderson reasonably hired more appropriate help for our new household, we offered your Mrs. Ghosh ten pounds to see her through the year and assisted her in seeking a new position by reading postings aloud to her, writing letters of inquiry for her, and ensuring she arrived safely at Captain Attree's residence. I confirmed that Captain Attree was indeed a sea captain for the East India Company these past

*thirty years. From there, I considered my obligation
to my dear departed uncle finished.*

*If you were so greatly worried about your mother's
welfare, I wonder that you did not long ago arrange
for her to hire a letter writer, or take her into your
household altogether.*

*Mrs. Anderson agrees with me that I am overbur-
dened with correspondence, and so I advise you that
after this letter, she will be your correspondent regarding my family. Rest assured that my brother
and sisters are well.*

Cordially,

G. Anderson

If he'd been speaking to John in person, he'd be scrunching his eyebrows in some facsimile of emotion. Making John think he cared. That this was the hardest conversation he would have all year.

When really, what he was saying was this: *You are not my family.*

John didn't reread the letter. He couldn't stand to. Even looking at it stabbed him with guilt.

Garrett was right, of course. If John did care about Amma, he would have started supporting her himself long ago. No matter that he could hardly cover his tailor's bills at the moment. He should be the one caring for his mother. Instead of sending money when he could and visiting even less frequently.

He hid the letter in his desk. At least he had other duties to distract him for the evening. Tucking his medical bag beneath his arm, he set out to discover what he could about counterfeit notes.

He went first to Mrs. Edwards's apartment, which was just down the corridor from his. He had a twofold plan: first, if there was no answer to his knock, he would let himself in and search for evidence of counterfeiting; second, if she answered, he would find a way to ask her about the counterfeiting situation to see if she betrayed herself.

Neither part of the plan was particularly strong, but it was best that John could come up with. After all, he was a surgeon, not a Bow Street runner.

Mrs. Edwards answered his knock. Though it was only seven in the evening, she had already changed into nightclothes. A thick cotton robe covered her body, her feet were swathed in woolen slippers, and her hair had been swallowed by a cap that was a hideous explosion of lace and lavender satin ribbons.

Her hand clutched the robe even closer at the neck. "Mr. Anderson. Is something the matter?"

John should have been used to this by now, but it always took him by surprise how someone who looked healthy and hearty by day seemed so vulnerable–so frail–at their bedside. Deprived of her hairstyle and gowns, Mrs. Edwards looked every day of her fifty-odd years.

He lifted his medical bag as excuse. "Both Lady Widlake and Miss Preston have complained of stomach ailments of late, so I thought I would pay you a visit. Have you been feeling well?"

Her gaze was harsh as it moved from the bag to John and back again. He thought she would deny him this ruse, and then he would have nothing except failure to report to Miss Preston. But then Mrs. Edwards stepped back, admitting him into her room.

"It is good of you to think of me, Mr. Anderson. It seems you are the only one who does. You are the third accoucheur to attend my daughter in these years and the first one to consider whether anyone else in the household feels the stress of the births. As her mother, I am unwell from worry about what she is to go through. You know a well as I do what I mean. It is her seventh confinement. In too few years. Lord Widlake gives her no time to recover. Too obsessed with his legacy, I suppose, without any concern for whether his wife dies in childbed or not. You must instruct him to take more than one month away from her this time. It is dangerous to her health. She must have at least six months to recover, if not a year."

This all said on almost a single breath. Mrs. Edwards retreated deep into the chamber to take a seat by her hearth. Her apartment had more furnishings than his, boasting two fireside chairs, a table with chairs for dining or cards, and a handsome chest in addition to a standing armoire. John sat opposite her by the hearth.

"Lady Widlake is in good health, all things considered," he assured her. "As long as the babe turns itself appropriately before birth, I have every hope of a safe and easy delivery."

"An easy thing to say now. What will you say when my daughter dies of puerperal fever because the child couldn't get its head in the proper position?"

John knew there was no response to this. He hovered his fingers over her stomach. "May I?"

She remained quiet only long enough for him to palpate beneath her ribs. "It is no secret to me that my daughter considers me a burden. I am not an idiot. She is embarrassed by me, always has been. That is my fault, I suppose, for raising her to be a class above me. It was her father's dream, you see, that she would marry into the peerage. And his luck that he was dead before seeing her catch Lord Widlake. Dead in the arms of his mistress, you know. I suppose you do, everyone knows. Though she wasn't his only mistress. At the time of his death, he was keeping two women in London and one in Bath. I pray that my daughter never has heard of it, though I have little hope that is true. Still, she was always naïve. Always anxious to love the men in her life, though they have done little to earn it. So perhaps even if she heard the rumors about her father, she refuses to believe them."

Her heartbeat sped up through this monologue, belying the ease with which she spewed the information.

John wouldn't be emotionless about his spouse's infidelity, either. Still, it was not about bygone woes that he wanted to hear. "It's a terrible business, isn't it, these fraudulent banknotes."

"It doesn't surprise me. The Preston family has always been clear-sighted on matters that the rest of Parliament is too greedy to see. You are likely too young to remember, but when Lord Preston announced he was closing Northfield Hall to goods touched by any form of slavery, the House of Lords nearly arrested him for treason. Creating fraudulent banknotes is an excellent experiment to illustrate the uselessness of paper currency. Although, it is the shopkeeper who loses out, isn't it? No one is going to reimburse the seller for the bad notes. That part is surprising to me. I always thought Baron Ashforth prioritized the common man. I suppose no one is perfect."

John gave up the pretense of checking her stomach. "You believe it was Miss Preston, then, who created the notes? I myself can't think where or when she forged them."

"Oh no, I imagine she utters the money that someone else forges. It must be manufactured at Northfield Hall. All sorts of people live there, you know. Likely Lord Preston recruited some of the fellows with a criminal history to run the operation. It is very clever, though

I imagine he never meant for anyone to be caught with the bad notes. Perhaps he meant for himself to be caught, since they can hardly arrest a peer, can they?"

Distracted as she was with her own thoughts, Mrs. Edwards didn't so much as glance at John as he looked about the room. There was no obvious equipment lying about. But she did have that chest underneath the window, large enough to store three sea trunks at least. If she were behind the counterfeiting, that might be where she hid the evidence.

"It is too bad about Miss Preston, of course. My granddaughters need a steady influence, and I was gratified that Lord Widlake consented to have them molded by the daughter of such an astute family. If only my daughter would let me take up the mantle. You will forgive me for finding it ridiculous that she prefers to have an accoucheur tutor the girls over their own grandmother. They need an education on being a woman, not to be quizzed on useless facts. But it is as I said; my daughter is embarrassed of me. I don't know what I do to deserve it, I must tell you, Mr. Anderson. I am a cheerful person, I can make conversation with anyone, and I offer every member of this household my entire heart. And this is how they treat me!"

She might be going off like this to distract him from the topic of the false banknotes. But John didn't think so. Passionate, radical, and annoying as she might be, he couldn't believe her to be the counterfeiter.

Packing up his kit, John extracted himself from Mrs. Edwards with the excuse that he must check on Lady Widlake once more before she went to sleep. This he did, a quick exercise in changing out her plasters and adjusting the pile of blankets to ensure she stayed at a healthy temperature.

Then, kit in hand, John passed through the family corridor into the service wing. He owed Miss Preston a report. A large part of him wanted to give it to her. Craved, in fact, the attention she would heap upon him with her intense eyes and grateful lips. John was no fool: the idea that he alone stood between Miss Preston and her hopelessness intoxicated him.

Yet his palms sweated as he entered the darkened corridor that housed Miss Preston, Nurse, and the other upper servants. Mrs. Edwards's complaints echoed through his head. Though her feelings of neglect were perhaps out of proportion, they nestled in her breast all the same. He could only imagine how his mother felt, being ejected from his cousin's home now after thirty years of keeping their house. Even Amma, the most cheerful person John had ever known, must be feeling lost. Alone. Exiled.

Regret consumed him again. Regret at how he had treated his mother. Regret at how he had allowed himself to trust Garrett. And regret that he might this very instant be willfully misinterpreting Miss Preston's intentions, too.

When he arrived at her locked door, John hesitated. An intoxicated man must at some point turn away from his drink, no matter how he enjoys its effects. If John were wise, this might be the moment he chose to turn away from Miss Preston. Protect his own heart. No matter the consequences to her.

He considered it. But, even knowing the danger lurking behind it, he opened the door.

———— ✦ ————

WHEN MR. ANDERSON ENTERED the room, Sophia's thoughts were still spinning from her last visitor.

It had been Lord Widlake, spilling into the room as Polly collected the dishes from Sophia's supper. "I bear good tidings," he had boasted, and Sophia's hopes had leapt, expecting to hear the true culprit had been apprehended. "I rode into town today to meet with Mr. Ord and his committee members myself. A good thing I did, too, for I was able to negotiate a favorable outcome for you. The Bank has agreed that, in exchange for a confession of your guilt in uttering false notes, they will grant you clemency for the crime based on the assumption that you were ignorant as to the notes' bad provenance."

"Confess?"

"Yes, and they will grant you clemency. It will be a few days of paperwork, perhaps, but by the end of the week, the whole matter should be sorted. You may resume your duties here, with no need for Lord Preston to intervene." Lord Widlake was close to grinning, so proud was he of finding this solution. But Sophia didn't see how it was a solution at all.

"But I have committed no crime. I did not utter bad notes, knowingly or otherwise."

At last, Lord Widlake noticed her lack of enthusiasm for his plan. "Someone paid Mrs. Chapple with bad notes, and you cannot deny that they were in your reticule."

"They were in my reticule when Mr. Ord searched it. I do deny that they were in my reticule while shopping in Boughampton. I would have noticed if I had a bad note in my hand." Too late, Sophia heard the edge sharpening her words. She cast her gaze down to the ground. "I do not mean to be ungrateful, my lord, yet I cannot in good conscience confess to a crime that I know I did not commit."

She considered saying more. If she explained her theory about Mrs. Edwards, Lord Widlake might be willing to entertain it–or even help investigate it.

He replied before she could decide. "Think on it. I am sure I can delay a day or two before delivering them your confession. If you are willing to concede you may not remember that shopping trip as well as you think you do, then we may all forget this episode ever happened."

It was his certainty that he was correct–that it was her *poor memory* that had landed her in this position–that outraged Sophia most. "Except I would not be able to forget. I would still be considered a criminal, even if I do not have to serve a sentence."

"If they conclude you are guilty without your confession, you will be considered a criminal and find yourself exported to New South Wales. If not worse."

Lord Widlake had locked her in the room with one last admonition to consider the proposal. In the intervening time before Mr. Anderson appeared, Sophia turned it over every which way in her mind.

There were practical reasons to confess. The ones that Lord Widlake had listed. The ones that guaranteed her a future, vague though it might be.

Yet Sophia knew herself to be innocent. She couldn't bring herself to lie about that, to tarnish her own name, just to satisfy the Bank of England that it had caught its criminal.

Mr. Anderson entered looking ready for a London drawing room. Crisp necktie, squared shoulders beneath his pressed coat, tan buckskin trousers that clung to his thighs.

Excitement thudded through her body. The distraction felt good, wiping away the anxiety crusting her thoughts, and she welcomed it.

While the door was still open, he asked, "How fares your stomach today?"

"The same."

"I'm sorry to hear that. I have brought a few more remedies to try." Shutting the door, he locked it, then tucked the key into his jacket pocket.

Protected by privacy, Sophia dropped the façade. She lowered her voice to say, "I rather liked last night's remedy, if you think we should try it again."

But Mr. Anderson did not return her smirk. In fact, he did not even look her in the eye. He moved the chair to the farthest corner of the room–three feet from her mattress–beneath the window. "I have had an eventful day."

She was not to be distracted for long, then. Sophia tucked her hands around her ankles to suppress a sigh. "As have I. The Bank of England has apparently offered me complete clemency if I confess to uttering false notes."

She waited, holding her breath between her lips, to see which side Mr. Anderson would land on. His first reaction was surprise, which swept across his face in a brisk expression of wide eyes and dropped jaw. Then he raised a hand to his cheek, as if to hide emotion. "Will you do it?"

At least he didn't take her participation for granted. "And be branded a criminal for the rest of my life? Lord Widlake said I may keep my position here, but I can't imagine many other employers will offer me opportunities when they discover this in my references."

"Yes, I can see it has its disadvantages." His gaze left her for a moment, growing dark and hazy. "Still, I didn't know the Bank could be so accommodating."

Sophia didn't need him to remind her that she was lucky to even have this opportunity. She could already hear it in a chorus of her family's voices: *Anyone else would already be condemned to the gallows, innocent or not.*

But it wasn't anyone else accused of this crime. It was Sophia, and these were the circumstances afforded her, and she would make her own calculations about what was best for her.

She needed distraction again. "Tell me about your eventful day."

Mr. Anderson cleared his throat. "I spoke with Mrs. Edwards."

"What said the blackguard?"

He played with the handles on his black leather surgeon's bag as he responded. "She had much to say, but none of it indicated to me that she bears guilt in this matter. In fact, she believes your father to be operating the counterfeit scheme and that you pass the notes into the market on his behalf." His gaze flicked up to meet hers. "Could there be any truth in her theory about your father?"

"Of course not." The denial came swiftly and automatically from her mouth. But this was the second time someone had thrust the possibility before her. And this time, she wasn't reeling from the shock of discovery. This time, she had spent a whole day ruminating on nothing but the question of fraudulent banknotes.

Papa believed in a better world. He believed in treating all people—men and women—fairly. He also believed in taking whatever actions were necessary to live life according to his own rigid principles.

If he were behind this, it wouldn't be the first time he had bent the rules of society to meet his needs. It wouldn't even be the first time he adjusted his own logic, since there had been the whole fracas with Berkshire linen not three years ago that had thrown Ellen and Max together.

But if Papa wanted to make a point about paper money, he would rail against it in the papers and at the House of Lords. At most, he might abolish currency within the realm of Northfield Hall.

He wouldn't risk anyone's life over it.

"Then I am not sure what to think. Mrs. Edwards didn't have any printing paraphernalia in her room that I could see, nor can I think when or how she would create the notes, any more than you could do so." Straightening in his chair, Mr. Anderson pressed his lips into a thin line before saying, "Perhaps you would be better off accepting clemency after all."

Sophia had been cooped up for too long for grace. "So you are here to say that you have fallen in line with Lord Widlake and Mr. Ord in believing me guilty, is that it? Especially since you know that I did indeed purchase contraception, and you know exactly how I was planning to use it. You have decided to conclude I am a lying slut, have you? You will leave me to face my fate without guilt because you tried your best to clear my name? Or is it because you had your fill of me last night that you are ready to desert me? Too bad you aren't man enough to fuck me properly, otherwise I might keep your attention at least one more day."

Her anger carried her on a wave long enough to enjoy watching the man flinch at her words. She relished how he ducked his chin. How he didn't dare look at her, not when she skewered him with what must be the truth.

But her righteousness evaporated with the last of her words. Once expressed, her fury deserted her. And she was left with nothing but her terrible accusations ringing in the air.

Oh, she had done it again. Let her tongue have its way and wrecked any hope of kindness. Mr. Anderson rose, as well he should. If she were him, she would flee, too.

Tears stung her eyes. Flooded them, more like, and her nose filled with pressure, and all of a sudden she was crying. He would think her a manipulative female. She was sometimes a manipulative female, but not now. This was a storm she couldn't help any more than she could have stopped herself from saying those awful things. Sophia slapped her hands to her face, as if that could hide it all. As if that could plug the dyke.

Let him leave. Let him desert her to her own meager devices. In his place, Sophia wouldn't stay to help a person who was such a wretch to her.

He owed her nothing. Therefore, Sophia would survive without him.

Except Mr. Anderson didn't unlock the door. He sat beside her, a sudden weight that made the ropes holding her mattress dip. He wrapped an arm around her shoulders. A loose embrace that asked for nothing, the kind of comfort her brothers Benny or Nate might offer. And he said, "Miss Preston, I am not that kind of man."

JOHN HADN'T MEANT TO sit on the bed. His plan had been to share the information he had gathered, collect new instructions, and be on his way. No physical touch involved whatsoever.

Yet she was in distress. And John was trained to aid people when they were in distress, no matter who they were or where their pain originated. If her foot bled, he would wrap it with a bandage. If her arm broke, he would set the bone in place. If a fever raged, he would cool her with every remedy he knew.

If he would do it for a stranger on the road, then it was natural that when Miss Preston wept, John held her in his arms.

Miss Preston was no frail and wilting flower, even now as her shoulders bucked with her hiccupping diaphragm. John's arm nearly couldn't span her frame. That felt natural, too, for she was a woman of far more personality and depth than he could ever hope to capture. He anchored his palm on the curve of her upper arm. The touch—more intimate than anything that would ever pass between him and a patient—did not spark dizzying waves of desire. Yet it upended the reserve to which he had hoped to cling for this interview.

He had meant to remove himself from her influence. He would help her as much as he could, but at a distance. Without the confusing addition of physical touch and personal confidences. That way, he would protect himself from feeling discarded when she no longer needed him.

And if there was anything he heard in that vicious speech of hers, it was that she intended to break with him as soon as he outlived his usefulness.

Yet here he was, holding her. Touching her. Comforting her.

"Anyone would be overwrought under such circumstances," he murmured. "I didn't mean to upset you. I know you aren't involved in this scheme. I will do everything I can to help you."

He reminded himself that he knew next to nothing about her, except the things that would break her away from him. She kept an independent mind. She fostered a fierce spirit. She indulged herself, in thoughts, in material goods, in sexual pleasure.

He should see those traits for what they were: warnings. Instead, John was intoxicated by them.

Eventually, she had let loose all the tears in her body. Her shoulders shrank into a stiff board. She removed a handkerchief from her bodice, blew her nose, and said, "How mortifying. I never lose control of myself like that."

His hand fell with her movements down to her elbow, which felt awkward, so he removed it entirely. Only it felt strange resting on his own knee, too. "We like to pretend we have control of our bodies, when really, I find, our bodies control us. Often for the better. After all, if our bodies didn't know to run a fever, how would we fight off illness?"

"I should like to have more control over my body, then. Sometimes I even feel that I am leashed by my own lust, rather than deciding with my own independence to be a lustful woman." A glob of mucus drooped from her nostril. She caught it just before it descended and blew her nose even more ferociously. "You shouldn't watch me. I am disgusting."

"I am an accoucheur, Miss Preston. It takes much more than nasal discharge to disgust me." In fact, her nose fascinated him, now that he looked at it closely, for it was almost a perfect forty-five-degree angle from her forehead, with a gentle curve at the end that was currently rubbed red.

He resisted the urge to chart his fingertip down its length.

Oh yes, he was in this woman's thrall. And it felt as awkward to call her by her formal name as it did to keep his hands to himself. He couldn't keep down the impulse to ask, "May I call you Sophia?"

Under the pretense of fetching a new handkerchief from her desk, she left him. Where her body had brushed against his was now frigid air. She remained on the other side of the room–though he could clasp her skirts in his fingers, if he stretched out his arms–and dotted the new handkerchief against her cheeks as if to wipe up tears. "I suppose so."

"And you will do me the same favor in return?"

He shouldn't have pressed. The victory felt hollow. It got worse, though, when she said, "I don't know your Christian name."

That was natural, he supposed. Whereas she was the daughter of a peer, listed in Debrett's and probably countless newspapers, John was a nobody. No one in the household would have used his first name, so when would she have come across it?

Except John didn't read the peerage books, nor did he follow the gossip columns in the newspapers. He knew her name was Sophia the way he knew she smelled of pears and disliked personal confessions and preferred coffee to tea in the morning: because all along, he had been so intrigued by her that every fact he could collect stuck in his mind like iron to a magnet.

Apparently, she didn't feel the same way about him.

"John," he supplied, though disappointment constricted his throat.

"John? Haven't you any nicknames that are more distinctive?"

"Why should I need to be more distinctive?"

"John Anderson has to be one of the most common names in England. Wouldn't you rather be known as something memorable like…I don't know…Rook, or Devil, or Duke?"

It felt like an argument. Her cheeks had turned pink, and her hands flew through the air emphatically, handkerchief waving like a red flag to a bull.

John had disappointed women before. He had rejected advances, put pause to physical encounters, and even once earned the ire of a widow named Jenny for declining her invitation to stay for Sunday roast. But this was the first time he had disappointed a woman by having the wrong name.

"I would prefer to be memorable for my actions rather than my name."

She deflated. "I'm sorry. I am not myself." With a sigh, she turned her back to him and fingered the detritus covering her table. John considered what he might say in response. His heart hammered too fast to sort through his thoughts. He waited long enough that she flipped open one of her enamel boxes, removed a tobacco pipe, filled it, and lit it with her taper. She returned to her seat beside him on the mattress. "Would you like to smoke, John?"

He accepted, though the offer startled him. Tobacco was one of the imports Lord Preston railed against in newspapers, Parliamentary speeches, and any other forum he could find. He wondered if she enjoyed it for its own purposes, or if she only smoked as a rebellion against her father.

Her blend was deep yet delicate, with a hint of the same bergamot orange that sometimes flavored tea. John recognized the taste from their kisses, so much so that his body reacted almost as if he were kissing her right then.

"So, John–" she leaned into the name again, drawing out the vowel and letting the *n* sing between her teeth "—what do we do next?"

The tobacco calmed his nerves but not enough to make him forget the tension of the argument. On an exhale, he handed back the pipe. "We must both get some rest. In the morning, perhaps the situation will be clearer. I shall think on who else might have the opportunity to produce the false banknotes. More and more, I believe it is someone outside the household." For good measure, he added, "Either way, you mustn't accept the Bank's offer unless it is what you believe is best for you."

John rose, almost expecting her to grab his hand and pull him back into her. But she nodded. "Thank you." Watching him, she sucked at the pipe, then blew out a ring of smoke towards the window. She waited until his hand was on the knob to say, "John, could you leave the door unlocked?"

He paused. He wasn't sure why he didn't immediately agree.

"I promise not to run off from the Abbey. I only want to stretch my legs. See walls that aren't these four. I'll be back in bed by morning like a good girl."

She blinked up at him, the picture of innocence. If innocence included a tobacco pipe, a crumpled dress, and teeth catching at her lower lip.

John could have lost his wits over any woman in the world. He didn't know why it had to be this one. He only knew that it was, no matter that even now, she used his name as a weapon to get her own way.

"Of course." Unlocking the door, he handed her the key. "I'll see you tomorrow."

There was no other answer for him to give Sophia. But as John took himself off into the night, he knew there were two ways this love affair could end: either he would earn her heart in return, or she would use him so badly that he ended up hating her.

He supposed it was up to her to determine their fate.

Chapter Eleven

Since confessing wasn't an option, Sophia resolved to find the culprit herself, even confined to her chamber as she was. If the nuns of yore could find God with nothing but their prayers, Sophia could suss out a common criminal with her wits.

She spent the following day at her window. Narrow as it was–and warped as the glass was in its lead strictures–it afforded a new view of Robin Abbey. From the schoolroom, her observations had always been inwards onto the courtyard. She had watched the kitchen maid Beula fetching water from the well, the groom Mr. Emery delivering Lord Widlake's horse for morning rides, and the Gibson brothers hauling this thing or that from delivery carts. Occasionally, Polly or Hattie or even Lady Widlake's maid Shaw scurried along the path beneath the cloisters on their way to a chore.

Her bedroom window afforded a different view entirely. It looked outwards to the narrow fields surrounding the Abbey, the forest stretching beyond, and the dirt road leading to the turnpike. A boring sliver, Sophia had thought when she first toured the room, but now that she had nothing to do but sit and watch, she discovered there was a fair amount to learn about Robin Abbey from this perch. Three tradesmen arrived at the Abbey that first morning, though two of them turned off towards Mr. Prewett's gardening cottage before reaching the household itself. Mr. Prewett himself crossed her view five times, his cart loaded with shovels and hoes and such, his horse moving more slowly with each sighting. And–most interesting of all–Mrs. Edwards rode a mare down the road. Un-accompanied. In a dark riding cloak that almost prevented Sophia from recognizing her.

But Sophia knew those self-righteous shoulders from even half a mile away.

"It is suspicious, don't you think?" she demanded of John that night, when he visited under the guise of delivering another stomach potion.

He hadn't yet sat down, not even though she had been spewing each instance of her observations at him for at least five minutes. Sophia wanted to grab him around the waist and toss him onto the bed for a good ravishing.

"Is it suspicious for a gentlewoman to go riding on her family estate?" John replied, though he managed to make the question sound like a statement. One that did not agree with Sophia.

"Why not use the riding paths through the woods, as Lord Wid-lake does? The road goes to the turnpike, and that is not a usual place for someone to go on a casual ride." Sophia was quite confident about this, although riding had never been a frequent pastime for anyone in her circle. In her family, they all busied themselves with far more important occupations than frolicking about on a horse for an entire afternoon. And as for her town acquaintances, a sedate saunter through Hyde Park to catch up on gossip seemed the main objective.

John pressed his lips into a thin line.

"Oh, fine, it is not enough to prove anything," Sophia admitted, "but I maintain that Mrs. Edwards is the one who put those notes in my purse, and this convinces me more. There is still the question of our midnight visitor in the bell tower, for which you have no other theory. Now, tell me what you have discovered today, or kiss me. Either will soothe my nerves."

She meant it as a tease. It came out more imperious than flirtatious, however, and she wished she could take it back, especially when John chose the former option. "I had a word with the valet Brooks, who I am afraid is quite satisfied to consider you the guilty party."

Sophia refused to feel the despair that knocked at her heart with that news. "Then tomorrow, you must suggest to Shaw that she is ill. Mrs. Hibbert, too. If anyone knows what is happening in this household, it will be the housekeeper."

John crossed the room. Not to get closer to Sophia, as she first hoped, but to go all the way over to the window. The night was dark and her room lit by a candle, so he wouldn't be able to see anything but their reflections. He looked at it anyhow. "At the risk of upsetting you, I have been thinking about that bargain the Bank offered you, and I wonder if it isn't better for everyone if you did accept it. Even though you didn't utter those notes. They're not likely to offer clemency to the person who actually did the counterfeiting."

It was only because he had already helped her so much that Sophia managed to respond with patience. "Why should I do that? I did nothing wrong. The guilty party should be the one to pay the consequences. That is the point of justice."

He turned from the window. His eyes were dark, glowing obsidian. "Justice isn't always fair. Do you want to reveal the culprit to be Mrs. Edwards, only to attend her execution?"

She pulled her wrapper against her skin. She burrowed under blankets, too. His words chilled her more thoroughly than the autumn night.

They were exactly the sentiment her father would express. *Sacrifice yourself in the name of balancing fortune's scales.*

She didn't want to hear that sort of thing from John. Even more, she didn't want to feel her heart unlock–just the littlest bit–to know he had the capacity for that kind of empathy.

She hadn't known she would find that attractive.

"Perhaps she should have considered the consequences before breaking the law. I can't account for the penalty being harsh. I can only account for my own actions, and I swear I did not utter any bad notes. Not a single one. I would answer for it if they charged me with fornication. But not this."

John softened. He moved close enough that she could see the candlelight reflecting off brown irises. Instinct told her to reach for his hand: feeling the heat of his skin settled her nerves. So did the relief when his fingers curled around hers.

"Lord Widlake negotiated this deal in the first place," Sophia said to prove she was not unfeeling. "Mrs. Edwards will not be hanged."

"No."

"Exiled to New South Wales, perhaps, but I'm not sure anyone would complain."

They remained in silence for a moment, Sophia on the bed, John standing before her, hand in hand. She longed for him to fall beside her. If his fingers alone soothed her, a kiss would obliterate the feelings pressing against her at all sides.

But he held himself apart. He had his own rules and rhythm to follow. Sophia was determined to honor that. So she did not ask for a kiss. She did not tip her head back or bite her lips or pull any of the other dozen tricks to distract him into a physical encounter.

She waited. And soon enough, he said, "Today I was thwarted, but tomorrow is a new day. I hope I return with better news."

"I would be lost without you."

He bowed, pressing a kiss to the back of her hand. Chaste as it was, it sent a thrill directly to the coil of her quim. But it was all he gave her. The next moment, he was gone, the key loose in the door.

His admonition rang in her head the rest of that week. Rain shrouded the Abbey and its grounds beginning the next morning, limiting visibility from Sophia's window and preventing Mrs. Edwards from taking any more furtive rides. Sophia decided to focus instead on gathering information from the few souls still within reach: Polly and Hattie, who alternately delivered her meals.

"How do you find Mrs. Edwards?" Sophia asked Polly as she collected the remains of the porridge and tea delivered as breakfast. "Is she in her usual boisterous mood of late?"

"I couldn't say, miss," was the reply. "I stay out of Mrs. Edwards's way as much as I can." Yet Polly hesitated at the door. "I was that sorry to hear of your troubles, Miss Preston. I was hoping...well, I suppose I was hoping you might give up the governessing and take me as your lady's maid back to London. Foolish, I'm sure. Anyhow, I wanted to say I am sorry."

"Lady's maid?" Sophia made a point of being familiar with the servants, and she and Polly had from the start shared a few bawdy jokes that endeared the maid to her. Still, she had never known Polly had pinned her own hopes for a future on Sophia.

And what a joke that was, when Sophia herself couldn't manage to decide what to do with her future. Though she didn't have much of a future to plan for now.

"Oh, I've been learning everything I can from Shaw, only she is rather prickly, isn't she? Still, I know how to remove a stain from silk, cotton, and linen, and I've subscribed to a lady's magazine that explains how to do all the latest hair styles. I was going to offer to show you, only..." Color flushed her cheeks. A few years younger than Sophia, Polly was the kind of blonde whose hair was almost white and whose skin burned under slightest contact with the sun. Her blush couldn't hide from a mile away.

Sophia hated for her to feel bad. She didn't mind aspirations, even if she doubted the wisdom of Polly planning anything around her. "Perhaps when this is all over. I didn't utter those notes, you know. Someone put them in my purse so that I would be blamed. Once I discover who that is, this whole matter will be cleared up, and perhaps I will need a lady's maid."

John's warning blared through her head even as she said this. The matter would be cleared up—for her. For Mrs. Edwards or Brooks or whoever it was that had actually done this, the chaos would just begin.

"Oh, do you really think?" Polly exclaimed in a rush. Her blush, rather than disappearing with relief, deepened. Balancing the food tray on one arm, she crossed to the armoire, whose door hadn't quite closed when Sophia last shoved a dress inside. "You'll want me to do some laundry, then, won't you. I can fix these dresses up nice for you so that when this is all over, you'll feel you have something new to wear."

Her own dress needed a little tending, as it was streaked down the sleeves with black stains, but Sophia bit back any criticism. The girl might help her, so long as Sophia remained friendly. "That would be too kind. Mind you get the rest of your work done first, though. I don't want you losing your position over me."

"I'll be careful."

"Oh, and Polly, if you learn anything about Mrs. Edwards, you'll let me know, won't you? I have a very strong suspicion she is the one who placed the bad notes in my purse."

"Of course, miss." Polly finally bobbed a farewell curtsy, her cheeks and forehead still a bright red.

Hattie was the one who came with Sophia's supper, a simple broth and bread served close to four o'clock. She was younger than Polly, no more than five feet tall, and incapable of bearing any expression on her face. Happy, angry, sad, she always looked the same: bored. Sophia asked her anyway, "Have you observed Mrs. Edwards coming and going at odd times at all these past few weeks?"

"Can't say as I have, miss."

"I noticed her riding out towards the turnpike yesterday," Sophia pressed on. "I wonder if she travels on her own off the Abbey grounds often, and if so, where she goes. I am not aware of her cultivating any relationships in the neighborhood."

"I'm sure I wouldn't know. My aunt–Mrs. Hibbert, I mean–told me not to mind anyone's business but my own."

Sophia hadn't realized that Hattie was related to the housekeeper. "Mrs. Hibbert is your aunt?"

"My father's sister. Frank and Jasper are my cousins by another of his sisters, Nancy. There are ten of them, in all, my aunts and uncles. We are a large family, and we do love each other, but it is a lot of mouths to feed, as my father always says."

"How wonderful that so many of you can work at Robin Abbey, then."

"Especially Frank and Jasper, now that Uncle George is gone. His shop was in debt, it turns out, and I'm not sure Aunt Nancy could feed the children if not for Frank and Jasper's positions here."

"Indeed." Sophia tried to think how to direct the conversation back to the question of banknotes. "Do you never clean Mrs. Edwards's room, then?"

"Of course, I do. Me and Polly together."

"And you haven't noticed paper and ink lying about?"

Hattie paused. Another person's expression in that moment would have told Sophia if they were thinking, worried, or curious. Hattie merely looked as if she had frozen with her lips partly open.

"Only paper and ink I can think of are the ones she uses for her letter writing," Hattie replied at last. "She posts a mighty number of them to that Mr. Corbett of the paper. Beula and I think she must be hankering to marry him, though he never writes back. But like I said, my aunt–Mrs. Hibbert, I mean–told me not to mind anyone's business but my own, so I'd better not say anything else."

Sophia let the girl go. It was an interesting point, and she said as much to John when he came by that evening. "Mr. Corbett has railed against paper currency from the first, you know. I wonder if he might be involved somehow."

"Now you think he actually engages with Mrs. Edwards as a correspondent?"

Incredulity stilted his words. Sophia defended herself, "He might be the conductor of the campaign, and Mrs. Edwards his agent. If he told her to utter bad notes in the name of politics, I have no doubt she would champ at the bit to do it. She quotes the man every day, doesn't she?"

John acknowledged this point with a lift of his shoulder. His visit was earlier than ever, just after the family finished their supper, which Sophia couldn't help but suspect was on purpose. With the household still awake, he couldn't stay longer than a few minutes without attracting attention.

She didn't know why he would want to avoid a lingering visit.

Before she could ask, John seized the conversation. "It could be. However, I learned more about Lord Widlake's campaign today. He needs to get Mr. Fenton elected over in Brackley to solidify Whig support for a bill he has proposed to establish a minimum wage for weavers. Essentially, he is buying Mr. Fenton's vote on the matter by paying for his election campaign. Only, he hasn't provided the funds he promised. I found a letter on his desk from Mr. Fenton threatening to switch allegiances to Lord Althorp if Lord Widlake doesn't send the two hundred pounds by the end of this month."

Sophia turned this information over in her mind. "You are suggesting that Lord Widlake decided to counterfeit the money in order to secure Mr. Fenton's loyalty. And when Mr. Ord came calling, Lord Widlake arranged for the bad notes to appear in my purse instead of his own."

From the other side of the room, John shrugged again. "It is as possible as your theory that Mrs. Edwards is working under Mr. Corbett's instruction."

"If it is Lord Widlake, then you have no qualms about proving it, do you? He is a peer of the realm. Only Parliament can hold him accountable, which they might, but it is not as if he will be executed like a common criminal."

"Yes. If it is Lord Widlake, I find I am very eager to expose him as the rogue too cowardly to face his own actions."

He leaned against the armoire as he said this. He wore his dinner suit, which cut around his arms in just the right angle to show off the slender muscles beneath. Sophia discovered a new fantasy in that moment: that she and John worked together to solve a puzzle, only to get so distracted as to pull off each other's clothes and fuck against the armoire. It was the feeling that he was on her side, that the two of them alone fought against the entire world, that made her want to take him deep inside her and never let go.

She aimed a smirk his way. "You read Lord Widlake's private correspondence, did you?"

John did not smirk back. "I have crossed many lines for you, Sophia."

Sophia could hear there were words he did not say. *And I will cross no more.* Or, *And I will keep crossing them until this matter is solved.* Or, *And I find I like it more each time.*

He didn't share with the thought with her. Instead, he changed the subject. "Is there any news from your family?"

It had only been a few days. Her letters were likely only reaching Northfield Hall now. Still, her note to Papa in London should already have arrived. "Not yet."

"I am waiting on letters from my mother and the monthly nurse, too. Perhaps the whole post got stuck in the mud."

She didn't appreciate how he rushed to say it, as if he thought her embarrassed that her family hadn't yet responded. They were miles away from here. They weren't forsaking her to reap the consequences alone, no matter how brash they might consider her choices.

Of this, Sophia was almost completely confident.

"I suppose you had better go before anyone asks what we are discussing," she said.

John hesitated a moment. "Yes, I suppose so."

It was the next day that the twins decided to target Sophia's door for their mischief. From her perch at the window–watching rain come down in sheets and turn the road into a slick, muddy mess–she could only guess at what they did to make such terrible crashes and thuds against her door. Since the commotion was accompanied by the gleeful shrieks of three-year-old boys, she concluded it was nothing more threatening than the Masters Cosgrove.

By the time Nurse caught up with them–"Naughty boys, the both of you, even if it was you, Harvey, who thought of it and Herbert was only following along!"–Sophia decided to play the distraught maiden.

"Oh Nurse, is that you? Whatever is going on? I feared a madman was on the loose!"

"Look at the mess you made, and disturbing Miss Preston, too! Bed without supper tonight, do you hear me?" Then Nurse cooperatively turned the lock. "Some of it has gotten under your door, Miss Preston. Do stay calm."

Sophia backed away to allow the door to open inwards. Braced as she was, she still wasn't ready for the sight of the corridor: broken glass everywhere, black ink staining the carpet and pooling in rivulets along the uneven stone floor. The twins boasted ink on their hands, faces, clothes, and even hair. Sophia could tell them apart only by their expressions: Harvey grinned at the chaos, while Herbert's mouth screwed up in preparation for a repentant sob.

"Gotten into Father's ink supply again, haven't you?" Nurse said to the boys. "Miss Preston, you don't by any chance have a towel, do you?"

Sophia fetched the towel she used for washing and also the catch-all wool cloths she kept on hand.

"They've done this before with Lord Widlake's ink?" she asked as she knelt to help Nurse mop up the mess.

"He keeps it in the lowest drawer of his desk. Harvey found it a few weeks ago, and now this is the third mess they've made. Though I have to say this is the most ink I've ever seen. You must have taken all his bottles. Is that what you did, you spawn of the devil?"

Harvey smirked. Lip trembling, Herbert clarified: "We took Grandmama's, too. We found it in her bag. The one under her bed."

Sophia tucked away the idea that Mrs. Edwards had a supply of ink hidden beneath her bed to explore later with John. Nurse continued chastising the boys: "That's stealing. Do you know what happens when you steal? You go straight to Hell. Do you want to go to Hell?"

"Yes!" Harvey declared.

"You've got your hands full, haven't you?" Sophia said in commiseration to Nurse. She meant it, too. If governessing was dreary and thankless, poor Nurse lived an existence that must be penance for a crime in some past life. Between the twins and baby Jacob, she could hardly get a single moment's peace.

"I count my blessings is what I do, miss. Could always be worse. I'm grateful to work for so fine a family, to be sure. There is none better than Lord Widlake. What he has done to remove the man-traps from the county saves lives, that I can tell you. And once he and Mr. Fenton win this election, he'll take care of the weavers, too. What I do is small compared to his work, and if it makes him sleep easy at night knowing his sons are in good care, then I can only flatter myself than I am contributing to good works, too."

"Still, you could use a hand. Two nurses wouldn't be amiss given there is another baby on the way, too."

"So long as Mr. Anderson delivers it healthy and blessed."

As if John alone controlled the outcome of a birth.

"To be sure, we all could use a little more help around the Abbey. Not enough maids, not enough footmen, not enough..." Nurse slid her gaze up from a puddle of ink to Sophia and let the words trail off. "Anyhow, the Gibsons might send a few more our way. They're on hard times, and Frank and Jasper have proved themselves well enough, haven't they. I hear there's a sister, but I wouldn't trust some unproven chit with the children. She could help Beula in the kitchen, perhaps. Of course, Cook has her two that she wants to bring on the property, doesn't she? Living in town with her sister now, which makes more sense to me, but who am I to have an opinion? I only raised five of my own children."

Sophia cut in before Nurse could prattle farther into the depths of gossip. "Where does Lord Widlake get his ink? Will he have to purchase more in town?"

"Cook whips it up, doesn't she? He has his particular recipe, and Mrs. Edwards has a different recipe, and between everyone, Cook spends more time making ink than food, if you ask me."

They had manufactured their own ink at Northfield Hall, of course, but ever since her Aunt Charlotte invited Sophia to London, she had taken great pride in buying ink from stationery shops. When she was particularly angry with her family, she bought inks made entirely of imported ingredients to write her letters home.

She wondered if Lord Widlake had ordered more ink made than usual recently.

"There, that's the worst of it, though this carpet will have to be replaced." Nurse declared them done, though Sophia still saw trails of ink in the mortar crevices of a few of the stones. She wiped those down, then added her rag to the pile Nurse had amassed. The other woman had already moved on, corralling the Masters Cosgrove toward their nursery.

Sophia almost didn't call her back. Except she knew she had to keep up the appearance of cooperation. "You'll have to lock my door again, Nurse."

Nurse smiled. "Of course, Miss Preston."

When the lock clicked behind her, Sophia discovered the ink had stained her sleeves and hem. She pulled off her gown, setting it aside for Polly to have a go at, and tried to make sense of everything she had learned so far. Lord Widlake and Mrs. Edwards both procured their ink from Cook; Lord Widlake needed money to win his campaign; Mrs. Edwards kept a bag of ink under her bed.

She wished she could make it all line up and point to a specific person as the clear counterfeiter. She wished she knew what John would think when she shared her discoveries with him.

Most of all, she wished she knew if John would even come visit her that night.

J OHN DECIDED TO TRY something new that night: stay away from Sophia.

It wasn't that he didn't want to see her. Every fiber of his being wanted to see her at every moment of the day.

Except for the moments when he actually saw her.

The toll of her purgatory was more visible every day. Dark circles beneath her eyes. Gouges around her fingernails from anxious picking. Even her clothes began to hang loose around her, though it had only been a handful of days.

Every symptom he saw on her body vibrated through his own. He couldn't eat, either, though he forced himself to swallow food no matter how ashen it tasted on his tongue. He couldn't sleep. He stalked Robin Abbey with his nerves in a constant staccato, plucking at him when he was seeing to Lady Widlake and when he was directing Mrs. Hibbert in setting up the birthing chamber and when he was in his own room puzzling over how to care for his mother.

No matter what he did, he was sure it was wrong. He expected each action to bare his true, ugly soul to the whole Cosgrove household: that he was so immoral a man as to dally with the governess, and that he was so selfish a man to leave his mother to destitution.

That he was, in short, a man just like his father.

Seeing Sophia didn't help. He looked forward to his visits every day, as if they were a balm to soothe his angst. But she was always shrunken on that bed, arms hugging her own knees. It consumed John with guilt that he couldn't do anything more for her. Anger, too, because even though she was going through the worst days of her life, he wanted her to see him there. To pause and ask him how he fared. To give him hope that he was not throwing his heart after someone who didn't even know how to catch it.

She never did. And when he tried to assert himself—to tell her that he worried because he still waited to hear from the monthly nurse in anticipation of Lady Widlake's great event and from his mother in Captain Attree's household—Sophia had batted his comment away.

Leaving him ignored and unvalued, and above all petty and selfish for feeling that way.

So that night, John decided to break the cycle. Instead of visiting her room to tell her the servants knew nothing, that he still didn't think Mrs. Edwards was the guilty party, that he had no new ideas, he decided to do something more:

He went in search of the mysterious sounds from the bell tower.

He waited for midnight. Then, with a lantern from the front entrance in hand, he snuck down the stairs, out onto the frigid cloistered path around the courtyard, and into the bell tower.

The door scraped against the floor as it had that night he met Sophia. John ducked inside and waited, counting to one hundred before moving another muscle. But no one came rushing from quarters unknown to investigate.

He fumbled with his flint, struck a flame, and lit the lantern. Then he lifted it to examine the bell tower's ground floor more thoroughly.

The square bell tower had been added to Robin Abbey after its initial construction. Its sole entrance came from the courtyard, though it butted directly against the service wing of the Abbey. John paced from one end to the other to measure its footprint: a full fifteen strides. Yet just like that first night, the ground floor was empty, save for the stairs leading up into the belfry.

John tried to remember the details of that night. They had heard the door scrape open. Then, there had been another thud, followed by the sounds of some kind of machine. The mystery interloper had definitely been inside the bell tower. Yet when John had come investigating, there had been no trace of them. And still, he saw no evidence at all.

He lowered the lantern. The light flooded the stone floor slabs, worn and uneven in age. Then it glinted off something else: an iron handle atop a trap door behind the stairs.

Excitement leapt in his stomach. John knelt to examine the discovery. A rectangular wooden door, not much wider than his shoulders, kept shut with a latch through the iron handle. He unhooked the latch, then pulled open the door. It landed with a resounding crash on the stone floor.

Beneath, John could see nothing but a dark hole. Even thrusting the lantern downwards, he made out a dirt floor some feet below and nothing else. John fumbled around to discover a rope ladder hanging just beneath his knees.

Descending into the abyss, knowing it could be a criminal den, without anyone to aid him was a dangerous proposition. But John wasn't about to close the trap door and go to bed.

This was his chance to put an end to this matter. To discover the true criminal, free Sophia, and find out what came next.

With the lantern in one hand, John managed his way down the ladder.

The cellar he landed in was no larger than the bell tower itself. The walls were dirt, the same as the floor. But John wasn't interested in the composition of the room. His attention fixed immediately on the machine occupying the bulk of the cellar: a looming, gleaming printing press.

Chapter Twelve

The letter arrived by a special messenger who rode all the way from London stopping only to change horses, and Lord Widlake himself brought it to Sophia in her room. It was late enough that she thought he was John, unlocking the door for an evening visit. Lucky for both of them that she was feeling too down in the mouth to whip off her gown and greet him naked.

"From your father," Lord Widlake said, while Sophia recovered from the surprise of seeing his sandy head instead of John's sleek hair. "Advice for how to manage a situation such as this, I imagine."

At last, word from someone in her family. Sophia rose to accept the letter, then rested against her desk to examine it. She paused, thinking Lord Widlake would leave her in privacy.

He did not. He waited in the threshold. One hand knocked against the stone wall as if to count the seconds marching by.

If she weren't at the mercy of his influence to keep her from prison, Sophia would have stared him down, one eyebrow raised, until he cowered under the awkwardness and disappeared back into the tomb that was Robin Abbey.

Unfortunately, Sophia needed his cooperation to remain in her room. Still, she noted his interest and the little beads of sweat gathering along his ruddy hairline. True, he might only be anxious to hear what her influential father had to say about her situation.

Or Lord Widlake might be waiting for a hint as to whether his scheme to frame her family for counterfeiting would be successful.

Steeling herself, Sophia turned her attention to the envelope. Papa's letters were usually untidy, with scrawls of ink climbing across the front and back of the envelope folds. It wasn't that they couldn't afford the extra paper, nor did he have to pay postage as a member of Parliament; Sophia sometimes thought he did it because he hated wastefulness and other times because he wanted to prove he was no different than the common man.

This letter blinded her with the glare of its bare white envelope. Too, it was a mere single page folded into itself.

She knew he had been writing in response to an emergency. Still, she would have hoped this emergency merited more than a few hasty lines. She broke the seal to see what her father had to say.

My dear daughter Sophia,

I enclose this letter in a packet that includes another message for Lord Widlake, whom I know to be a kind and reasonable man. It is with that knowledge that I trust you are being well treated despite these accusations and that the matter will soon be a distant memory.

I am sorry you have been swept away by our family's reputation. As a whole, I am very proud that the Preston family name is known throughout Britain for courage, kindness, and a willingness to challenge the status quo in the name of a better future. In matters such as this, I begrudge the human nature which twists our intentions into a braid with any nefarious motive. A scheme such as counterfeiting notes only injures all participants in the economy. Though I recognize the common man is struggling to pay for the price of bread, there are other ways to effect change that have nothing to do with illegal paper currency fraud.

Let me stop myself, for I know you neither want to hear my arguments nor need to. While I must remain in London for a negotiation with the prime minister, your sister Ellen is on her way with Max in tow. Between the two of them, I am confident that your portion of this fracas will be sorted. So let me say this, since for once I believe you might read my letter: I admire your strength of character. You follow your own North Star, just as I attempt to and your mother succeeded in doing. You do it fearlessly, joyfully, and purposefully. We may disagree on many points, but as I watch your life unfold, I have no doubt: you are a Preston, through and through.

More to the point: you are your mother's daughter, through and through, and my soul warms knowing she lives on in you.

You are in my heart, my thoughts, and my prayers.

With great admiration,

Papa

"Has he any useful advice?" Lord Widlake's question interrupted Sophia as she read those last few lines again. She discovered her thumb following along the line of text; she yanked it back. The letter fell to the surface of her desk.

"The viscount and viscountess Berwick will be arriving soon to advise us on the matter. My father is confident they will sort it out. Without requiring me to confess to a crime I did not commit." Sophia squared her gaze on Lord Widlake, watching for a reaction that might betray his true intentions. "He mentioned he included a letter for you as well."

"Ah, yes." Lord Widlake cleared his throat. "I only wondered if he included more detailed advice for you."

"He did not."

Lord Widlake cleared his throat again. "Then I shall bid you goodnight."

How she wished John had been there to witness the interaction. Sophia felt sure there was something strange in Lord Widlake's reaction. But even she had to allow that after three days cooped up in the small cell of a room, her judgment was skewed to suspect every glance that landed her way.

If only John had been there, he would have told her if her instincts were right.

At the very least, he would have *been* there. Within arm's length of her. Filling the room with his calm presence and steady gaze.

Sophia turned back to the letter. She had known Papa wouldn't come himself. He was preparing for the first parliamentary session in years that wouldn't be tied up in the war with Napoleon. He nursed grand hopes that he could finally push through a bill banning slavery itself from all the realms of the Empire. With the glory of Britain pulsing through everyone's veins, he might even have a hope of actually achieving the law this year.

Still, she was his daughter. She was locked in a room, facing transportation or execution.

She would have thought just the once, he would put family ahead of the nation.

We were born with great luck, and the price is that we must do all we can to spread that luck to others, rang Mama's voice in Sophia's mind.

She knew the justification. She knew Papa loved her, even though he couldn't come himself.

She still wanted him there, if only to wrap her in a hug and offer her a handkerchief and promise that everything would sort itself out.

Sophia folded the letter back into its envelope and tucked it into her enamel box of correspondence. Ellen and Max were on their way. Ellen would do the hugging and handkerchiefing and promising that everything would sort itself out.

If John visited her that night, Sophia promised herself, then she would have all the comfort she needed.

⁂

S NEAKING THROUGH THE ABBEY was more difficult with metal type clanging in his pockets. John kept pausing, muffling the noise with his palm, sure that he would wake a family member or servant or one of the children and be found out.

He made it to Sophia's room without incident. Across the corridor, the soft orange glow of candlelight seeped from behind Nurse's door, so he let himself into Sophia's room without so much as a knock.

She sat at her desk. When their eyes met—hers cast at an angle over her shoulder—she smiled, a gesture that began as a twitch of the lips and ended as a grin.

"I feared you had forsaken me."

John offered a palmful of type in response. "There is a printing press in the cellar of the bell tower."

Sophia stared at him. Then she leapt, seizing his hand in hers and wrapping its closed fist into the nook between her breasts. John clapped his spare fingers over her mouth to muffle the squeal erupting from her throat.

"Don't let anyone overhear."

"What does it matter if anyone overhears? You did it! You found the proof!"

The joy in Sophia's eyes was impossible to look at. If only John had done as she believed. If only he could deliver her the freedom she deserved.

"Look at what is in my hand." His whisper rasped like a sore throat. He forced his fist open despite the clasp of her fingers.

He had grabbed the type at random as easy proof of what he had discovered. The letters spilled against each other: two *t*s, an *e*, and a *p*. Latent ink stained his palm.

"If it were for counterfeiting, it would have copper plates, not type. I found a printing press, not an engraving press. It is for printing text onto paper. A secret newspaper, perhaps. Not bad notes."

Sophia still clung to his hand. She had twisted into his body so that her back pressed against his chest and groin and legs.

If he knew she wanted it, John would wrap his spare arm around her waist. But that would be an embrace, and he wasn't at all sure she would welcome it now, with their plan falling to pieces around them.

"I'm sorry, Sophia."

"Sorry?" Releasing his hand, Sophia pushed away, landing again at her desk. "Do you not think a printing press a significant discovery? Someone at Robin Abbey is organizing secret activity. If they are willing to print newspapers beneath the bell tower, it is not a stretch to imagine they might also be involved in counterfeiting bank notes."

She tripped over her words, glowing. John took a step backwards, reaching for a response to cut through the excitement eclipsing her judgment. "What would you have me do? Show Mr. Ord the printing press and claim that you cannot possibly be the person using it? If anything, finding this printing press on the premises of Robin Abbey makes it easier for the bank to hold you accountable for the notes."

"We will have to find the person responsible for the press. Did you search the area for evidence of who it was? Or what they were printing?"

"Yes, of course." Although at first, he had wanted so badly for his discovery to end this ordeal that John had seen nothing except the press. Then he had gathered himself and his presence of mind. The press sat within the small footprint of the bell tower, surrounded on all sides by solid dirt walls. It was a portable press. In drawers beneath its top surface, he had found the type, ink, rollers, and paper. Circling the press, John had walked into a series of strings nailed between two of the walls, where he assumed broadsheets dried after pressing. There were paper trimmings, too, proof that something had been printed and cut down.

Beyond that, there had been no clue as to who used the press or what they printed.

"You'll have to go back." Sophia's fingers danced along her lips as she imagined a plan. "Lord Widlake has a store of ink in his desk. Perhaps he uses it for printing rather than correspondence."

"Why would he need keep any print secret?"

But Sophia didn't seem to hear him. "Or there is still the question of Mrs. Edwards. Hattie said she writes a fearsome amount of correspondence. Perhaps she is doing the printing and mailing it out in the guise of letters."

"She would only be able to send a few pamphlets at a time, if that is the case."

"Do you think you could intercept her next letter?"

John stared at her. He waited for her to hear what she was asking. This was more than inquiring into family dynamics or descending into locked cellars.

Intercepting a letter was, in itself, a form of crime.

Sophia didn't take back her request, not even when he let the silence stretch between them. At last, John had to say something. "Perhaps we should discuss what will happen if we cannot find any proof of some other culprit."

This cut through her single-mindedness. Though John hated to see apprehension freeze her features again. "If you found a secret printing press, you can find the person who is trying to pin this crime on me. I know it."

"And if I can't?"

Her gaze dropped. Lifting a letter from her desk, she responded, "I heard from my father at last. My sister and her husband are coming to assist in the matter." With a ghost of a smile, she added, "She married a viscount who is very large and intimidating. Lord Berwick should ensure Mr. Ord's cooperation."

Relief ballooned John forward. "Then we needn't worry further. Viscount Berwick will handle Mr. Ord, and you may go home safely with your sister."

"Go home?" Sophia evaded his hands as he reached out. "Why should I not stay at Robin Abbey? I have done nothing wrong."

"Would you want to stay here, knowing someone bears you enough ill will to risk your arrest?" John had always assumed she would return to Northfield Hall just as soon as Lord Widlake and Mr. Ord agreed to it.

"That is why we must find that someone. I have every right to be here, as you do."

Anger glittered in Sophia's eyes. John didn't blame her, except he didn't understand why it was directed at him. "Of course you have a right to be here. Yet the reality remains that you have been falsely accused, and we still don't know by whom. At some point, you must stop complaining to the dealer and play the cards you have been dealt."

Sophia recoiled as if he had slapped her. "I did not realize my protestations tired you. My apologies."

"That's not what I am trying to say." John reached for her again. If only he could touch her, he thought he could calm her.

Sophia danced away from him. "If you do not think this merits further investigation, then you mustn't overextend yourself. My sister will be here any day. I will await her assistance."

He hadn't meant for this to happen. John had only wanted her to face the situation for what it was. To put aside wild expectations and make a plan that grappled with reality. "I want to assist you, Sophia. I want to see you through this."

"And then you want to see me safely home, far away from you and your precious reputation."

He had talked himself into a corner, and John didn't know how to get out of it. From the way she glared, fingers curled, John wasn't sure Sophia even wanted to let him try. He handed her the fistful of type. "I think we had best bid each other goodnight and revisit the subject tomorrow."

"You needn't revisit anything for my sake. I will manage perfectly well without you."

John reached for the door. Its handle rattled at his touch. "I didn't mean to upset you."

She didn't reply to his parting words.

Chapter Thirteen

Next morning, Ellen and Max, Viscount Berwick, finally arrived. From her perch at her chamber window, Sophia saw the flash of their carriage as it wound around the last curve of the road. A quarter hour later, she heard the hubbub of their arrival: the call of grooms' voices across the courtyard as they rushed to take the team of horses, the clatter of footsteps down the corridor as the maids hurried to find clean linen for guest rooms, the children's voices gushing into excited pitches at the prospect of visitors.

Sophia had to wait in her room, which each day felt more cell like. She imagined this was how the nuns had felt, cloistered so much from the world that they could not even use the strength of their voices to communicate. What terror they must have felt, when they awoke one morning and understood the depth of the vows they had made as girls of fourteen or sixteen or however old they had been when their families steered them into the convent. A life in the safety of stone walls, with guaranteed shelter and food and community, must have seemed such a boon until that moment–which must certainly have arrived for each and every sister—when one realized there was no escape. This room, this life, this group of people who did not even speak to each other was one's destiny because one had made it so.

In the doldrums of the afternoons, Sophia believed that she, too, would never leave this room or Robin Abbey or the endless existence as prisoner.

She used the wait to tidy her room. Ellen wouldn't be shocked by a mess, but she would tilt her head in disappointment the exact way Mama used to, and Sophia didn't care to earn that reaction when she needed her sister's support. She made sure each of her gowns hung in the armoire so that the cabinet door shut properly. She closed up her tobacco kit and perfumes and cosmetics and buried the boxes under her bed so that Ellen wouldn't be overcome by the presence of imported goods. She even changed into a wool dress so Ellen wouldn't catch her in cotton. By the time the key turned in her lock, Sophia's room looked as spartan as it had the day she arrived at Robin Abbey.

Lord Widlake himself pushed open the door. He was looking ill compared to the last time Sophia had seen him. Sophia knew she shouldn't find that satisfactory. Still, she indulged in a tingle of pleasure.

That was nothing, however, compared to the joy of beholding her older sister for the first time in months. Ellen wore a gray wool traveling costume, her red hair pinned up in an unforgiving braid, her skin as pale and freckled as ever. The sight of Ellen–smile sneaking onto her lips–overwhelmed Sophia with delight.

She leapt forward to pull her sister into a hug, decorum be damned.

"You were overdue to cause trouble again," Ellen whispered into Sophia's ear. No judgment or disappointment in her tone, either. She squeezed Sophia closer before releasing her. Loud enough for all to hear, Ellen asked, "Are you well? Have you had enough to eat? You are looking pale. Are you ill?"

"I haven't been outside in days, nothing worse." Sophia made a point to look gratefully and obsequiously in Lord Widlake's direction. "His lordship has been very generous to me, all things considered."

The man stood ill at ease beside Max. Most men did. Ellen's husband was one of the most imposing of the peerage, both in size and personality. He towered over the average Englishman, and, from helping Ellen in her carpentry shop, he boasted broad shoulders that promised victory in any duel or fistfight or whatever physical altercation a foe might imagine. On top of that, he was witty, smart, and almost never lost a philosophical debate–though Ellen was always willing to take him on, especially in her never-ending quest to radicalize him to her own extreme progressive views.

As son-in-law to Papa–and a member of the House of Commons in his own right–Max represented an invaluable ally to Lord Widlake. Which made Sophia's current state that much more complicated for her employer.

Max angled his body toward Lord Widlake as he said in that imposing voice of his, "I have been closed up in the carriage for three days and am going out of my mind. I cannot imagine how you have been coping, Sophia. Perhaps we could all go for a walk through Lady Widlake's garden while we sort out this situation."

Lord Widlake, of course, could give only one answer. Ellen linked her arm through Sophia's. "You mustn't leave out a single detail."

They descended as a group to the garden. The Misses Cosgrove congregated in a most unladylike fashion on the threshold of the schoolroom to watch them pass. On the stairs, they encountered the maids Polly and Hattie, who scurried out of the way despite being overladen with fresh linens. On the ground floor, they cut through the formal drawing room, where Lady Widlake and Mrs. Edwards sat by a tray of food with embroidery in their laps.

Sophia wondered where John was, and whether he had purposefully made himself scarce. Then she banished the thought; it didn't matter to her where he was or why he did what he did.

He wished her gone from Robin Abbey. No doubt, he was off rejoicing that she was no longer his burden.

"Now," Ellen said when they stepped onto the garden's gravel path, "your letter said this is all about counterfeit banknotes. Do explain further, because I can't wrap my mind around the situation."

Sophia explained as best she could. First, about the outing to Boughampton and her purchase at the stationer's. Then, about the terrible moment when Mr. Ord had removed from her purse the false notes. "I am quite sure I would have noticed them if I handled them. Someone placed them in my reticule, Ellen."

Ellen, being a level-headed and honest person, nodded along. Keeping at least ten paces behind, Max and Lord Widlake were also engaged in conversation, and from the way Lord Widlake seemed to be in a permanent red flush, Sophia assumed he was telling Max his version of the story.

"It is quite the mix-up," Ellen said. "One that shouldn't be a problem in the first place. The Bank of England has no business prosecuting anyone. Nor should the punishment be execution. If only our government had more sense, this predicament would not be so dramatic."

Sophia lowered her voice so that not even the robin nestled in the overgrown hedge could hear. "Lord Widlake has suggested that since the notes are signed by *The People of Northfield Hall*, perhaps Papa is the one behind their printing."

Pink rushed up to Ellen's ears. She glanced backwards. Sophia watched as she and Max caught each other's eyes in some deep, unspoken, marital communication. It was the type of secret look that Sophia had always scorned as trite; it was, she had always thought, decoration that might look like a silk scarf but actually operated as a noose ever-tightening around one's neck.

After watching Papa break into pieces without Mama, Sophia had promised herself she would protect herself from such heartbreak at all costs.

Strange, then, that jealousy speared like a mace in messy jags through her heart.

The moment lasted half a second before Ellen's gaze and attention returned to Sophia. "Papa wouldn't do such a thing."

"Yes, but…"

The benefit of so long being siblings was that Sophia didn't need to finish her sentence before Ellen replied. "This is entirely different than the matter of Berkshire linens. That was obfuscation of the truth. This is a criminal enterprise. Papa would never condone such a thing."

"You're right, of course." Papa never would. But then again, Papa was only one of nearly two hundred people living on the estate. How hard would it be for someone to set up a counterfeiting operation at Northfield Hall without anyone in the family ever knowing?

"We shall sort this whole thing out one way or another." Ellen used her soothing, older-sister voice, patting Sophia's hand where it sat on her forearm.

Sophia wanted to protest that she didn't need soothing. Yet apparently she did, for she was almost overcome by tears at the gesture. She pulled out her handkerchief and pretended to sneeze into it. "Anyhow, I'm sick and tired of talking about this. Distract me with news from your life. How is my darling Rosalind?"

"A troublemaker, through and through. I've no doubt that when we return, Mrs. Chow will report to me that Rosalind has broken a dozen dishes or sicked up on all her clothes or some other such horror. She hates it when Max is gone, even if it is just to Thatcham for the afternoon. He indulges her, of course. He made her a notebook of scrap paper, and now she follows him around and pretends to write her own letters while he does his work."

Sophia knew Ellen better than to believe the chagrin she pretended to. "At a miniature desk made specially for her by her mother, perhaps?"

Ellen grinned. She did that so often in these years since meeting Max that Sophia had forgotten to keep noticing. It really was something, when a person was so happy that they let sunshine beam straight out of their soul.

"We cannot help ourselves. We need you to come be governess so that our children don't end up completely full of themselves."

"Children?"

"If all goes well." Ellen's palm slipped towards her midsection, currently hidden behind the heavy drapes of her traveling dress.

"Is this the moment you decide to be coy?" Sophia teased. "Are you trying to tell me you are expecting another child?"

Ellen's grin faded into bewilderment. "I told you in my last letter. Did you not receive it?"

Her words reverberated between them. Sophia knew she hadn't read Ellen's latest missive. The truth was, she rarely read her family's letters closely. She was always too busy worrying about what version of her life she would share with them in her reply to focus on the minutiae of what they shared with her.

Though in this moment, with Ellen's disappointment welling between them, Sophia could admit to herself that news of an imminent niece or nephew was not minutiae.

"It must have been lost." She pulled her sister into a hug. "Delightful news. I cannot wait to turn another child of yours into a selfish boor in my own image."

Ellen returned the hug, but barely. Sophia kept talking in a rush, as if more words would erase her bad behavior. "Oh, but you must allow Mr. Anderson to examine you while you are here!"

The gentlemen joined them as they reached the end of the garden. Max, looking even more smug than usual, looped an arm around Ellen's waist. "Who is Mr. Anderson, and why should he examine my wife?"

"Mr. Anderson, the accoucheur." Lord Widlake made this reply with acute gravity, as if trying not to embarrass Max with information he should already have. "He delivered the Countess of Gresham her child earlier this spring, and Lady Georgina Barrows her twins last year, if you'll recall. If you are so inclined, Lady Berwick, I insist that you consider Mr. Anderson at your service for as long as you remain at Robin Abbey."

"That is too kind. I am quite countrified, you see, and have thus far put my trust in the local midwives. How exciting to encounter a trained accoucheur." Ellen looked at Sophia, a question dancing in her eyes. "Is his family here with him?"

She knew Sophia well enough to guess that where there was a man in want of companions, there was a flirtation of one kind or another.

Were they younger–or unobserved by anyone except fami-ly–Sophia would stick out her tongue in response to the taunt.

She almost missed Lord Widlake's response. "Not at the moment, although we do expect his mother to arrive soon for a visit."

That was the moment the garden doors opened and John himself appeared.

At no point in all their secret meetings had he mentioned his mother coming for a visit. And now Sophia felt as if she had never seen him before. He wore a new suit, this one of vibrant, freshly-dyed black. His jaw bore no subtle shadow of a beard, instead cutting a harsh, clean line. Instead of the tired, cautious intrigue that normally shaded his eyes around her, he wore a mask of open obsequiousness.

Unease surged like nausea up Sophia's throat. Was this a man who misrepresented himself, or was she a woman who only read what she wanted of him?

J OHN BOWED HIS HEAD as expected upon introduction to Lord and Lady Berwick. He had known, of course, that Sophia came from aristocratic stock even richer than the Cosgrove family. Yet that was easy to dismiss as a quirk, no more or less off-putting than how, in her chamber, he always seemed to be poked by an errant corset or box or letter. Until now, with the viscount and viscountess here in the garden.

They were tall, the both of them, and stood in that way of aristocrats with stiff spines and squared shoulders. The viscount had a thick head of hair that fell about his face in a style that none could get away with except a peer of the realm. His arms brimmed with muscles beneath his fashionably tight coat. John wanted to grip the man's hand—as he would upon any other introduction—and squeeze it until he flinched. He wanted to flex his chest and stare the viscount down and exert his right to exist within three feet of Sophia.

He could do none of that. Especially since, in the aftermath of their quarrel the night before, John wasn't confident Sophia wanted him to pollute her visit with her family. He waited for Lord Berwick to say, "Ah yes, the famous accoucheur," before opening his own mouth.

"It is my honor and privilege to be presented to your company."

"The honor is ours," said Lady Berwick. Surprisingly, her voice sounded nothing like Sophia's. Where Sophia spoke in low and gravelly syllables, as if summoning the tones from the bottom of her throat, Lady Berwick's voice was clear as a bell. Her words, too, were shaped differently, leaning into a country accent instead of adhering to the strict tonnish enunciation that Sophia modeled. "Lord Widlake has been telling us your recent accomplishments. How fortunate for Lady Widlake to be under such care."

John had no response for that. He didn't trust aristocrats when they heaped praise upon him. It never was about him, after all.

Even Lady Berwick, who actually was looking at him, meant for her host to hear the compliment. In flattering John, she flattered Lord and Lady Widlake, just as bragging about John's accomplishments served Lord Widlake in elevating his status for having procured top talent.

He was impatient for the exchange to be over, though he was the one who had stepped out into the cold garden of his own volition. That had been pure instinct: with word whistling through the Abbey that Sophia's family had arrived, that she was out of her room, John's feet had walked him downstairs before he could think through his strategy.

"Mr. Anderson has been very kind to me in these recent days," Sophia said, tucking her chin in imitation of a chastised child. "I'm afraid with all the dramatics, my stomach has been upset. Mr. Anderson has tended to me without complaint."

He didn't miss the way her sister lifted an eyebrow at this. A suspicious eyebrow, John guessed. She would know Sophia's temperament; surely Sophia's claim was as good as declaring to her sister that she and John were lovers. The lady replied, "I am glad to hear it. We Prestons are a hardy bunch, but even we need allies in times of trouble."

Lord Widlake ushered the party back inside to the formal drawing room, where Lady Widlake had hot cider waiting for them. John wasn't sure he was invited to join the party and hovered in the corner until Lady Berwick called to him, "Mr. Anderson, won't you come sit by me and tell me all about why a woman should need an accoucheur?"

"Yes, do," drawled her husband, though John couldn't tell whether he was being sarcastic or not. "Lady Berwick doesn't believe any of the arguments I have presented to her."

"It is a matter of principle, dear, that I do not agree with you if I can choose not to," she replied, and the two exchanged a private smile.

As ordered, John took the chair beside Lady Berwick's. She and Sophia sat together on a two-seated sofa, leaving him a chair upholstered with a woven scene of Cupid aiming his arrow at errant Roman lovers. Sophia ladled him a cup of cider.

"My sister anticipates the Great Event this winter," she said as she placed it in his hands. It seemed to John she took care not to brush her finger against his.

She was still upset with him, then.

"Ah, my felicitations." John had suspected as soon as he saw Lady Berwick. Beyond the conversation topic of choice, there was a certain look to her that suggested to him a *grossesse*. "Are you feeling well so far?"

"It kept me from my work the first few months, but lately, I have been feeling nothing except euphoria." She went on to explain that she kept a joiner's workshop at Northfield Hall and spent most of her days at woodworking. Her hands, John noticed, were disguised in linen gloves, which perhaps was to keep Lord and Lady Widlake from being offended by calluses and scars.

Sophia chimed in, "Mr. Anderson thought it odd that I chose to be a governess. I'm sure you are recalibrating that assessment now that you know how my sister chooses to spend her time."

"Next thing I know, you'll tell me your brother is a lawyer," John quipped without thinking, then tensed. It was one thing for Lady Berwick and Sophia to make light of their family's eccentricities, but another thing entirely for an unknown surgeon to add his own comments.

Luckily, Lady Berwick smiled. Sophia replied, "No, not yet anyhow, but both Benny and Nate still have some years before we may declare them uninteresting."

"And then we will wait with bated breath to see in whose footsteps Caroline chooses to follow." Lady Berwick settled her gaze on John. Unlike Sophia, who was always so full of energy that one sensed her attention darting this way and that even when she looked straight at you, John felt pinned by Lady Berwick. This was a woman who would notice his every expression and measure his every word. "I understand your mother is coming to visit soon, Mr. Anderson."

Cider splashed from John's cup onto the saucer and his hand. It was still hot, hot enough that it stung his bare skin. It began to drip onto the floor; he moved it above the hardwood instead of the imported carpet until he fished out his handkerchief and mopped up the mess. "I have invited her to join me, yes. If all goes as I hope, she will be here within the fortnight."

John stole a glance at Sophia. She watched him, her expression schooled into polite interest, as if it was of no import to her whether his mother visited or not.

He had tried to introduce the subject. But she had dismissed it. Perhaps John had hesitated in forcing her to hear him because he feared her response would be, *And why should I care? What else have you learned about the banknotes?*

"That will be nice," Lady Berwick prodded. "How long has it been since you last saw her?"

"Eighteen months." An unconscionable amount of time. John had never meant to let it get so long. Except it seemed each time he finished an engagement with one family, the next one awaited him with great impatience, demanding he travel as soon as possible lest anything go wrong with the mother. And John did not have the luxury of making his own demands. Perhaps in a few years, when he was established. For now, he existed at the whim and mercy of his patients.

"How nice that she can visit." This from Sophia. She pitched her voice high and breathy, as if she were trying to do an imitation of her sister. Lady Berwick cut Sophia a glance, and John saw that eyebrow rise in suspicion again.

"I am grateful to Lord and Lady Widlake for making her welcome." Although they had been vague about what accommodations they could offer her; John rather feared they would take one look at Amma and banish her to some frigid room in the servants' quarters.

Whatever they offered would be better than leaving her on Neptune Street with Captain Attree.

Meanwhile, Sophia had turned frosty at John's reply. She turned away, angling her body towards Lady Widlake and Mrs. Edwards across the room. Her chin lifted, and John had studied her profile long enough by now to read the anger lining her cheeks.

He had not yet told her about his invitation to Amma. Apparently, that omission hurt Sophia. And now her family was here to help free her of these accusations.

If she didn't need his help and didn't want his company anymore, was this the moment when John lost Sophia's esteem altogether?

Chapter Fourteen

Lord Widlake announced the family would be taking supper in their rooms, which was really to avoid any awkwardness over hosting Ellen and Max at his table while leaving Sophia in her cell. Still, he did not shut her in when he returned her upstairs. Sophia listened to the door click shut without the telltale turn of the lock; she waited to feel relief.

It did not come. Relief would have been being freed from this nightmare altogether. Relief would have been discovering who had actually counterfeited the notes and seeing them locked in a room no larger than ten paces in any direction.

Relief would have been knowing whether John cared for her at all.

She changed out of her wool dress, swapping her corset and petticoats for a cotton shift beneath a poplin morning gown that wrapped around her waist like a robe. It was a cast-off from Aunt Charlotte, the Countess of Pemberly, and Sophia usually eschewed it because it made her feel like a fifty-year-old dowager rather than a vibrant and attractive young woman. Tonight, however, it gave Sophia the feeling of an embrace.

She was surprisingly fatigued. After days locked in solitude, spending the entire afternoon abroad in the Abbey had drained her of energy. Even though she should be bouncing with hope and excitement that at last her cavalry had arrived.

Still, Sophia did not go to sleep. She should have. What did it matter if John came to visit her? What would he have to say that she cared to hear? He was no more than a man whose body she found attractive. A person whose kiss set her body on fire. He was hardly the first person to do so, and he wouldn't be the last. Unless he managed to use the interval between cider and midnight to discover something new about the false banknotes enterprise, there was no reason for him to bother her that night.

She read her correspondence from Ellen—discovering that, indeed, Ellen had mentioned her condition in her latest letter—and then every note she had received since arriving at the Abbey. Once-a-week letters from Papa, short notes every month or so from Benjamin that focused mostly on whichever soulmate had enthralled him that day, schoolgirl letters in careful calligraphy from Caroline whenever her governess had prompted them. One letter from Aunt Charlotte, inviting Sophia to stay with her in London should she ever come to town, and one from Nate from his regimental training in Portsmouth.

Sophia wished she hadn't ignored the letters. She wished even more that she had written back. At the time, she had been so afraid to admit that she was unhappy. As if she expected her family would rejoice in that news.

When in reality, perhaps they would have lent her the wisdom to know what to try next.

John didn't knock on her door at ten, when most of the household would already be asleep. Nor at midnight, when he usually came. At one o'clock, Sophia had to assume he would not visit her at all that evening.

She should welcome it. If he wanted her to leave Robin Abbey, then they had nothing to say to each other. Except she had worked herself into a lather, and Sophia couldn't very well fall asleep when indignation ran hot through her veins.

And besides, Lord Widlake hadn't locked the door.

Morning gown fluttering like a queen's train, Sophia flew through the dark and silent corridor. At John's door on the opposite side of the Abbey, she did not bother to knock.

He was not in bed. She interrupted him sitting in a stiff wooden chair, legs stretched before him, staring moodily into the dying fire. He wore his smallclothes, stockings, and shirt, which hung down past his knees. When he jerked up to his feet at her entrance, the collar flapped open to show most of his bare chest.

"Is something amiss?"

A ridiculous question, since she wouldn't be banging into his room if there were nothing amiss. She wanted to scoff at him. She wanted to ridicule the question, pick it apart word by word, make him feel the fool until he squirmed backwards and cried defeat.

"Kiss me."

He blinked. Well, she did, too. Sophia didn't know where that command had come from, except that the anger didn't last when she looked at him. He was too good, his eyes too kind. And if he wanted her gone, then the very least he could do was kiss her one more time. Or fondle her with those expert fingers.

Would he ever let her fuck him?

John closed the distance between them. He shut the door, which Sophia had neglected to do, then caught her fingers in his own. Holding her hands–almost as if they were schoolchildren–he tipped forward and pressed his lips to hers.

It was chaste and innocent. The kind of kiss Papa used to give Mama in the morning before taking himself off to whatever he did during the day. Not the kind of kiss that should satisfy Sophia.

She clung to his hands. Her eyes were closed, and she kept them that way. She didn't want to discover what she would do next if she looked up to see him. Clearly, he had her bewitched. He had turned her into a woman whose heart–not her loins, not her nerves, but her metaphorical heart–leapt at so sweet a gesture.

Sophia did not want to learn what came next in this experience.

"I never meant to imply I wanted you to leave. I assumed it was the natural end to this ordeal." He was close enough that his words expelled breath against her cheek. She smelled the peat of whiskey over the aroma that was uniquely John.

Strange, how she wanted to turn her face into that breath and gulp it up, as if consuming it into her lungs would bring her that much closer to him.

"I suppose it is too much to expect Lord and Lady Widlake to keep me on after all this."

"Lord Widlake wants to stay in Lord Berwick's good graces. That much is clear. If you want to stay, perhaps he can arrange it." John released her fingers. He backed away; Sophia finally opened her eyes so she could keep track of him. He crossed to his nightstand, where the whiskey bottle stood. He shook it in the air, as if to ask if she wanted some.

Sophia nodded. A little whiskey couldn't hurt. In fact, it might cut through her confusion. It might restore her to her usual, uncomplicated self: a lusty woman who wanted one thing from a man, and nothing more.

He only had one cup, a tin affair that likely came from his own travel kit rather than from the Robin Abbey household. They shared a double portion, one leisurely sip after another as they sat beside the fire. The whiskey was quality, smooth and smoky as it surged through her innards. John watched her when she drank. His gaze was steady, his pupils and irises indistinguishably black, and his eyebrows drew together almost into a frown. Sophia realized on her third sip that, if she was tracking all these details, she must be watching him back.

She willed herself not to look away. In fact, she leaned forward and propped her chin on her fist. "Are you looking forward to seeing your mother?"

And here came the satisfaction: John broke the stare. He turned his entire head towards the fire. "I tried to tell you."

There was a hesitancy to his words that told Sophia he was sorry–and that the topic made him uncomfortable. That was enough for her. She was uncomfortable, too, for if they stayed on the subject, she might have to explain why she cared whether he told her or not. Now that he had acknowledged his error, Sophia wanted to forget the entire affair as fast as possible. "I do have a way of distracting you, don't I?"

He smiled, but barely. It was more of a twitch at the corners of his lips. "The truth is I still await confirmation. She hasn't arranged a reply since my letter. I wish she would."

Sophia tried to remember what John had told her before about his mother. She was the source of his Indian heritage; she had been the senior Mr. Anderson's mistress in India before he brought her and John back to join his English family; she had been put in the service of someone else's household. What kind of service, Sophia didn't recall, nor did she know whose household it was. She wasn't even sure whether John had been put in that household, too, or not.

She should have listened better. At the time, she had only cared to make him feel comfortable. She hadn't thought she would need the facts of his life stored in her long-term memory.

Still, she could guess at what might be bothering him. "You fear she is being mistreated in her new situation."

"However she is faring, it is my fault. I trusted my cousin to care for her as if she were his aunt. Or at least a cherished housekeeper. I should have known better. I should have seen to her welfare myself."

Sophia wanted to curl her fingers into his. For the moment, she kept her hands to herself. "It is not your fault your cousin lacks family feeling, nor is it your fault for believing better of him. If there is a guilty party, it is your cousin, not you."

The smile she earned this time was genuine. It flooded his face in a way that took Sophia's breath away.

She had never lost her breath, not like that. She had to remind herself to inhale. To not gape in the middle of a conversation.

Dimly, she heard a part of herself protesting that this was not a healthy way to respond to a man. Yet she was too lost in John's aura to listen. She leaned closer, so that she could smell him as he asked, "And you do not find fault with me for being the bastard son of a housekeeper?"

"There are many negative things that are true about us Prestons, but scorning people who have been cheated by life is not one of them. I look forward to meeting your mother, in fact. I'm sure she has interesting stories to share, not least of which are embarrassing secrets about your childhood."

This time when John kissed her, it lasted. Sophia had time to sink into him, tasting the fresh coating of whiskey on his lips. She breathed in his skin. She ran her fingers along his jaw, feeling each barb of stubble. He cupped her cheek in kind, the soft pad of his thumb curving beneath her face to better fit their mouths together. They neither sparred with nor explored each other. They had kissed enough by now to know what made the other purr.

This kiss, Sophia realized, was the reason she had stormed into his room. She didn't care if he ever let her fuck him. Let her quim soak in want. Let fire rage across her skin. She hadn't stayed up all night waiting for John to come slake her lust.

She had been waiting for him to embrace her in this quiet way of his. To use the tools of a novice lovemaker to make her feel as no other lover ever had: cherished.

Sophia felt the kiss coming to its natural end. She didn't fight it, nor did she unwrap her dress or press John's palm onto her breast or do any of the other things she might once have done to stoke their mutual desire.

She opened her mouth to excuse herself. So content was she that Sophia almost didn't understand when John rasped, "May I take you to bed?"

J OHN KNEW HE WAS ready because every part of his body agreed. His stomach didn't clench, his armpits didn't sweat, his lungs didn't constrict. In fact, he wasn't even aware of them. He was doing his thinking with only his lips, his fingertips, and his cock–and it felt like heaven.

Sophia flushed when he asked the question. He had learned today that her sister was a ginger-haired, pale skinned person who blushed at the slightest provocation. Sophia wasn't like that. Her skin wore the olive burnish of French or Italian blood somewhere along their heritage, so her cheeks didn't flare often. But she did flush now, deep enough that John could watch the blood rushing behind her ears and across her forehead and down the gape of her voluminous morning gown.

"Are you quite sure?" was her response. She said it with such little breath that John understood her by watching her lips move.

She had the most enchanting lips.

"Quite."

"I didn't prepare myself." This with enough volume to qualify as a whisper.

"Good thing I am what I am." He wrapped a curl of her hair around his finger because he could. "What do you prefer? A pessary? A French letter? Onan's sin?"

The latter was not a device but a method, one that would require him to spill his seed anywhere but inside her. In fact, it was his common practice, as an extra precaution and courtesy to his partner.

But he wasn't surprised when Sophia replied, "The pessary. I want to feel you come inside me."

"Your wish is my command."

Together, they rose from their chairs. They had been face-to-face, chest-to-chest, hand-to-hand long enough that John felt as if his own body tore away when Sophia stepped backwards. She glided to the bed. John watched her climb the footstool to the top of his pile of six mattresses. A snake charmer's song could not have been more mesmerizing than her hips swaying beneath that voluminous wrap dress.

She knew she commanded his attention, too. Atop the bed, she untied the belt keeping shut her gown. She wore a shift beneath–John had already discovered that much–but it was white and thin. Even in the firelight, John could see through it to the shadows of her breasts and stomach and treasure box.

"I await your ministrations, Mr. Anderson."

Like an idiot, John had been standing there staring. His cock was harder than surely it ever had been before, and Sophia could see that well enough. Her words jolted him back to the moment.

He went to the armoire, where he had stored his medical supplies, and unlocked the box in which he kept contraceptives. He did not travel with a large quantity, since he was not in the practice of taking lovers himself. Rather, John kept a selection of devices available to counsel his patients after they delivered, especially those who needed to keep further pregnancies at bay or risk their health.

Still, he had a pessary for Sophia.

He removed it from its jar, in which it had been soaking in a solution of myrrh, honey, and coriander. The pessary itself was a wad of linen tied with a clean cotton string for easy removal.

John turned to Sophia, who still waited in repose on the mattress. "Would you like to insert it, or shall I?"

She spread her legs into an open vee. "I think you had better, doctor."

It took mere seconds to cross the room. Another heartbeat to bound up the stool onto the bed. John slowed then. Drawing her shift to bunch around her hips, he ran his fingers up the length of her legs. Her hair there was dark and soft, even more so as he neared the insides of her thighs.

Sophia shivered. "Your hands are cold."

John lifted his fingers to her mouth. "Warm them for me, then."

She sucked three fingers. Her tongue and cheeks were soft like velvet. Her eyes met his, glowing, and he knew they were both imagining his cock in place of his hand. He had thought it impossible to grow harder, but he did, until it was almost an ache.

He didn't have the patience for any more games. He wanted to see Sophia without a stitch of clothing. He wanted to kiss each inch of her skin. He wanted to discover which parts of her body sweated the most, where hairs sprouted surprisingly, how her smell changed.

He wanted to thrust himself straight through her center.

Reclaiming his hand, John stroked his fingers—warm from Sophia's mouth—against her wet pudendum. Across the ridges of her labia, around the ring of her vagina, up for a quick tease across her nymphae and clitoris, and then back to her vagina. The sponge slid right in, and he followed it with a finger until he felt it nestle against her cervix.

With John's hand still inside her, Sophia lunged forward and caught him in a kiss. She nipped his lip between her teeth. For that briefest of seconds, John believed they would never part, that they were now fused together and would die without ever again separating.

It was a thrilling, terrifying idea.

Then she let him go. "Do you like that?" she asked, moving her teeth to scrape against his jaw. "Do you like it when I bite you?"

John didn't know the answer. Instead of replying, he wrestled off her wrap and shift. She leaned back cooperatively, hands above her head. Her breasts bounced a little when the cotton drew up over them, and John watched her erect nipples settle back into their lopsided places.

He almost forgot to free her wrists of the shift before he caught her breasts in his mouth.

John didn't know which was better: losing his entire consciousness in physical sensation, or listening to Sophia do the same. She gasped at the initial contact of his tongue to her nipple. Then, as he tasted the salty dew of her skin, she let out a moan. "Oh yes, I like that, Mr. Anderson," came next, as he moved from her right nipple to the one on the left that rolled outwards like an errant pupil.

John had explored this territory before. But this time, he didn't feel the buzz of anxiety encroaching. This time, too, Sophia was completely nude. He reached around and clasped her bare buttocks in his palms, even as he continued to flick her nipple with his tongue. He could only get a portion of her flesh in his hands. She gasped anyway. When he felt her muscles clench, he adjusted his grip and came up for air.

Sophia grabbed him now. In great impatient fists, she unbuttoned his shirt and pulled it over his head. It hadn't even landed on the floor before she moved to his smallclothes. She tucked her fingers between the fabric and his skin so that as the smallclothes moved down his legs, her palms replaced them. John had never before felt so on fire. He barely even heard himself panting–like a dog, or some untried youth–as she rolled his smallclothes and stockings off his feet.

Now they were both naked. On the mattress. For the barest of moments, they were still, regarding each other. Taking each other in.

Sophia was miraculous, as John knew she would be. Those tantalizing breasts. The luscious hair curling over her pubis. And great heaps of flesh curving this way and then that. John couldn't wait to make her whole body heave in pleasure.

The moment ended. Sophia leapt upon him. Her palms pressed his shoulders into the mattress. Her knees squared off around his hips. And her quim descended onto his cock. Wet. Hot. Tight–and getting tighter as she squeezed her muscles around him. At first, she tortured him with long, slow movements, rising up as if to release him from her sheath then sliding back down to claim him again. John lost his breath and his brain. Then she settled in. She leaned forward. Her breasts dangled just out of reach of his mouth. Her clitoris dipped close to his skin. And Sophia rode him at a canter–no, a gallop–fast enough that the bedframe squeaked and the pillows quaked. John knew he should care about the noise. But he didn't. Not even a little. She bucked against him with such fervor that he could think of nothing but her vagina and his cock and the sensation that his whole body belonged to her and –

And, of course, he didn't last long. He came in a great spasm of blinding light. Relief, release, rejuvenation.

John wasn't sure he had ever orgasmed this hard.

When he returned to his body, Sophia was still on top of him. Still riding him, as if he had never come. She had straightened, and her right hand plunged down to her clitoris. She opened her eyes, discovered him looking back, and grabbed his palm. She sucked three of his fingers into her mouth. Her tongue lapped against them in rhythm with her hips, a desperate, needy suck that at the last moment turned into a bite.

John cried out–in pain, but also in pleasure, though he couldn't quite tell the difference–in the same moment that Sophia peaked. She vocalized her orgasm into his fingers, a hum that vibrated straight to his heart.

Her orgasm lasted longer than his. It rolled through her body in free-flowing waves. John wished he could get hard again already as he watched her breasts and stomach and hips undulate.

But he was a man, not a fantasy. A man nearing thirty, who needed at least an hour's rest–if not more–before being ready to go again. When Sophia finally lifted herself from him, his cock was already half-soft. She grinned at it, then at him, and kissed his lips one more time. "Regrets?"

Half of him wished he had seized her earlier, that very first time she propositioned him, so that he could already have had a dozen of these heady experiences. The other half knew he couldn't have enjoyed it until this moment. He laced his fingers through her hair. "None. You?"

"None," she agreed.

John was glad to hear it.

Chapter Fifteen

"**A**s to your affair with Mr. Anderson, is it helping or hurting in the case of this accusation?"

This Ellen asked in the privacy of her chamber, to which Sophia was allowed a visit the following afternoon. There were many wonderful things about the escape, including that Sophia had another opportunity to leave her room and see her dear sister.

Unfortunately, it also meant she was subjected to Ellen's tastes, meaning that instead of being served a nice imported black tea, Sophia was forced to choose between a peppermint or chamomile tisane, and instead of snacking on sugar-laden tea cakes, they ate plain scones without even the improvement of marmalade.

It was almost as dreary as a visit back to Northfield Hall.

Still, Sophia did not complain. To spend the afternoon with her sister, to know that at least this one person in the world trusted her to have not counterfeited money, and to still have John Anderson ringing through her bones from the night before, Sophia was far too cheerful to let moral principles knock her into a foul mood.

"Helping. He has been investigating on my behalf, although it has not yet borne any fruit." Sophia explained their theories about Mrs. Edwards and Lord Widlake, as well as the question of the printing press in the bell tower.

In her chair opposite, Ellen shook her head. "I can't think why you would take the risk of an affair here in the Abbey. If you were found out, Sophia...I daresay Lord Widlake would not be as considerate if he found you to be an adulterer rather than a counterfeiter."

"Don't preach at me." Sophia picked up a scone, as if to prove that she was amiable to good behavior. "Mr. Anderson and I are quite discreet."

"Then why did Lord Widlake tell Max that you used the counterfeit money to purchase a box of 'inappropriate materials'?"

The tea churned in her stomach at the idea of Lord Widlake whispering to Max about contraception. That had to have been an uncomfortable conversation, and she didn't know which man would have blushed more.

Served them right. They had no right to discuss it in the first place.

"Mr. Anderson explained that. Those were ingredients for a potion against menstrual cramps."

Ellen gave Sophia the look.

Well, there was only one way to deal with Ellen when she climbed onto her high horse. "You ought to have let that expression die with Mama. It makes you appear much older than you are."

"Mama would urge you to be more careful, and you know that is true. I thought you wanted a career as a governess. How will you keep it if you are caught in an indiscreet position?"

"Fucking, you mean. You may use the word, Ellen. It's just the two of us in here."

Sophia wished she derived more satisfaction at driving Ellen onto her feet with a great sigh of disgust. This type of diversion used to be enough for Sophia to shake off the shame Ellen foisted upon her.

Perhaps this whole affair was scraping rather too close to danger for Sophia's taste. She didn't like feeling that she couldn't proclaim complete and total innocence to Lord and Lady Widlake, since she was lying to them about John.

Neither did she like knowing she was putting John at risk. She had never before taken a lover who risked his reputation as much as he did. When she had first approached him, she hadn't thought it would be complicated: a few midnight fucks in quiet parts of the house when no one was looking, and then they would go their separate ways when Lady Widlake delivered the baby.

She hadn't expected it to take so long to seduce him. Nor had she expected all eyes in the household to be on her.

Pacing, Ellen said, "Lady Widlake suggested we take you home to Northfield Hall. I don't know if Lord Widlake would agree to it—or whether it is even legal—but if we could arrange it, would you come?"

It was just as John had predicted: instead of regaining her independence, Sophia was expected to retreat.

She had stewed over the idea long enough to see the wisdom of it. Removing herself from Robin Abbey meant the scandal could die down without threatening the reputations of anyone in the Cosgrove family or that of Sophia. Buttressed by her family, she would spend a year or two living a quiet, respectable life. And then, if she were lucky, she could find herself a new position and start her quest for independence all over again.

"Would you take Mr. Anderson on as your accoucheur so he could come with us?"

Ellen pursed her lips. "Don't you think you have risked both his and your reputations enough already?"

This, Sophia remembered too late, was why she was always so desperate to get away from her family. As much as she loved them, and as much as she craved their attention and admiration, she never could feel like a fully realized, independent Sophia with them. They made her feel like a caricature.

As opposed to John, who seemed to see Sophia as a lustful woman, an intelligent individual, an independent adult, and a worthy partner, all in one.

"I will stay at Robin Abbey, if Lord and Lady Widlake will have me. Though I do appreciate your offer."

Ellen sank back into her chair. "As you wish. I shall put in a word for you with Lady Widlake when I get the opportunity."

"Thank you." Sophia waited. Her sister had another scold tucked just beyond her tongue; Sophia could feel it in the air like a gathering storm. She had a good idea what it was, too. The same kind of reprimand Sophia had earned her whole life long. When she begged for silk gowns and snuck away into town and didn't share her sack lunches with the other children: *You are thinking too much of your-self.*

Ellen said nothing. She poured herself more chamomile tea. Behind them, the clock ticked, growing louder each second.

Better to toss the matter between them than to keep waiting. "Mr. Anderson suggested that I take the Bank's offer of clemency in exchange for a confession, since whoever did make those notes will be hanged if they are caught."

Across from her, Ellen blinked. "Mr. Anderson would have you brand yourself a criminal?"

"Only because the Bank guaranteed they would not force me to serve a sentence." Sophia picked up the peppermint tea again. "It is what you would do, after all."

Ellen reached over the table, plucked away Sophia's tea, and took her hands. "The law is unjust. No one should be hanged for making bad notes, nor should they be transported for uttering them. What I *would* do–and what I try to do–is fight to take that power from the Bank of England as much as possible. But fighting for change does not mean sacrificing ourselves in the process. I draw the line at offering up your name like some sacrificial lamb. We shall force a change some other way."

"I am not being selfish in insisting I am innocent?"

"No." Her sister's smile looked almost exactly like Mama's. "Besides, sometimes being selfish is exactly what a person needs to be."

Sophia hadn't started out in life wanting to be selfish. It came naturally to her. And when she couldn't be less so—no matter how many scolds she earned from Mama and Papa—she embraced it as her personality. The defining characteristic that separated her from her family.

She hadn't realized how desperately she needed Ellen's words. "I'm sorry I didn't read your letter. I'm sorry I don't write more. I didn't want to admit that I hate being a governess. I'm no good at it, and I get no joy from it, and I haven't the faintest idea what else I can do. But I didn't mean to ignore you. I am so happy you are happy. Truly, I am."

"That's all we want for you, Sophia. Happiness. Even if we don't understand your particular version of it." Ellen smiled. "You will find a wonderful adventure, once this ordeal is behind you. I have no doubt."

Sophia retreated back to her tea. "Whatever happens, I will write more. Even if I hate it, I will tell you so."

"We would all like that." Ellen chewed on her bottom lip. "You might begin with Nate. I'm worried about him. His letters were cheerful. I thought he might even be courting someone in Portsmouth. But then he stopped writing. And when Papa went to visit, Nate refused to see him altogether."

Sophia and Nate had long ago allied against being devout idealists like the rest of the family. Still, she couldn't imagine her eighteen-year-old brother refusing to receive anyone's visit. "I'll write him with my newfound wisdom. Though I can't promise it will help."

"At the very least, it will remind him that his family loves and cares for him. Even if his first letter home in a month is the news that he has been accused of uttering bad banknotes."

Their conversation was interrupted by a knock on the door, which Ellen rose to answer. It was the Misses Cosgrove, all three of them in a bunch. Misses Francesca and Mary clung to each other's hands, while Miss Cosgrove stood proudly in the threshold. "Begging your pardon, Lady Berwick, but would you like a tour of the Abbey now? We finished our embroidery, and my mother said we could ask you."

Ellen had spent the morning with the girls, overseeing their lessons in Sophia's stead, and apparently, she was now their favorite person in the world.

"Oh, how lovely," Ellen exclaimed. "Will you be able to answer all my questions about the Abbey? Such as who lived here before your family did?"

Miss Cosgrove launched into a rote recital. "My great-grandfather purchased it in 1701 from the Earl of Colchester. Before that, it was an abbey for Cistercian nuns, who had to take vows of silence in service to God, but they were Catholics, so King Henry VIII seized their property. Back then, it was called Cherubin Abbey, but my father changed the name to Robin Abbey."

"After all the robins in the garden," Miss Mary added.

"No, because Robin Hood is Father's favorite story," batted back Miss Francesca.

Ellen, having retrieved her shawl and gloves, interjected, "You will be the perfect tour guides. Do you think Miss Preston may come along with us?"

The three girls peered into the room, as if discovering Sophia there for the first time. They frowned in unison, all of them perfect imitations of their grandmother.

"I don't need a tour," Sophia answered for them. She rose. "You may begin by escorting me back to my chamber. Then you must be sure to show Lady Berwick every nook and cranny of the Abbey. The servants' quarters, the kitchen, the bell tower."

"And the crypts!" Miss Mary agreed. "Those are the best part of the whole house."

"The crypts?" Sophia couldn't stop herself from echoing it back—even though she should have done. She wanted to clap the word back into her mouth, for she couldn't let on even to the Cosgrove children that she was trying to investigate the counterfeiter herself.

Only, she hadn't ever heard of crypts in Robin Abbey. As far as she knew, the building ended on the ground floor without so much as a wine cellar.

Miss Cosgrove frowned at her sister. "We would have to get the key from Father to go down there, and he is out riding."

"No matter," Ellen said, as if there were no import to the idea of a secret part of the Abbey. "I don't much like the idea of a cold, dark crypt anyhow."

"But they're haunted!" Miss Mary replied, as if that were a decisive argument.

The girls debated the merits of a haunted Abbey all the way along the corridor that led to Sophia's room. There, Ellen did the honor of locking Sophia in. She pressed a kiss to Sophia's cheek before doing so. "I'm sorry to have upset you earlier. I'm concerned for you, that's all."

If she were a better person, Sophia would have responded in kind. But her mind was still latched on the crypts, on the key, and on what they could mean for proving her own innocence.

"I forgive you, as always," she said instead, and kissed her sister back. Then she listened to the lock turn and settled in to wait for nightfall.

I T WAS THE KIND of day when nothing could go wrong. John woke to a healthy fire in the hearth, so that his fingertips and toes did not need five minutes of vigorous rubbing before functioning. In honor of Lord and Lady Berwick, breakfast included kedgeree, kippers, and sliced apples from the storerooms. His patient was in good health, spurred by her visitors, and didn't need extra cajoling to walk outside with Mrs. Edwards for exercise. He even received word that the monthly nurse, who would assist in the delivery and tend Lady Widlake afterwards, expected to arrive within the fortnight. By afternoon, John retreated to his room with the contentment of a job well done.

He grinned to himself as he slipped into his bed for an afternoon nap. Sophia's smell lingered on his bedclothes. Some of it was her pear perfume. Some of it was sweat. They hadn't cuddled for long after the event, since John had been slipping into slumber and Sophia had mustered the presence of mind to return to her own room. Yet here she was, dyed into the starches of his quilt. And there on his pillowcase lay a long strand of her dark hair.

John wrapped it around his index finger. He needed a nap after a night so magnificent.

When he awoke, his finger had gone nearly white from the loss of blood flow.

The sun, too, had disappeared. Beyond the windows, the sky was a growing mass of storm clouds. John had meant to sleep for a half hour or so, but the darkness overwhelmed him, and he feared he had missed out on an entire afternoon. He stumbled down from the bed and checked his watch in his discarded jacket: it was only half past three.

A tap at the door revealed Mrs. Edwards. "Do you have a moment, Mr. Anderson?"

He admitted that he did. Rather than step into his room, she led him back to the sitting area in her own apartment. "I'd rather not ring for a maid, unless you are parched or starving?"

"Neither." Though his stomach did growl a little; so full had he been from breakfast that he skipped nuncheon. John preferred to follow Mrs. Edwards's lead, since he didn't know if she wanted to ask for medical advice, share family gossip, or discuss something else entirely.

She assumed the same fireside chair as during their previous interview. This time, she was much more herself: her gray hair pinned up beneath a simple cap, her gown a brown silk with an amber brooch, her chin lifted in anticipation of a fierce debate. In some ways, her temper reminded him of Sophia's. Except Sophia lashed out to protect herself; Mrs. Edwards seemed to lash out because she enjoyed it.

"Mr. Ord returned."

Perhaps that explained why, upon waking from his nap, the very chemistry of the Abbey seemed altered. "Has there been a development in his investigation?"

Mrs. Edwards narrowed her eyes at him, with the same impatience of a teacher with a slow pupil. "Of course there has been. Lord Berwick arrived to wield the power of a viscount against that of the Bank of England. Mr. Ord's investigation will change entirely now."

"You mean to suggest that Lord Berwick will require that Mr. Ord declare Miss Preston innocent of these charges?" John knew how he felt about that prospect: relieved beyond belief. He couldn't tell, however, what Mrs. Edwards felt or—more important-ly—how she wanted him to feel.

"He will do whatever is necessary to protect the Preston family in this matter. You can be sure of that."

This, John knew, referenced her theory that the Prestons themselves were the counterfeiters. He did his best to keep any reaction from his face. "An interesting turn of events to be sure, madam, yet I fail to see what it has to do with you or me."

Her hands flew through the air in a claw of frustration. "If Mr. Ord can no longer accuse Miss Preston, then he will find someone else at fault. He already searched your rooms, and he was about to do mine when the notes were discovered in Miss Preston's. It only follows he will turn to us when he needs to decide whom to blame next."

"Perhaps he will let the whole matter drop."

"Don't be naïve, Mr. Anderson. After all this fuss, they can-not let the matter disappear without anyone paying the conse-quences, else the whole countryside will take up counterfeiting."

The last time John had sat in this chair by Mrs. Edwards's fire, he had decided she had nothing to do with the affair at all. Yet now he wondered if that had been his moment of naïveté. Surely an innocent woman would not be so excited by the prospect of further investigation. As surreptitiously as possible, he swept his gaze across her room again: the giant chest beneath the window, the bed whose silk skirts hid the gap between its bottom and the floor, the armoire.

Perhaps Sophia was right; perhaps Mrs. Edwards was hiding something in plain sight.

"I say this to warn you," the older woman continued. "If you have anything to hide, see to it now. I doubt Mr. Ord will leave Robin Abbey without another dramatic scene."

"Thank you for your consideration, Mrs. Edwards, but I have nothing to hide. Have you?"

She narrowed her eyes at him. "Only my pride and dignity, Mr. Anderson. To think Lord Widlake would allow an intrusion of his own mother-in-law's privacy. It is a shame."

John murmured his agreement in order to end the interview. He was just heading towards Sophia's cell–with a stomach potion in hand by way of excuse–to share his observations when he spotted Mr. Ord departing to town beneath a cloud-studded sky. In the main hall, Viscount Berwick gathered the family to explain that since Sophia had been unaware the notes in her reticule were bad, the Bank of England had declined to charge her with a crime. Lady Widlake declared that they would celebrate with a feast. Everyone dispersed to prepare.

By suppertime, the dining room sparkled with candles, the whole Abbey smelled of roasted meat, and Sophia herself was in the drawing room for the pre-meal sherry.

She glowed. John knew that was because she was free–and Lord and Lady Widlake had agreed she could stay on as governess. She wore a gown too elegant for her position, two strands of pearls around her neck, diamonds in her ears, and pristine white gloves up her arms. She brought down a collection of fans and offered one to each of the Misses Cosgrove so they could play dress-up, too; the eldest Miss Cosgrove wore her silk evening dress, and even Lady Widlake had gone to the trouble of a formal dinner gown.

Still, Sophia glowed, and John liked to think he was one partial source of the endless wit and smiles and laughter that propelled her through supper. What they had gotten up to in the wee hours of the morning. The warm, thrilling safety of knowing he was in the room admiring her.

He restrained himself from interacting with Sophia, for fear he would reveal to the whole group his true feelings. She was the belle of the party, anyhow, and didn't lack for attention. John sat at his place at the table—demoted to the sagging middle between Mrs. Edwards and the young Miss Cosgrove, so that the viscount and viscountess could occupy the seats of honor—without much conversation at all. Sophia and her sister laughed over harmless stories from their youth, while Viscount Berwick sparred with Mrs. Edwards over the Corn Laws.

John fancied that Sophia stole glances at him throughout the meal, though he never did catch her in the act.

After supper, Lady Widlake suggested they reconvene in the drawing room for dancing. "Tonight is too splendid to let it end in the humdrum of conversation, don't you agree, Miss Preston?"

"I could certainly use the exercise." At last, Sophia looked directly at John.

He wished immediately that she hadn't. For she bit her teeth into her lip, and all he could see was her naked and on top of him.

They separated by gender long enough to relieve themselves. Then Miss Cosgrove took up the harpsichord and the rest of them took up dancing.

John partnered first with Lady Widlake. Achy as she was, she was eager to dance, so they began with a minuet that allowed her to parade about the room in time to the music. John kept a careful eye on her ankles, for his biggest fear was a fall that would bring on the delivery too early, but the dance went well, and at its end she agreed that it would be best to watch the rest of the evening.

"I should like to dance with my wife, if you don't mind," Viscount Berwick said, reclaiming his viscountess from Lord Widlake. "Mr. Anderson, if you would partner with Miss Preston?"

John couldn't quite tell for sure, but he thought the viscount winked at him with this suggestion.

He didn't dwell on it. Sophia presented herself to John with a formal curtsy, dipping low enough that John could see straight down her bodice to the lace decorating the rim of her corset. When she rose, she was biting into her lip again.

Mrs. Edwards took up the harpsichord so that Miss Cosgrove could dance with Lord Widlake. She called out the name of the song, a reel. John gripped Sophia's hand for the starting position. And then, after an initial chord, they were off.

It was the type of dance that flew. One step after another–swirl, promenade, turn-and-cast–and if you couldn't remember, you didn't have time to find out before you were on to the next. In the small expanse of the drawing room, they had to stay close to each other even as they whirled from one partner to another and back again. John looped an arm around Sophia's waist to keep from falling–he didn't know if it was he who had lost his balance or she. He couldn't take his eyes from her or he would lose the dance. Her hair fell from its pins; her pearls bounced along her collarbone; her dress flashed in the candlelight.

When the song ended, John was all sweat and no breath. Somehow, despite that, he was laughing, and so was Sophia, and so was everyone else, and yet that didn't terrify him. If everyone saw the truth in his heart, let them.

Let them hope with him that Sophia might agree to keep this fire between them alive for the rest of time.

Chapter Sixteen

Euphoria didn't last long. Next morning at breakfast, Sophia's appetite spoiled when Ellen announced she and Max would return to Northfield Hall that very afternoon. "We've got Rosalind waiting for us," she explained.

"The roads will still be muddy from the storm." Sophia wasn't sure why she so desperately wanted her sister to stay, except that the visit had been too short, and their conversations had revolved around Sophia's own poor decisions. She wanted Ellen to stay at least long enough for them to discover one of Ellen's imperfections, too.

"This is England," Max replied. "The roads are always muddy."

Then, Sophia had to herd the girls into the schoolroom, even though John hadn't yet come down to breakfast. They hadn't visited each other the night before; Sophia had stayed up late talking with Ellen instead.

She regretted that now, when she didn't get even a glimpse of him at breakfast.

Having gone a week without a proper governess, the girls were unruly, unfocused, and undisciplined. It took all of Sophia's energy to corral them from one activity to the next. Her only break was to see Ellen and Max off in their carriage, which the Robin Abbey grooms had cleaned to a gleam for its return journey.

Ellen clung to Sophia for several moments longer than necessary. "Look after yourself, sister. I know there is no governing you, but do try to be somewhat sensible, won't you?"

"As long as you try to be somewhat interesting." The thing about Ellen's embraces was that they were always exactly what Sophia needed. When Ellen stepped away, her whole body went cool as if a gust of wind shivered down her spine.

"I expect the next scandal to involve even more intrigue and even higher crimes," Max said by way of farewell.

Ellen turned back once more before climbing into the carriage. "You will write to Nate, won't you?"

Sophia nodded. "I promise."

And then Ellen and Max were gone, trundled back to their boring life of bliss. Meanwhile Sophia returned to her day at Robin Abbey.

She ordered herself to enjoy her position. Compared to being locked in the same room for days on end–or being transported for a crime she hadn't committed–governessing should be no chore at all. Sophia returned to the schoolroom determined to find the joy in her role. The optimism in molding young minds. The humor in the girls' childish antics. The power in instilling them with her own values of independence and intelligence.

Her resolve lasted an hour. And Sophia admitted to herself it was no fault of the Misses Cosgrove. They were well-intentioned children.

The problem was her. The problem was that she was bored out of her mind. The problem was that she itched for each day of her life to be different from the last.

Standing in the schoolroom, instructing the girls on French grammar, Sophia knew she couldn't last another month doing this every day, even though she had just fought a battle to stay.

Picturing her future was too depressing. And too puzzling, since she knew only what she didn't want and had no answers as to what she could do next that would make her happier.

She let her mind turn away from reality. And back to the question that remained unanswered: who had planted those bad notes in her reticule, and why?

It was at supper that Sophia finally saw John again. The merriment from the night before had dissipated: Mrs. Edwards seemed ripe for another argument while poor Lady Widlake listed sideways in her seat as if even the concept of a meal was too much for her to face. "Perhaps you would prefer supper in bed," John suggested, but Lady Widlake insisted on remaining.

"I shall feel too sorry for myself if I am deprived of common daily tasks already. There will be enough of that once I am in confinement."

Still, Lord Widlake rushed through the meal. Sophia had only time to take a few bites of each course before he signaled the footmen to replace it with the next. In sum, she had a quarter bowl of pumpkin soup, three forkfuls of beetroot, half a haddock, one piece of jellied ham, and a gulp of stewed apple. Then Lord Widlake declared the meal over. Helping his wife from her chair, he declared, "I think it best if we each retire to our own occupations, rather than sit up in the drawing room."

"I quite agree," Mrs. Edwards said. "My daughter is looking peaked in service to you, my lord."

Sophia watched the reactions sweep across the room: annoyance in the baron, mortification in the baroness, confusion or ignorance in the children. Chagrin twisted John's eyebrows, and Sophia suspected he felt sorry for Mrs. Edwards, as he much as he condemned her for the comment.

At least, that was what she imagined of her lover. A man with the capacity for emotions more complex than hers.

For her part, the tension in the room choked her like a hand to her throat. She fought back: "I shall take a turn in the garden to walk off that excellent meal."

"But it is already dark out!" Mrs. Edwards objected.

"Then Mr. Anderson will escort her," Lord Widlake replied with the least amount of grace Sophia had ever heard from the man. Belatedly, he looked to John. "If you don't mind, that is."

John had already bowed his head in obedience—or perhaps in subterfuge, for his chin was tucked so low that not even Sophia could see his expression, and he kept his reply short: "Certainly."

The garden was not the only place to walk at the Abbey, but it was the most accessible from the house, and after dusk, it seemed safest for walking by lantern light. Sophia retreated to her room for her cloak, then met John at its entrance off the formal drawing room, where he waited with a lantern.

Her body ached when she drew within reaching distance of him. In an instinctive, carnal way. She had to fight the urge to step directly into his arms. Which was different than how she usually reacted to lovers. Sophia was accustomed to seeing a man and wanting to take him between her legs; this tenderness was new and not entirely welcome.

He smiled at her. "Miss Preston, it is good to see you out and about again."

"If you can call being abroad in the household 'out and about.'" She accepted his hand to step down from the Abbey onto the garden path half a foot below. It had drizzled again that evening, and the gravel was slippery under her boots.

"How is your stomach feeling?" John's voice dipped low with the question. "Have you need of another dose of medicine?"

Heat rushed from her core. "Here?" It was a little cold, granted, but the yew hedges guarded them from the worst of the wind. Sophia had sucked one earl-to-be's cock at Vauxhall Gardens in London; there was no reason why she and John couldn't find a little joy in Robin Abbey's gardens now.

"In a bed, rather." John drifted a pace or two away from her as he glanced over his shoulder. "Anyone looking out from the family bedrooms can sight our lantern. I should hate for them to wonder why we stopped walking."

A disappointment, but Sophia supposed he made a good point. Still, she tucked the fantasy away for a later date. "Who do you imagine would be marking our progress?"

He hesitated before answering. Long enough for Sophia to notice the concern knitting his forehead. "It could be anyone, couldn't it? One of the maids preparing the beds, one of the children, Lord or Lady Widlake..."

And yet, Sophia suspected his comment did not come from a general anxiety of being caught with her. "Or it could be whoever placed the banknotes in my purse."

"Yes, I suppose so."

They had executed the full, small square path. Sophia carried onward for a second loop. "Have you heard of the Abbey's crypts?"

"No."

"Neither had I, until Miss Mary mentioned them yesterday. Apparently, Lord Widlake keeps the key. It occurred to me that the forger might be doing their work down there."

John walked in silence for a few steps, so that the only sound between them was the crunch of his boots against the gravel.

That, and their breaths, whose smoky exhales twisted together in the air.

"Perhaps it would be better to forget the matter entirely. No one plans to investigate you further. It might be wisest to live and let live, so to speak."

"And yet, you worry that someone is watching from the window."

John let out a little sigh. "I rather hoped that our conversations would no longer revolve around this intrigue."

She stepped forward. Not close enough that anyone looking out the window would find cause for complaint. But close enough that she could see the curve of John's lips. He had done so much for her already. She knew the number of favors he had done her was far out of proportion to those she had done him. She should follow his lead and let the matter die with Max and Ellen's departure.

She should let their relationship return to her favorite activity. Except the question remained. Someone had arranged for her to be accused of the crime. Therefore, that person was owed the same courtesy.

"Search the crypts with me. If we discover nothing, then I will stop worrying about the matter. I will go back to being a perfectly ill-behaved governess."

John's eyebrows arched. "And if we discover something?"

Sophia thought that answer was rather obvious. "Then we shall follow where that trail leads."

THEY MADE A PLAN, since exploring the crypt was not so simple as waltzing downstairs under the cover of midnight.

Sophia would discover its entrance from the Misses Cosgrove the next day in the schoolroom. John, meanwhile, would borrow the key from Lord Widlake.

His was the more difficult task. Perhaps impossible. John woke at dawn from a nightmare in which he tried to remove the key from the baron's neck, only to find himself entombed in a cold, dark crypt with no one the wiser.

He began by applying to Lady Widlake during her morning examination. "I heard from Lady Berwick that the Abbey boasts historical crypts. I wonder if it is possible to take a tour? I confess, I have an amateur's love of Tudor history."

Lady Widlake smiled at him in that long-suffering way of hers. "Of history, Mr. Anderson, or are you one of those men who seeks ghost stories?"

He forced himself to play along. "When it comes to the Tudors, are those not one and the same?"

"Indeed. We don't allow anyone into the crypts, however. Not since last year, when the footman Jasper got himself locked in. With the twins so determined to slip through Nurse's grasp, we can't take the risk of them endangering themselves down there." Lady Widlake shifted her dress to reveal her swollen ankles. "Isn't there anything you can do for me about this? I feel I can barely walk, though I desperately want to take exercise."

For her ankles, he instructed her to lie with her feet propped on pillows with cold towels wrapped around the joints, changed hourly. It was unlikely to make a difference, he knew, but sometimes the best way to address a problem was to give the appearance of addressing it.

As for the crypts, he approached Lord Widlake in the afternoon. It was raining again, so the baron had retired to his study with correspondence. He was a man who looked comfortable behind a desk, more natural in the leather seat than he ever appeared in the saddle or even at his family dining table. For once he looked his proper height, and the creases across his forehead appeared as natural reactions to his circumstances rather than permanent features.

"How may I help you, Mr. Anderson?" he asked by way of greeting, and even this sounded looser and less guarded than his manner outside the study.

"I am indulging in some personal reading, my lord, and wondered if you have any histories of Robin Abbey that I might peruse."

Lord Widlake pursed his lips in thought. "If you're looking for insight into the estate management, I can offer my late father's secretary's personal journals, which track the crops and harvests and tenants."

"Actually, I am interested in the Abbey itself. When it was constructed, who the architect was, that sort of thing."

The lord's eyes glazed over even before John finished his sentence. "You are at liberty to review the collection; it is very possible my grandfather purchased a book on the topic that I have willfully ignored all these years."

John had no choice but to continue the charade. Following Lord Widlake's gesture, he ventured to the corner of the study with the oldest books and began taking them off the shelf, one by one, to discover their titles and subject matter.

"How fares Lady Widlake?" the baron asked.

"Very well." All things considered—her age, the number of children she had already delivered, her disposition, and her health—John was very happy with her physical state. "A few weeks yet, I do believe, and God willing, you will have another healthy child."

"The baroness is the heart of my family. I hope we will not need to have any difficult conversations during the delivery..." Lord Widlake took a deep breath. "If we do, I shall want to save her life at all costs."

John had only ever had to have that difficult conversation a handful of times in his career: when the delivery had lasted days, the mother was exhausted, and the baby was still in the birth canal. At that point, the question became whether to let the mother keep attempting a natural birth—and likely die in the effort—or use the crotchet hook, sacrificing the baby to save the mother's life.

If he was forced to have that conversation during a birth with one of his high-profile clients, John could assume his career would be reduced to delivering babies to the poor with little pay for the rest of his life.

The trouble was, no matter how healthy the mother was during pregnancy, there was no predicting when a baby wouldn't come into position properly, or when the uterine pushes would not be strong enough to expel the child. John was no god: the most he could do was respond to the situation as it developed.

To Lord Widlake, he replied, "I understand. And, if I may say it, Lady Widlake must count her blessings to have a husband so invested in her health."

John didn't mean Lord Widlake's commitment to choosing her life–that wasn't uncommon, since a mother would likely recover and bear another child sooner rather than later–but the solicitousness with which Lord Widlake treated his wife every day. He could not tell whether the two loved each other, yet Lord Widlake exhibited more consideration towards his lady than most of the aristocratic husbands John had witnessed previously.

"Do you plan to marry?"

John let the idea blossom for a moment: Sophia as a wife, following him from one assignment to another, sparkling with conversation at the end of the day, ensuring his shirts were mended and dazzling his clients with her wit and class.

The idea evaporated. Sophia wasn't a woman who would fold herself into the role of wife. She wouldn't be herself if she had to align her days to his.

And John wasn't sure he would be himself, if every day he worried whether his wife resented her choice in marrying him.

"Perhaps one day," he answered Lord Widlake.

"It was a matter of course for me. I find it a peculiar experience, at least from this vantage point with fourteen years behind us. The courtship is filled with emotion. Anticipation, apprehension, awkwardness, hope, even love." John glanced over to see Lord Widlake blush at this. "Lady Widlake and I were engaged for a year before we married. I wrote her every day, can you believe it? There was something about her...I suppose I believed that a man's life partner should be a partner to all his thoughts and feelings, too."

Uncharitable though it was, it was hard for John to imagine anyone finding Lord Widlake interesting enough to read daily letters detailing his internal monologues.

"Then you marry. You see the object of your affection every day. You discover the answers to all the mysteries that kept you up at night before." Lord Widlake wilted in his chair. "I thought it would be simple to provide us a happy life. I would give her children; I would pursue a career that would keep the family name powerful and proud; I would model good behavior with my own. And I have done all that. Yet I look back at these fourteen years and I wonder whether she has been happy at all."

It was a startling confession, until John considered that a person rarely said what they truly felt. Which made him wonder whether Lord Widlake actually worried about his wife's happiness at all, or if it was his own he questioned.

"Her ladyship has always struck me as very content."

"Content, yes. Is that the same as happy?"

John thought of his mother. Always without complaint, even when she was forced to work fourteen hours by the hot fire through the long summer days. Even when his own kin turned her onto the street. Always ready to remind him life could be worse.

Amma hadn't raised him to expect happiness. That was too fleeting an emotion. He would take stability: a steady income, a home, a future he could rely on. If happiness befell him a time or two, then the luckier was he.

"You must forgive me," Lord Widlake said, interrupting John's thoughts. "I always worsen with introspection as my lady approaches confinement. Fear of loss, I suppose."

"It is natural."

The study heated with awkwardness for a moment. Then, Lord Widlake cleared his throat. "Any luck with those books?"

"Alas." John hadn't even been looking at their titles these past ten minutes. "I'm afraid if I am to find anything on the history of the Abbey, I shall have to examine the building itself. I confess, I was hoping to discover whether there were hidden chambers or sealed cellars with ancient booty."

Lord Widlake did not smile. "There are the crypts, but I do not allow anyone in them. They are far too dangerous."

"Dangerous? Even for an adult?"

"Indeed. It is too easy to get locked in. Just ask poor Jasper."

"As you say." There wasn't much more John could do at this point, beyond stealing the key.

He met Sophia after supper in the drawing room. She sat with a book held up to the firelight, for all to see a perfectly-bred young lady. John leaned against the mantle for the disguise of polite conversation.

Without looking up, Sophia greeted him, "I found out where the crypt entrance is. Did you get the key?"

He told himself the ache creeping around his stomach was from the cream sauce at supper. Not from Sophia's single-mindedness.

She didn't mean to come off that way. It was only that they didn't know how long they had alone in the drawing room before Mrs. Edwards or Lord Widlake came to accompany them.

"I did not. The entire household is forbidden, out of fear the twins will get themselves locked down there."

At last, Sophia lifted her gaze. "Or because Lord Widlake is hiding his counterfeiting operation?"

"I don't suppose we'll find out either way."

Now she frowned. The last time she had looked at him that way—like he was being a perfect fool—was when she assured him she didn't care one way or the other that Amma worked as a housekeeper. That frown had been the key to unlock John's anxiety. To make him feel that she cradled his heart as carefully as he did hers.

This frown did the opposite. Especially as she followed it with, "Why shouldn't we? All that's left is to steal the key."

"And put both our positions at risk?" John couldn't stay at the mantle. He pulled a footstool beside her chair and sat. As if being close enough to breathe in her scent would calm him. "It doesn't matter now that you are free of charges. We can put it behind us."

Hearing the words out loud, John wished they were true. How he wanted Sophia to look at him and smile and not follow it up with anything about the bad notes or even flirtation. He wanted her to see him, the way he wallowed in her presence, without requiring anything more.

Sophia shut the book in her hands. "You agreed to help me search the crypts."

"Yes, I did, but—"

"So we will search the crypts. Then, if we don't find anything, we'll put it behind us. We can talk about anything at all you want. Assuming we don't find anything." With a smile–a little flirtatious, a little condescending–she patted his hand. "You've been such a help to me. Whatever would I do without you?"

John didn't have the heart to summon a response.

S OPHIA DRESSED IN HER dark gray wool, the better to sneak about the Abbey, and arrived to meet John at the base of the main stairs at midnight. At least, that was the plan. Yet even minutes after the clock stopped its chimes, she remained alone. The first few moments she dismissed as accidental. Each passing minute, though, her heartbeat drummed louder in her ear.

Perhaps he wasn't coming after all. She knew he wanted to put the matter behind them. He wanted to pretend that she hadn't been locked away for days, her name dragged through mud, saved only by the weight of Max's influence.

Sophia wanted to put it behind them, too. She wanted to be sneaking through the Abbey to slip into John's bed, not to descend into dusty old crypts. But she couldn't put the matter behind her until she had answers. She needed someone to blame, or at least some explanation with which to frame the chaos she had just survived.

Once she had that, she could focus on John and her future.

Still, as she waited, she began to fear John had at last forsaken her. Perhaps asking him to steal the key from Lord Widlake's study had been the last straw. She should have volunteered to do that herself, since she had seen even in the hazy firelight that he didn't want to do it.

She was so on edge when he finally arrived that she greeted him with, "You're late." Immediately, she wished she could take back the words. What she meant was: *You're here! Thank God! I need you!* She cleared her throat. "Did you get the key?"

He stepped close enough for her to see a heavy metal key in his palm. "You know where to find the door?"

Miss Mary had been all too happy to provide detailed directions on how to find the non-descript door beside the scullery. "The door is mighty heavy," Miss Cosgrove had added in that world-weary way of hers.

Sophia led John down the corridor per the girls' directions. Sure enough, the door awaited to the left of the scullery. Checking that they were alone, she struck her flint, lit the taper she had brought along, and affixed the candle inside a lantern. The door thus illuminated proved to be some old wood–polished but warped–with heavy iron hinges and fittings. John fumbled a little with the key, and then he had to wrestle the door to turn the lock.

In short measure, however, they descended into the crypts.

Sophia had prepared herself for an encounter with filth and decay. She was braced for dust to assault her nostrils (with three handkerchiefs tucked in her bodice as preparation); she expected cobwebs to catch her hair and stone sarcophagi to leap at her from the darkness.

Instead, they were greeted by clean and order. The packed dirt floor did not sprout clouds with each footstep. The corridor boasted burial alcoves, to be sure, but the stone tombs were simple rectangles without any decoration. Sophia lifted the lantern to discover an inscription on one of them: *Here Lies Mother Superior Johanna Lowell.*

Beside her, John asked, "Are you frightened?"

"No." Not even a little. "Do I seem frightened?"

She swung the lantern back around in time to see the chagrin in his smile. "I don't know how you would behave when frightened. I imagine you have too much pride to swoon or scream; that's why I asked, to make sure I wasn't missing your signs of fright."

His tone was teasing; she mimicked it even as she sensed there was something lurking below his words that was not a tease at all. "I may be proud, but I am also a woman of passion. I suspect you would know I am frightened the same way you know when I am aroused to other emotions."

They continued down the corridor. It followed the U shape of the rest of the Abbey. Sophia paused in the corner to examine the alcove, but it was the same as the others.

"And can you tell whether I am frightened?" John asked. "Or when I am aroused to other emotions?"

A clear invitation to smirk. "I can certainly tell when you are aroused, sir." And she paused long enough to cup his groin in her palm.

He was not hard–she did not expect him to be–but instead of leaning into the invitation, John broke away from her. He even took the lantern into his own hand. "I wonder if you can."

Sophia followed him further into the crypt. This was the type of scene she had always hoped to avoid. Stuck with John in this cellar, surrounded by nothing but dead bodies, she couldn't very well walk out. Because then she would be above stairs, surrounded by nothing but apathy. Free of the murky waters of an argument, to be sure, but bereft of friends.

Bereft of John. If she was being honest with herself.

"I can tell you are not happy with me right now," she said. "Perhaps you would be so kind as to tell me why."

"I am not unhappy with you. I am not unhappy at all."

"Your tone implies otherwise."

With a great heave of breath, John whirled around. The lantern swung wildly with his movement, scattering light across the tombs. They were almost to the other side of the Abbey now, with one last branch of the crypts in which they might find any evidence of the counterfeiter.

Sophia didn't much care in that moment if they ever found the culprit.

"I am not unhappy. I question what is in the scope of your notice. We have spent an equal amount of time in each other's company. I know the scent of your perfume. I know that you prefer silk over any other fabric. You bite into your lip when you are interested. I can tell when your smile is unrestrained or when you are humoring a person. I know the exact moment when I have asked too many questions and made you angry. And what I wonder is if you could recite a similar list about me."

Once a gauntlet was thrown, Sophia always rose to the challenge. Except within her, reactions warred. Even though John vaulted the words at her like they were lances, she absorbed them as she would kisses. It was beyond flattery. Her heart glowed; an impossible sensation, yet true. She wanted to wrap her arms around his neck and press her skin to his.

She felt the same as him. Beneath the specifics of the list, she knew what he described: that feeling that when John was in the room, the rest of the world melted away. And that when he wasn't there, he was still her center. He was her compass north. At all times, hovering along all her thoughts, she tracked where he might be, what he might be doing, and when she might see him again.

She wanted to respond to his list with one of her own. To prove that she could, since he didn't believe in her. And to bestow upon him the same glow.

Only Sophia didn't have such a list. She would barely even be able to create one for Ellen, whom she had known her entire life. She wasn't a physician trained to notice people's bodies or reactions or emotions. She was a governess—a poor one, at that—who need only concern herself with ideas and comportment and arranging a pleasant life for herself.

And that spiked anger across her body, despite the beauty of John's words. For if he knew her the way he claimed to, he shouldn't ask such a thing of her. "I am selfish. I told you that from the start."

"So you did. I suppose it is my fault for thinking that in the case of love, your definition of self might extend to include me."

Never had she heard his voice so cold. So remote. Even his accent changed, carving out each word in the frigid tones of the overly-educated instead of his usual London drawl.

"Who said anything about love?" she fought back. "I am sure I never gave you any reason to believe I am interested in an affair of the heart."

Lies. Lies so strong and sharp she could hear them tearing through the air even as she said them.

Sophia knew they were a poor man's shield. She owed John more than to cower behind them. She lied anyway, and she forced herself not to wince when they drained his face of color.

"You are correct. The error is mine. After all, you were happy to fuck me without ever asking my name." John thrust the lantern back into her hand. A splinter from its handle dug into her finger. "I beg your leave. Having procured your key, I believe I can provide no more service to you tonight. I trust you can see yourself upstairs safely."

He didn't wait for her to respond. And Sophia could think of nothing to say that would bring him back. She watched him march the corridor until he turned down the other end of the U. He would be walking in darkness now. Climbing up into the Abbey without so much as a taper light to guide him.

His choice. All of this was his choice. She had been honest with him from the start about who she was and what she wanted. This was his mess. His hurt. As for herself, Sophia was absolutely fine.

There was nothing for it but to carry on. Dabbing at her eyes—stinging from the splinter in her finger—with one of her spare handkerchiefs, Sophia continued further into the crypt. At the last corner, she paused again. This was her final hope to discover the counterfeiter. If she turned down this corridor and found nothing, she would have to resign herself to a black, permanent ignorance.

She took a deep breath. Swung the lantern to her right.

And illuminated the entire operation. Paper, ink, copper plates, printing press, drying lines. Crates stacked with completed bills. Even at a glance, even in the dim light of the lantern, she could read the signatures: *The People of Northfield Hall*.

Strange, how victory broke her heart.

Chapter Seventeen

John didn't see Sophia for three days. A small miracle, that, considering they occupied the same house. And for a great house, Robin Abbey was tiny. It had hardly enough rooms to separate him from the woman.

Still, he managed it. He took late breakfasts, after waiting to hear the pitter patter of the young girls rushing off to the schoolroom. He ordered suppers to his apartment. When Lady Widlake dismissed him for the day, he left the Abbey altogether and stalked the soggy forest surrounding it as if on the hunt.

He searched for something, to be sure. Not a wild animal but some kind of peace. A miracle solution that would heal the wound festering in his heart.

If he were to describe the symptoms to a physician, he would not call it a clean break. It seeped: a slashed vital organ leaking pain into the rest of his body. His chest was heavy. His lungs struggled to draw full breaths. His stomach seized in cramps whenever he ate more than a piece of toast. If he allowed himself to lie still, the pain pooled all the way to his fingertips.

He loved Sophia. Yet to her, he was nothing more than a body with which she enjoyed playing.

The morning after the crypts, she had sent him a note by way of the maid Hattie:

I found the engraving press, etc. Proof of the conspiracy, but no proof of who is behind it. I will let the matter drop. Please accept my apologies.

He read it a dozen times. It never changed to say: *I love you, too.* It never morphed to promise: *I will do better if you give me another chance.*

And so he avoided her.

Who said anything about love?

She was right, of course. From the very beginning, she had been clear about who she was and how she felt. She wanted to fuck, not to fall in love. She wanted someone who would not linger in her life. She most definitely didn't want a man who picked an argument with her over emotions in the middle of the night.

John was supposed to have kept a stiff upper lip. He was not supposed to have desired anything beyond her quim and tits and arse.

Now that he had bared his heart to her, she was anxious to be rid of her plaything.

It was the walks through the forest that helped John the most. The movement dissipated the pain that otherwise weighed down his limbs. The air–cold and moist from constant autumn rains–shocked his lungs so he could feel nothing else. Neglecting gloves and a hat, John let his fingers and ears go numb. This was what summer had felt like as a boy when he and Amma first arrived to England: so cold he thought he would never be warm again.

His body had adjusted then. His heart, too, shifting allegiances from his father to his uncle and then to Garrett. And now to himself and Amma and no one else.

John would adjust to this break with Sophia. If he took enough walks and ate enough meals alone and left Robin Abbey at his first opportunity.

When he did leave, John would focus again on his priorities: to be England's foremost accoucheur. To set up his own practice in London, to purchase his own country home where Amma could live out her days in fresh air, to own a coach and four, to be solicited for his opinion on the most complex of medical matters.

One day–once he left, he hoped–that dream would feel full again. One day, he wouldn't have to forcibly remove Sophia and her flirtatious teeth from his own imagination.

It was on the return from one of his walks on the fourth day that John next saw her. He saw the whole family, in fact, the moment he walked in. They were all assembled by the stairs: Lady Widlake in the rear, baby Jacob in her arms; Nurse with a firm grip on an arm of each of the twins; Lord Widlake halfway up the stairs; Mrs. Edwards just behind him; and the girls clustered at its base with Sophia at their center.

She wore a ruffled white gown with an orange cashmere shawl around her shoulders. When he entered, she was the first to see him: a curl of hair fell loose against her neck as she turned her head his way.

John's heart burst with joy at seeing her.

Alarm flashed across her eyes.

"Ah, here he is," Lord Widlake exclaimed. There was a strange energy to his words: he spoke too loudly and enounced his words too perfectly. "Mr. Anderson, perhaps you can explain yourself."

John tore his eyes away from Sophia. Miss Preston. She was the only matter upon which he had need to explain himself.

If he didn't look at her, perhaps he could get away with the lie. *I have never engaged in inappropriate behavior with Miss Preston.*

That was when John noticed Mr. Ord at the top of the stairs. The man was as tall and narrow as John remembered. His moustache drooped more dramatically than on his last visit. Those details distracted John from processing what he saw in the man's hands: an engraved copper plate, an ink-stained sack, and a stack of banknotes.

"It is as I thought." Mrs. Edwards clutched at her neck as she spoke to Lord Widlake. "Did I not say you must search his quarters again? Think how he allowed poor Miss Preston to take the blame for so long."

Her words skated across his skin like ice. She had warned him this would happen. Except she had never mentioned that she would be the one pointing Mr. Ord his way.

Ignoring his mother-in-law, Lord Widlake said, "There have been more false banknotes in town. Mr. Ord returned for advice and found these instruments in your apartment. How do you account for that, Mr. Anderson?"

John felt the weight of all their eyes, even the footmen at the door and the maids passing in nearby rooms. Mrs. Edwards waited for him to fall for her trap. Nurse gleamed with the excitement of an incurable gossip. Lady Widlake watched, and at least there was horror in the way she clasped her child to her chest.

It was Sophia he cared about. And for once, he couldn't read her. She might be angry or frightened or disgusted. John didn't have the time or the heart or the courage to interpret the crease of her brow.

"I cannot account for it, my lord. I have never seen those items before."

Lord Widlake looked to Mr. Ord. "Those are the same banknotes that have been circulating in Boughampton, are they not?"

"They are. There were more of these, too, in the back of his armoire. I brought out this stack to show you what I found."

"They are not mine." John reiterated the defense before Mr. Ord could even finish his sentence. At this point, it was all he had. "I know nothing about counterfeiting banknotes. I could hardly even sketch the human body for my anatomy lecture, much less engrave a design in copper. This is another attempt by whomever cast doubt on Miss Preston to now accuse me. It won't work. I am not a counterfeiter. I haven't the time, have I, since my days are devoted to the welfare of this household?"

He forced himself to stop. He knew that the more he said, the more desperate he sounded. And the desperate were often confused with the guilty.

His mind raced, trying to see a way out of this. If he were arrested, he could write to his cousin. Garrett had the money to pay for a solicitor. But the scandal alone would ruin him. Assuming his innocence could be defended in court, being removed from Robin Abbey a presumed criminal would be enough to ensure the only mothers who allowed him near them were the mothers confined to Fleet Street prison.

If he could not nip this in the bud, then this was the moment when all of John's dreams died.

"Miss Preston, did you not believe someone deliberately placed those banknotes in your reticule?"

"Yes, I did." She lifted her chin. John still couldn't tell what she thought. He knew what he wanted her to say: *It wasn't Mr. Anderson. I can vouch for him. If you touch him, I'll set my family on you same as if you touched me.*

A coward's desire. He was supposed to be able to fight for himself. Yet he craved that protection. If only someone–anyone–cared enough for him to defend him beyond the point of reason.

Mrs. Edwards elevated herself up a step. That much closer to Lord Widlake. "And it was you who did so, wasn't it, Mr. Anderson? After all, you also are the one who thought to inscribe the notes as guaranteed by *The People of Northfield Hall.*"

"Which made us all think it was Miss Preston," Mr. Ord added unnecessarily.

Sophia pulled that orange shawl closer around her shoulders. John waited, though he knew the defense was imaginary. It was to her advantage to blame him. She could rest easy at night, believing she at last had the answer to the great mystery. And she would need not worry about an errant lover demanding her heart in addition to her body.

She might even believe it. That look in her eyes might be horror as she narrated a story in which John had spent all these weeks lying to her—toying with her—while making her the scapegoat to his scheme.

John couldn't live with her thinking that. She could choose the easiest course of action and let him take the blame. She could forget him entirely. But he couldn't stand to let her go believing that he had betrayed her. It was to her that he pleaded one more time, "I know nothing about this matter. I am innocent."

Her teeth sank into her lower lip. She turned away from him. Now he couldn't see her face at all. Couldn't read anything except the back of her shoulders and spine.

But he did hear her voice—strong and true and typically defiant—when she said, "It wasn't Mr. Anderson, Mrs. Edwards, and you know it because the truth is the counterfeiter is you."

F OR THE FIRST TIME in days, fire surged through Sophia's veins. She shouldn't take pleasure in how Mrs. Edwards paled, but she did. The woman was all too happy to accuse John. And before that, Sophia's family. Now it was her turn to stand accused, no matter the truth. Let panic sweep her off her feet; let nausea squeeze her gut; let the old woman die of fright right there on the Abbey's steps.

"I found equipment much like that a few nights ago in the crypts. By the oldest tombs, just under the state rooms." Sophia continued with her voice pitched loud enough that Parliament itself might hear her. "I cannot help but wonder what you might find, Mr. Ord, if you look in that great chest underneath Mrs. Edwards's window?"

"You confess to lurking in the crypts yourself yet dare accuse me!" Mrs. Edwards gasped.

Lord Widlake nodded at Ord, however, and the man turned for Mrs. Edwards's apartment.

Sophia called, "Search under her bed, too. I hear she keeps a great bag of ink there."

Mrs. Edwards drew her spine into a straight line. "Even if you do, what can you conclude? If you will not take the paraphernalia found in Mr. Anderson's room as proof that he is the guilty party, why should you use anything from my room against me?" Then she took another tack. "Really, Lord Widlake, that you would allow a mere governess to speak that way to me."

Never had Sophia been gladder to be more than a mere governess. For she needn't cower, nor bite her tongue, nor even look down contritely as Mr. Ord returned.

His eyes darted between the lord and lady before he announced, "It is as Miss Preston said. Paper and ink and...well, and this, my lord."

He handed Lord Widlake a stack of papers. These were not banknotes; they were larger, and they boasted no fancy engravings. The print was big enough for Sophia to see the headline from the base of the stairs:

LORD WIDLAKE FAILS AGAIN TO TAKE ACTION

If Mrs. Edwards had been pale before, she was white as chalk now. Only her nose retained color: the burnished red purple mottle of skin ill-used. She cried out to her daughter, "Agatha, you must see..."

Lord Widlake blocked her from even looking at his wife. "I knew your complaints against my politics, dear Mother, but I never imagined you would make them so public. Or act so rashly as to create a criminal scheme here in my own home. What is your goal, then? To ruin my name and therefore the future of your own grandchildren? Or will you take it a step further and burn down the Abbey while we sleep inside it?"

Mrs. Edwards let out a strangled noise. Sophia heard outrage in it, the same emotion they had all heard from the woman a dozen times. Mrs. Edwards looked desperately about: up at Mr. Ord, down at Sophia, beyond to John. But finally, she did face Lord Widlake eye to eye. "I printed the handbills, I admit it, but I had nothing to do with the counterfeiting."

He scoffed.

"No, you must believe me, my lord. I wanted to rouse you into action. You have the power to take a stance. You have the opportunity to lead us towards a better future. I wanted to force your hand to do something about the Corn Laws. Inaction will not create a legacy. Your current course will guarantee that no one remembers you even in a dozen years." Caught up in her own tirade, Mrs. Edwards regained her color. It was only when Lord Widlake interrupted–"Good God, woman!"–that she returned to the matter at hand. "I paid Frank to print the handbills for me. I distributed them in Boughampton. I wrote letters to Mr. Cobbett, too, though he hasn't yet deigned to publish them. I did not produce counterfeit banknotes."

John asked, "Is it Frank's printing machine below the bell tower, then?"

"Below the bell tower?" Lord Widlake lost a little of his bluster as he turned to John. "What's all this then?"

Sophia feared John would equivocate from the way he blinked under Lord Widlake's examination. She wondered what lie he could spin and hoped it would be convincing enough.

In the end, he told the truth: "I heard mechanical sounds coming from the bell tower one night. After Miss Preston was accused, I thought I might be able to clear up the matter and went to investigate. There is a printing press underneath the trap door."

Lord Widlake skewered Mrs. Edwards again with his glare. "What have you to say to defend yourself?"

"I don't know how Frank printed the pamphlets. I don't know anything about the crypts." Mrs. Edwards stepped backwards. "Please, Lord Widlake, you must believe me."

"If not you, then who?" Lord Widlake cast his scowl from Mrs. Edwards down to all of them. Even his children. "Do you maintain that it is Mr. Anderson? Or Miss Preston? Whom would you like to accuse now, madam?"

It came to Sophia in a rush. The stains on Polly's sleeves. Nurse complaining that Cook spent half her time making ink. How the crypts boasted not even one cobweb, despite being locked to the entire household. How evidence had ended up in Sophia's own locked room.

And then there was the question of how the banknotes were distributed in town. The first accusation had come directly after the family's trip to Boughampton, but no one from above stairs had left the Abbey for days. Which meant the bad money was being transported by a member of the household.

Or members. All along, Sophia had pointed out that she was incapable of running such an operation by herself. That was true of John, too, and Mrs. Edwards, and even Lord Widlake. False banknotes required an engraver like Frank; distributing them required someone with regular access to the market like Cook; keeping it secret from the rest of Robin Abbey required collusion.

The culprit was not an individual, but a cooperative. And in that instant, Sophia understood: it was the entire household.

Now that she knew, she saw the guilt in Nurse's eyes; she noted the way Frank and Jasper stared at the ground rather than at the accused Mrs. Edwards on the stairs; she saw Polly slip away.

They had all been anxious to assign a political motivation to the scheme. But in the end, it was simple. Someone had discovered a skill for counterfeiting among the group, and the household colluded to create the money. They needed it for an ailing relative, perhaps, or one of them was saving up to strike off on his own with a new wife, or they were greedy.

They saw an opportunity to change the system within which they operated, and they took it.

Sophia couldn't blame them for it. She couldn't even blame them for invoking Northfield Hall. If it weren't illegal, it was the kind of scheme her own family would endorse.

Mrs. Edwards replied, "Are you so naïve as to believe Mr. Anderson's denial? We had none of this trouble before he arrived here, and you have found proof in his room. What more do you need to be convinced of his guilt?"

Sophia admired the scheme, now that she had figured it out. But she would not let John be their scapegoat. If someone had to be hanged for the crime, it would be the actual criminals. No matter how sympathetic their motivations.

Not John. Never John.

"He is not the counterfeiter. Or should I say, he is not one of the counterfeiters. Don't you agree, Mrs. Hibbert? Jasper? Nurse?"

It was that last one, Nurse, who gave them away. She crumpled into a wail, "Oh, and I'm that sorry about it, too! I never should have agreed to go along with it!"

Hubbub reigned for a moment as Frank and Jasper tried to deny her and the twin boys erupted in sympathetic sobs and Hattie rushed in to silence her. Then Mrs. Hibbert stepped forward and hushed them all. "Lord Widlake, Mr. Ord, I must take full responsibility."

Sophia watched as Lord Widlake reached the obvious conclusions. She braced for the ugly scene that must follow. Would Mr. Ord allow Mrs. Hibbert to fetch a cloak before carting her off? Would she scream or argue or struggle? Would they ever hear from her again?

Lord Widlake surprised Sophia. "No, Mrs. Hibbert, it seems it is I who must take responsibility." He faced Mr. Ord. "It is my household, and it has been mismanaged. The fault is mine. You must hold me accountable for all wrongdoing."

Mr. Ord could not arrest a peer of the realm. Yet Lord Widlake would face other consequences, should word of this scandal get out. Embarrassment. Public shaming. Parliament could even order him locked in the Tower of London.

So they watched, every one of them holding their breath, to see how Mr. Ord would decide to respond.

It was in that moment that Lady Widlake rent the air with a great cry of pain.

CHAPTER EIGHTEEN

O F COURSE, THE BABY did not arrive immediately.

Even for a woman whose body was accustomed to delivering infants, John knew it would take at least an hour from her first unbearable pain. Yet her scream did the trick: everyone reacted as if she was about to die.

John leapt to her side. She had mentioned a stomachache that morning, but he had assumed it was digestion, not reckoning on cramps–especially since he expected she knew the difference. He took the one-year-old from her clutch and handed him to Miss Cosgrove. Then, wrapping an arm about Lady Widlake to support her, he drew her through the crowd and upstairs. "Come, my lady, we must make you comfortable."

He had anticipated another three weeks before confinement, though the date was always guesswork. Mr. Pool had once expected his patient to deliver in April only to have her gestation last through June; more often, John heard stories of the reverse. Either way, Lady

Widlake was earlier than expected, and the monthly nurse had not yet arrived to assist the birth.

He led Lady Widlake to the lying-in apartments. Originally the state bedroom and dressing room, the unused chambers were kept in pristine condition to show off the baron's status as a peer. Now the state bedroom was crowded with the lying-in cot, an endless stack of linens, and a table for John's medical supplies. A jumble of sofas and chairs filled the adjoining dressing room for family members or visitors throughout the delivery.

The room was too cold, especially with night coming on. John rang for a maid to build a fire. Lady Widlake whimpered with another cramp. "Would you like to lie down, or walk about?" John asked. "Or perhaps a game of cards?"

She opted to walk. Mrs. Edwards, who had trailed them to the chambers, seized Lady Widlake's arm. "You mustn't overdo it. Easy now, especially if you feel a pain coming on again."

Anger seethed beneath John's skin at the ease with which the woman resumed her role. Only minutes ago, she had pointed Mr. Ord in *his* direction. Tried to frame *him* for a crime punishable by hanging. If she wasn't going to face any consequences, at the very least John could ask that she remove herself from the room.

He pushed the wish away. In any other event, he would have demanded she leave. In this moment, however, she was the mother of the woman about to birth a child. Lady Widlake's mental state mattered more than his.

John distracted himself by preparing the room. He closed up the window shutters and stuffed rags in the keyholes of all the cabinets and doors. He laid out a rug on the stone floor of the dressing room to muffle any footsteps. He set a pot to boil on the fire once it started so there would always be boiling water to wash instruments and hands. Then he rang the bell again to order up a tray of barley water and bread, in case the lady grew hungry.

He tried not to think about the problems facing this delivery.

First, the child was coming early. Never mind that he always accounted for a margin of error. John knew from the mountains of anecdotes swapped between himself and his colleagues that when the birth came early, it was more likely to be difficult. And a difficult birth meant a higher likelihood that he would lose either the mother or the child.

Second, he was supposed to have more assistance. For an ac-couchement, he usually had both a monthly nurse and a wet nurse in the chamber with him. They helped calm the mother, gave her in water and broth, and managed the parts of her body he couldn't when maneuvering the infant from the birth canal. Mr. Pool had always said that the major portion of the accoucheur's job was to keep the mother calm: without the efficient ministrations of the nurses, John didn't know if he could keep Lady Widlake in the proper mental state to produce her child.

And then there was the other problem. The fact that his head and heart still pounded. He had just been accused of counterfeiting, for God's sake! He had almost been arrested. His veins pulsed with icy adrenaline. He knew what this meant for his body: he would do too much, too fast, and then lose all energy. Which was the exact opposite of what was required of him. This was the moment when he needed to focus and withstand days without sleep, if necessary.

If John couldn't get ahold of himself, he wouldn't be able to serve Lady Widlake in these hours of need. That not being an option, he needed to whip himself into shape–and fast.

"You must understand, Agatha, what it is for me to live in this world. I was not born to be silent. I couldn't be if I tried, and oh, how I tried when your father was alive. Did it do me any good? No. So I swore to myself I wouldn't keep down my words, not if all it got me was...well, you needn't know those details." Mrs. Edwards was almost shouting, so passionate was she, as she and Lady Widlake returned to the room. John yanked on the bellpull. He still needed that barley water, and he could do with a pot of coffee for himself. Especially if Mrs. Edwards was to stay in the room until the delivery started in earnest.

"Lord Widlake has so much power at his fingertips. Yet he refuses to use it! Am I to sit here and watch him idle? I try speaking to him about it. I try prodding him with literature from greater thinkers than I. He doesn't listen. He doesn't do anything. So, like a mother with her child, I must guide him somehow. I hoped these pamphlets would at last turn his attention to the matter at hand."

"Enough!" Lady Widlake shook free of her mother's arm, leaning against the wall instead. "You do not hear yourself, Mother. You humiliated him. You humiliated *me*. All for what...so that you could feel a part of the political process?"

"We must not stand silent when our countrymen suffer."

"Then start a sewing circle, rather than use our money in our home to say nasty things about us." With a whimper, Lady Widlake suffered through another pain. "I do not want you here, Mother. You will apologize to Lord Widlake and see to the girls. Once this is over and the babe is born, then I will decide if I can forgive you."

"But, Agatha, I am your mother—"

Lady Widlake turned to John. "I should like to rest now. Will you see my mother out?"

"She is beside herself with pain, Mr. Anderson." Even as he took Mrs. Edwards by the elbow, she protested. "You must give her opium. It is too much agony for one person to bear."

"Perhaps, ma'am, the pain would be less if she were not grieved over family matters."

It felt good to say. Even better because Mrs. Edwards harrumphed, without words to respond. John heralded her from the bedchamber, through the visiting room, and into the corridor.

Perhaps one day he would speak his mind to Garrett, and perhaps it would fill him with this same invigorating joy.

"Oh good, Shaw," Mrs. Edwards cried as she turned into the hallway. "You're just the one to calm her down. She is overwrought. Remind her I am here, won't you? I am here for when the pain gets too bad."

John leaned out the doorway to beckon the maid in. Only it wasn't Shaw alone. Behind her was Sophia. She had lost the shawl; she stood in regal glory in her simple dress, her hair gleaming beneath its cap, her hands clasped just beneath her breasts.

John wanted to pull her into his arms. He wanted to breathe her in, then kiss her, then free her of her clothes and lose the entire afternoon in her body.

But after that, he also wanted the promise of a hundred years spent exactly the same way. And that was what she couldn't give him.

He forced himself to focus on the maid. Yet another member of the household all too happy to throw him into the gaol to protect herself.

That could matter again once the babe was born. For now, John needed an aide in the room. "Lady Widlake could use some assistance."

He wanted to measure her cervix. And he needed to get her into a birthing shift so that they didn't spoil her gown.

All of this necessitated female helpers. If not for Lady Widlake's sensibilities then for propriety's sake. It was his deficiency: he should have arranged for the monthly nurse to arrive early. If he offended anyone, John was the one who would be blamed, not nature or the baby or Lady Widlake.

A tall woman, Shaw carried herself with pride and reserve; John wasn't sure he had heard her put two words together before that day.

Yet she hurried into the room as if a fire chased her. "My dear Lady Widlake, what do you need?"

John felt Sophia following behind him. He tried not to notice. It didn't matter if she was there to see to Lady Widlake or to speak to him. He had one purpose from now until the babe arrived, and it had nothing at all to do with Sophia Preston. No matter that she had stood up for him. Without her, he would be in Mr. Ord's gig that very moment on his way to the county gaol.

She was still Sophia. The woman who didn't return even a fraction of his feelings.

And he still had a child to usher into the world.

"I can't imagine what you were thinking." Lady Widlake's tone–even harsher than the one she had employed with her mother–yanked John's attention back to the matter at hand. "To engage in so criminal an act..."

"And to expect innocent people to take the blame," Sophia added.

Shaw knelt beside Lady Widlake's cot. "I never meant any harm by it, my lady, please believe me. My father wants my brother to take an apprenticeship in London with a merchant, and it costs two hundred pounds. I thought this was a way to earn the money. Who does it hurt but the bank?"

"You spared no thought to the reputation or position of this family, of course," Lady Widlake chastised.

"I never thought we would get caught. Frank and Jasper's father was an engraver. They knew how to make the notes look real. All I had to do was take some of them to market once a month. No one the wiser, us that much richer, and none of us were doing it to be evil. We're each of us only looking for a way to make sure our families have a future."

Behind him, Sophia let out an angry exhale. "Until you were discovered. Then you had no qualms about letting myself or Mr. Anderson face the consequences, did you?"

At last, Shaw turned, raising red-rimmed eyes over her shoulder to meet Sophia's gaze. "We knew your father wouldn't let you hang, Miss Preston. He is a hero of the people, but he is still a lord. That's why we signed the notes the way we did."

"What of Mr. Anderson? Were you the one who put the engraving plates in his armoire, and who did you think would save him from the hangman's noose?"

John's heart pounded in his throat. He knew he did not deserve to be cast under suspicion for the crime. He felt that anger himself. Yet hearing Sophia say it–feeling the tremor in her voice from sheer emotion–swept him nearly to his knees.

If only she could give him more than righteousness.

"That was Hattie who placed the plates. She thought he was more believable than Mrs. Edwards. I'm sorry." Shaw didn't look at him. She turned back to Lady Widlake. "Won't you let me assist you, my lady?"

John needed fire in the hearth, barley water, bread, and coffee. He needed a woman to protect Lady Widlake's privacy. He needed at least one other person to grasp Lady Widlake and keep her spirits up and help her survive this incredible ordeal.

If Lady Widlake wanted it to be Shaw, then so be it. "The monthly nurse hasn't yet arrived," he conceded. "We'll need someone in the room to assist."

"Let me, my lady. Haven't I served you well all this time?"

Shaw reached out, trying to fix the pins in Lady Widlake's hair. Lady Widlake batted her away. "I cannot blame you for needing money, Shaw, but I cannot trust you anymore, either. I cannot trust anyone in the scheme, and apparently that means there is no one in this entire Abbey I can trust except my own family, Mr. Anderson, and Miss Preston. Now, leave me be. Miss Preston can be my attendant. Can't you, Miss Preston?"

All eyes turned to Sophia.

"I suppose I can help, if Mr. Anderson thinks I am fit to."

She looked from Lady Widlake to him, eyes shining. How he wanted to imbue that gaze with meaning. He forced himself not to.

What John thought was that he needed focus. And so far, when in Sophia's presence, he had only ever been able to focus on her. If she was his assistant, it might not be any better than if he went the next fifty-six hours without another sip of coffee.

Besides, she might faint at the first sight of blood. She might argue with him about his methods. She might get Lady Widlake more agitated rather than calm her down. She wasn't trained; she wasn't even a servant accustomed to taking orders and dealing with unpleasant odors. She was a baron's daughter.

But she was Sophia. And John needed her. And Lady Widlake didn't leave them many other options.

He threw her an apron. "If you care about that dress, you'd better put this on."

SOPHIA DIDN'T KNOW MUCH about childbirth. Among her siblings, the only birth she remembered was that of Caroline, who had come along when Sophia was ten. Mostly, Sophia remembered Papa taking them all into Thatcham for the day and letting them watch a troupe of actors perform a bawdy play. Other women gave birth at Northfield Hall every now and then, of course, but Sophia avoided wherever that was happening. She knew the process took a long time, longer than seemed necessary. She knew it was painful, and that most women took pride in bearing that pain in the name of their husband and child.

She didn't know how much blood was involved. Or sweat. Or how purple a woman's face could turn as she expelled a child from her nether parts.

Most of it wasn't blood, though. Most of those fourteen hours were spent waiting. Sophia helped John build a fire in the hearth. She played two-person whist with Lady Widlake. She read the lady letters sent from friends in London, and when those disappeared, recited poems. Lord Widlake stopped in every hour or so, and all the children came to kiss their mother goodnight.

"I didn't get to write my letter," Lady Widlake sighed as their father escorted the children away. "If something should happen...you will tell them I love them with all my heart, won't you, Miss Preston?"

Sophia promised she would.

The drama of the afternoon disappeared in the birthing chamber. Sophia had no idea if Mr. Ord had carried away Mrs. Hibbert after all, or whether he had accepted Lord Widlake's pseudo-confession. She knew Polly had run off in the first wave of commotion, and apparently even Beula was in on the scheme.

What she would give to turn and run, just like Polly. Sophia couldn't stand the waiting around for the baby to come, and she wasn't sure she could face the gore of what came next.

But she had seen the look on John's face. He needed help. Therefore, she would provide it.

It was just before dawn that the timbre of the room shifted. Lord Widlake napped in the dressing room while John washed his hands for the hundredth time in a basin of hot water. Lady Widlake herself seemed close to dozing as Sophia read aloud from *The Mirror of Graces* about the best potions for removing freckles from skin.

And then she let out a cry louder than ever. Before John could even return to his position at the end of the cot, she let out another. "Mr. Anderson, I believe it is time!"

"Miss Preston, help her into position."

He had explained this earlier, when he had previously checked the lady's cervix: Sophia helped Lady Widlake to curl onto her right side, knees up. She remained there, by the lady's arms, while John sat on a stool beneath her legs. Lady Widlake's entire shift was wet with sweat, and she whimpered as Sophia drew a cool cloth across her forehead.

Then came the screaming. And the pushing. And the purple face, and the blood, and more sweat, and something else that smelled terrible that Sophia feared very much was shit. She held onto Lady Widlake's shoulders, offering whatever she could, while the lady pushed. John the entire time focused on the baby.

He was the picture of cool confidence. Even as blood spurted at him from the woman's fanny, he hardly blinked. He moved with precision, gave clear orders, and even made time to praise Lady Widlake for her strength. "This child is having an easy time of it because of you. Just a little bit longer. Just a little bit more."

It was enough to make Sophia long for praise, too. For John to look up at her—even for just a moment—and smile. Or nod. Or do anything to acknowledge that she was there. She was helping. She was making a difference in bringing this child into the world.

His focus remained on Lady Widlake. Sophia's focus was claimed by her, too, as the lady crushed Sophia's hands. It seemed this part would go on forever. But before the sky had even pinkened with the sun, it was over.

The room filled with a new, deafening wail as John withdrew the baby from Lady Widlake's vagina.

"Miss Preston, I need your assistance now." He still spoke in that calm, efficient tone. Except now Sophia saw the hint of a smile on his lips.

How long it had been since she had seen him smile. How much she had missed it.

She followed his instructions: hold the child while he cut its cord, wash it with a clean rag, swaddle it in the awaiting blanket. Euphoria–dangerously close to what she felt after a good fuck–fueled her. She took her time to make sure she did each task properly, then finally, at John's direction, placed the child on Lady Widlake's breast.

"There you are. Another girl for your collection."

John cleaned himself up while Sophia removed Lady Widlake's birthing shift and repositioned the lady into the center of the cot, where the linens were still dry. Then there was nothing to do but alert Lord Widlake to the birth of his child.

Sophia didn't know if the man would hold the infant himself. He was so stiff and removed on a normal day. But he entered the lying-in chamber without his jacket, his hair askew, and went directly to his wife's side. "All is well, madam?"

"Your daughter, sir."

He lifted the baby in his arms. Sophia couldn't see his face, yet she could feel the love enveloping him and the child and Lady Widlake. When he bent to kiss his wife's lips, Sophia turned away.

For so long, she had thought that to be inside a love like that would break her heart from the very start. That the threat of losing a partner more dear to her than herself would be far too painful to bear.

But here she was, about to lose John, and the joy of knowing him far outweighed the ache of his silence.

Sophia loved him, without meaning to, and she didn't want to deny it anymore.

John stood less than a foot away from her, yet it felt as if he were all the way in London. He, too, averted his eyes from the scene before them. But instead of looking at her, he looked down at his hands.

Sophia knew this wasn't the time or place. But now that the child was born, John would be on his way in a matter of days. She might never get a chance to put things right between them. So she decided to ride the wave of euphoria before she lost her nerve.

She touched his arm. "I'm sorry I don't have a list. I didn't know you did. I didn't know that is how a person loves someone else. I only know how I love someone. I love you. This is what it feels like for me: I am happiest when you are in the room. I am fascinated by who you are. I am addicted to being the object of your attention. You see me in a way no one else does. You like me in a way no one else does, in a way that encompasses me entirely and not just one part of me. It is intoxicating. And I want to make you feel the same. I want to make you feel like the most interesting and important person in the entire world. It's just that I'm not you. I don't catalog the way you behave or the nuances of your smiles. It's not how my mind works. Perhaps that means I'm incapable of love. Or I'm incapable of loving you the way that you want to be loved. But I do love you. Please believe me that I love you."

John stared at her. He was exhausted. She noticed that suddenly, in the circles beneath his eyes and the droop of his mouth. He hadn't shaved, either, and the stubble she loved so much blackened his jaw. She wanted to run her fingers through it. Not for sexual gratification but for intimacy. She wanted to be the woman he allowed to touch him under any circumstance.

From the cot, Lady Widlake said, "Lord Widlake, I believe we have a scandal on our hands."

Sophia dropped her hand. Fear jolted through her, and she saw terror seize John. But Lord Widlake laughed. "Robin Abbey is a house of scandal now, my dear lady. Better a scandal of the heart than of another crime."

"I did always think you would make a better wife than a governess," Lady Widlake said to Sophia. Then she lay back. "Now, if you don't mind, I should like to rest."

They acquiesced, of course. Lord Widlake kissed his wife again, Sophia took the baby, and John cleared away his instruments. They shut the door.

And still, John didn't answer her.

Chapter Nineteen

JOHN ALWAYS FELT THIS way after a delivery: elated, shaky, and like he might at any moment shit his pants.

Add to that a confession of love, and John considered it a miracle he hadn't yet vomited.

He stumbled out of the lying-in chambers. His portion of the work was done. He would stay another week or so to ensure Lady Widlake recovered properly–or to tend to her if she descended into fever–but then he would leave. Farewell to Robin Abbey. Farewell to Sophia.

She trailed him from the room. She wanted a reply. She deserved one. That was quite the speech she had delivered. He had felt the tremble in her body as she soldiered through it.

She meant what she had said. That he believed. The trouble was that John didn't know what to do with it.

Sophia loved him. As an individual fact, that was wonderful. Like breaking free from a wool cloak on a hot summer day. John was not too stiff or unsure or attached after all. He did not overreach. He loved Sophia, and she loved him back.

A miracle was what that was.

But he didn't know what it meant. In a week or so, his duty to Lord and Lady Widlake would be complete. They would show him from Robin Abbey. And he would be on his way: in two months' time to Colonel and Mrs. Hipswaite, and after that to the Baroness Aveline, and from there, he could only wait and see.

Meanwhile, Sophia would be here.

All he had wanted that night in the crypt was for her to say she loved him back. That she was as obsessed with him as he was with her. Now that she had confessed to it, John realized it wasn't enough. It would never be enough.

He wanted a life with her. Anything less would break his heart over and over again.

"John?"

He blinked. Somehow, they had ended up in his apartment. Somehow, Sophia had followed him in and shut the door and he hadn't objected. Even though the whole household must be up with the arrival of the baby.

She was beautiful, this woman he loved. The birthing chamber had not been kind to her: she had lost her cap, her hair frizzed from its pins, and her dress and apron alike were spattered with bodily fluids. Still, he could stare at her for hours. That face, so perfectly oval until an emotion overcame her. Those eyes, gleaming and flickering and tricking. Those lips, pink and curved and teasing. And then there was the rest of her, broad and warm and full. Her lop-sided breasts and overwhelming bottom and soft curves everywhere in between. She was everything he wanted bound in a perfect earthly wrapper.

John didn't have a reply for her yet. He pulled her into his grasp anyway. One hand up her neck, fingers snaking through the wreckage of her coiffure. The other around her waist. For four days straight, he had needed this kiss. He took it now greedily. She opened her lips to his as soon as they touched. She tasted of hard work. John's whole body responded. He pressed closer, tongue to tongue, chest to chest, groin to groin. His cock was hard, felt like it had been hard for eternity, and he couldn't keep track of time anymore. She removed his jacket; he ripped her dress over her head; they fell together to the floor, legs entwined; then they were naked and his knees scraped against the carpet. John dipped between her legs and tasted all of her: the length of her pudendum, the peak of her clitoris, the folds of her nymphae, the silk opening of her vagina. She wasn't sweet, this woman of his. She was savory salt, a string of false starts, a series of gasps. But she was his, and he was hers, and for this moment, John didn't need to think beyond that.

When she shook with orgasm, John framed her body with his. She pulled at his hips. And how he wanted to be inside her. But she didn't wear a pessary, and his supply had gone with her to her chamber. He bent his head to whisper in her ear, "I don't want to put you at risk."

They could have paused. His wooden box of condoms sat only a few paces away in his armoire. But John was afraid that would break this moment. And it was this moment he wanted: the cotton safety of being in Sophia's arms. Of knowing he was her whole world. That, for now, she had no fears and neither did he because they held each other above anyone or anything else.

If he paused to get a condom or fetch a pessary, he might return to find a different Sophia. Or he might be the one to change. Return with desire fragmented by thoughts. Even inside of her, he might not find pleasure, having given himself time to worry about the future. Reminding himself of all the babies he had delivered even when the mother had taken precautions. Fearing that one day soon, Sophia would regret this.

He couldn't break this moment. He was too exhausted to do anything but revel in it. So instead of entering Sophia, he took his cock in his own hand. He palmed her wayward breast. He kissed her mouth, letting his tongue make clear how much he loved her.

She kissed him back as if this were her last breath. Her ten fingernails dug into his arse, sharpening his pleasure as a whetstone to a knife blade. She raised her quim against his thigh. Her wet desire smeared across his skin. John imagined that wrapping around his cock. He imagined pounding into her so hard that her skull shook. He imagined kissing her like this while fucking her, and that was better than being inside her wishing he could kiss her, and it took but a moment for him to spill into ecstasy.

When he returned to reality, Sophia's arms wrapped elbow-to-elbow around his neck. He opened his eyes to find hers a breath away. She smiled. "I love you so much it hurts."

Only she would smile in the face of pain. Fierce, foolish, fantastic Sophia. John closed his eyes again. "I know exactly what you mean."

***

SOPHIA HAD ENOUGH SENSE to leave John's apartment. She covered him with the quilt from the bed, then slipped into her abused clothes and hurried back to her room. She didn't think anyone had observed them—not when most everyone still slept, except Lord Widlake and Miss Cosgrove, and they were consumed with the new baby—but she knew a reckoning was coming. She couldn't profess her love in the hearing of her employers and expect to retain her position guiding their daughters into chaste maidenhood.

Soon, she would have to discover what came next. Lady Widlake would expect John to offer to marry Sophia. She would expect Sophia to accept.

Sophia didn't know what John wanted to happen. He was a dutiful man. One with a reputation to protect, too. He likely would offer marriage, knowing it was what the respectable world expected of him.

She didn't know if he actually wanted to marry her. And worse, Sophia didn't know if she wanted to marry him.

She wanted to be with him. She wanted to collect days with him like butterflies in a jar, so that every now and then they could open it up and say, "Oh, remember that frolic?" or "How could you ever get so upset about something so frivolous?" or "Which of those was your favorite day?"

But that fantasy lived in divorce from reality. She had once wanted to be a governess, too, fancying herself the mistress of little minds and influencer of a generation of young ladies. Only to find it was this: a life of rules, early mornings, and family dynamics that were more tiresome than her own.

What if Sophia accepted marriage to John, then discovered it too was a life she couldn't stand?

And worse—what if the true problem was that there was no lifestyle to satisfy her? What if she denied John, found some new position as a companion or artiste or whatever else she could get, and only then realized the problem was her expectations?

Peeling off the layers John had so recently torn from her body, Sophia washed with the tepid water waiting in her basin, then donned her nightdress and climbed onto the creaking mattress. Exhausted as she was, she didn't think she could sleep, not with so many questions racing from her mind to her heart and back again. She was a woman who didn't know what she wanted, who didn't know how to make the man she loved happy, and who didn't know whether she would even have this roof over her head come the next morning.

Sleep was out of the question for her.

And yet, next thing she knew, she woke to a rapping on her door.

The room was dark; Sophia realized immediately she had slept the day away. From the other side of the door, Hattie called, "It's Lord Widlake, Miss. He would like to see you in the study before supper."

She dressed in a hurry: shift, corset, and her green dinner dress that only required her to fasten five buttons up the side. She wished she hadn't slept. Or, if she had to have slept, she wished she had woken up with a brilliant solution for all her problems.

Instead, she answered Lord Widlake's summons with the same muddle around her heart as before.

John stood by the window. She had expected to see him, yet Sophia's heart leapt at the sight of him. He wore his best dinner suit, and his hair was freshly cut close to his scalp. Sophia wanted to run her fingers across his head and chest and lips and ruffle him entirely.

She tore her attention away from him to curtsey to their host. "I apologize for keeping you waiting."

"Not to worry." Lord Widlake was the most cheerful Sophia had ever seen him. His usually stiff upper lip actually stretched into a smile. "First, I should like to thank you both for ensuring the safe delivery of our Letitia. Lady Widlake and I are beside ourselves with joy. In particular, Miss Preston, I must thank you for stepping up when no one else could assist Mr. Anderson."

Sophia was too nervous to acknowledge this with anything more than a nod of her head.

"I owe you both a deep apology on behalf of Robin Abbey for involving you in the bad notes scheme."

John asked, "May I ask what the truth of it all was?"

With a sigh, Lord Widlake confirmed Sophia's suspicions: "The household colluded in the operation, it seems. Frank and Jasper's father, you may know, was an engraver. When he died, he left them in debt, and they moved his printing presses to the Abbey to hide them from creditors. Apparently from there, Mrs. Hibbert had the idea to supplement everyone's income. Frank and Jasper did the engraving and pressing. Polly and Hattie helped with the drying and cutting. Cook made the ink, Shaw and Nurse purchased the paper, and even Beula assisted by uttering the notes when she went shopping."

Her stomach sank with each detail. If Lord Widlake knew each person's role, then Mr. Ord likely did, too. Which meant the Bank of England would prosecute them all. Beula might be lucky enough to get away with transportation, and Shaw and Nurse and Cook might be able to find their way out of the charges, but Frank and Jasper would be facing the hangman's noose.

For the first time, she wished she had issued a false confession when she had the chance.

"As far as Mr. Ord is concerned, they acted under my instruction. Therefore, I will be the one to face the consequences. At the very least, I expect Mr. Fenton will lose the election. At the worst, the House of Lords may see fit to prosecute me." Lord Widlake squared his shoulders. "In any case, I am prepared to accept the punishment. In the meantime, the presses will be destroyed, I will repay any merchants who were fooled by bad notes, and the whole of the household will be dismissed."

Sophia knew she had gotten her position in large part because Lord Widlake wanted Papa's favor. She hadn't paid much attention to whether or not he had earned it until this very moment. "You may count on support from my father and Viscount Berwick, I am sure."

Lord Widlake accepted this with a nod. Then, with a new smile, he said, "Mr. Anderson has requested my permission to speak with you alone. In the absence of Lord Preston, I am happy to give my blessing. For a quarter hour and no longer." He took himself to the door. "I do hope you will be on opposite sides of the room when I return."

A Sophia of earlier days would have taken that as a challenge to discover all kinds of carnal games to play from afar.

This evening, however, she didn't have the appetite for even a smirk. She drank in the sight of John as he turned from the window. His thick brows knit into that frown of his. His hands clasped formally behind his back. It was almost like when they had first met and she had wanted nothing more than to flirt the clothes off him.

Except now she wanted nothing more than to figure out what sort of future wouldn't break both their hearts.

"Did you rest?" John asked without taking a step closer to her.

"Yes. All day, apparently. I didn't expect to." She forced herself to stop; she didn't want to waste their quarter hour talking about herself. "Did you?"

He nodded. "For a little while. I like to tend to the mother every few hours in the days after birth to ensure she doesn't catch a fever." Pausing, John fiddled with his white gloves. Then he said, "I never gave you a proper reply this morning. Here it is: I believe you, and I love you, too. Nothing would make me happier than to make you my wife, though I have no title or fortune to offer. If you should like it, my life is yours."

She supposed she had expected him to say, "Well, darling, the game is up. We've been found out, and now we must pay the price." Something that would make her laugh and make her angry all at the same time, so that she would have an emotion to latch onto for her response.

Sophia hadn't expected him to say it like this. So sincerely. So quietly. So much like he was bracing for her to reject it.

The way John said it made her want to say yes.

"The trouble is I'm not sure what kind of wife I would make. I've always said I would never marry. And I do want to spend my life with you. It's just that I don't know what I want my life to be."

He smiled. It wasn't quite a full one, though. "I do have difficulty imagining you following me from one client to another. Always being polite and pleasant and…"

No, she wasn't the candidate for a wife who would be obsequious to whichever client they needed to pay John next. She agreed, "I might be miserable no matter what I do. That might be my punishment for being a willful woman with high expectations. But I should hate to make you miserable with me."

John shifted closer by one step. "If we don't marry, what will you do?"

She wouldn't stay at Robin Abbey; that much Sophia knew. Even if they allowed her to keep the position, she couldn't live in these halls haunted with the ghost of John. "I'll go home for a time, I suppose, and then sort out my next adventure. Perhaps I can convince my Aunt Charlotte to take me on a Grand Tour. Or I could fund a printing company for scandalous writing by women. My mother would have loved that."

"You deserve whatever grand adventures you wish for."

Neither option sounded very appealing at the moment. Not with John so close. She didn't know quite how, but they had closed the distance between them.

"If I were a decade older," she said to fill the air, "I would be an eccentric spinster, and I could take myself on my own adventures without worrying that people would talk. Then I might take myself to India and visit your Calcutta and picture you there as a very young boy."

He reached out. Not to kiss her but to cup her cheek. His palm was smooth, though she knew his hand was strong and his fingers capable. She could press her face into his skin for the rest of her life. That was a future she wouldn't mind.

"You could wait until you are ten years older. Or..." John's hand slid down her jaw and neck and arm—setting every nerve on fire—until he clasped her fingers in his. "The one advantage of marriage is that you could have so many more adventures if you were a Mrs. instead of a Miss. Marry me, and you can do whatever you want."

Sophia couldn't tell if he meant it, or if he was keeping himself from kissing her, like she was. "What if I leave you the very next day for a tour of the continent and never return?"

He cast his eyes downwards so she couldn't see his reaction. "Whatever you want."

"What if I start publishing fantastic claims of science in the London newspapers and make a fool of myself?"

"Whatever you want."

"What if I take a lover?"

John's hand tightened around hers. He held her gaze in his own. "Whatever you want."

"What if I have a dozen children by other men and ask you to deliver them?"

"I ask for no commitment from you, Sophia. Only your name as protection to me against scandal. And in return, that is what I offer you."

Oh, he meant it. Sophia couldn't stay apart from him any longer. She wished she could make him feel this way, for it was such a gift. To be seen. Accepted. Embraced.

She lifted her free hand to his cheek. "What if I decide I love you too much to ever part, and I spend every day with you, and every night we fuck, and you can never rid yourself of me no matter how hard you try?"

John beamed. "Then you would make me the happiest man alive."

"It does seem like the selfless thing for me to do, to save you from scandal by stepping in with my good name."

Sophia still didn't know what she wanted from life. She couldn't map out what she would do in the next month or year or decade. But in that moment, she knew what she didn't want: to exist another second without locking John Anderson to her side.

"You had better marry me, Mr. Anderson, or Lord Widlake will be terribly shocked by our behavior."

And indeed, no kiss had ever been more shocking than the one she and John shared just as Lord Widlake returned to the room.

The wedding, everyone agreed, would take place by special license as soon as possible.

FIRST EPILOGUE

MR. AND MRS. ANDERSON found Captain Attree's residence was almost impossible to locate. John and Sophia walked arm in arm down the entire length of Neptune Street twice before they noticed the black door of a two-story house tucked in the recesses of two larger buildings. This, John hoped, was where the letters marked Small House arrived at the end of their postal journey.

"How quaint," Sophia said as they climbed the three steps that protected the house from the street. "With those window coverings, it makes one think of a country home, does it not?"

She teased. The window coverings were wooden shutters, painted as tar black as the door. They would do a good job of blocking out sunlight, except the sun didn't find its way to Neptune Street in the first place, on account of how narrowly it cut between the city buildings.

When the time had come to leave Robin Abbey, John and Sophia agreed their first adventure would be to retrieve Amma. They would take her to Northfield Hall for a brief visit to Sophia's family before John had to report to Colonel Hipswaite.

To think Garrett had reduced his mother to such circumstances that she had to accept this position. John channeled the outrage into his knock, as he would do into his conversation with Captain Attree, as he would do in the face of any obstacle until he liberated Amma from this mess. At his side, Sophia squared her shoulders and put on the expression he had come to recognize as her Preston face. The one that marked her a noblewoman by birthright and a fighter by instinct.

If John's outrage didn't work to save his mother from whatever employment contract she had signed, Sophia's accent and silk gown and father in the House of Lords would do the trick.

He raised his hand to knock again when the door swung open. And just like that, he was face to face with his mother.

"Amma."

John hadn't realized how much he missed her until this very instant. She looked just the same: her hair tied back in a thick braid, her strong arms and waist bursting in a plain English gown, her eyes and mouth lined with memories of different days. The reserve holding back her smile disappeared as soon as she saw him, and then she was unbridled joy.

Same as she always was.

"John Anderson, give me a kiss at once!"

How she loved to call him by his full name. He had forgotten to warn Sophia of that. He stooped down to press his lips to her cheek. She smelled of the kitchen fire.

"Are you well?" John couldn't stop himself from asking, though he knew there were a hundred things they needed to tell each other. But he couldn't wait one more second without reassurance.

"More than well. You must come in. I have the kettle on for tea already, and fresh almond cakes from the store down the corner. You'll like them. They're better than the almond tea cakes at Gracechurch Street." Amma pulled him into the house and, as if noticing her for the first time, averted her eyes from Sophia. "May I welcome you to Small House, ma'am?"

Sophia blushed. It blossomed so fast on her cheeks that it took John by surprise. She looked to John, teeth plunging into her lower lip.

"Amma, may I present..." John wasn't used to her new name yet, though it had taken only a few hours to become accustomed to her at his side these past weeks. "This is my wife, Mrs. Sophia Anderson, formerly Miss Sophia Preston."

Sophia bent her knees into a quick curtsy. "I'm honored to meet you, Mrs. Ghosh."

She had worried that his mother would be upset that they had married so quickly and without telling her in advance. But in this, John knew how to predict his mother. Amma erupted into another smile. "Mrs. Anderson. I lived to see the day. Come in, come in, you must have the tea cakes, too."

Amma took them to a sitting room in the back of the house. It overlooked a courtyard that actually boasted a sliver of sunlight. John spotted a tool shed, a stone well, and even a raised garden over which presided a lush rosemary bush. In the sitting room, they had their pick of spindly wooden chairs. Amma bustled in with a Wedgwood teapot, matching ceramic cups, and a tray of the promised tea cakes. "Now, you must tell me everything."

"There is not much to tell. Miss Preston—that is, Mrs. Anderson now—was the governess at Lord and Lady Widlake's. We fell in love." John found he couldn't say the words without touching Sophia. He reached over and closed his gloved hand over hers.

Sophia laughed. "Oh, is that all that happened? I must have imagined the rest."

For a second, from the way her eyes flashed at him, John feared she was about to tell his mother about how they had kissed in the dark of the bell tower. But she only launched into the other part of the story: the bad notes, the accusations, the drama of delivering a baby. "I wasn't sure your John would ask me to marry him after I made such a muck-up of things," Sophia said, "but I did tell him I loved him, and I suppose we are both hoping that is enough for the future. What do you think?"

It was in that moment that Captain Attree entered the room. John shot out of his seat. His outrage was not with this man, of course, who had done a reasonable thing and hired a talented woman for his open position. Still, John was here to liberate his mother, and he was ready for a fight.

"Who have we here, then?" the man barked in a gruff, overused voice.

In person, Attree lived up to the idea of a retired sea captain: average height, leathery skin from long exposure to the sun, white hair, and a bit of a limp as if his legs or back ached.

Although, John realized, the tan of his skin might not be from the sun but instead from some heritage similar to his own.

"My son, Captain Attree." Amma stood, still smiling, and came to stand behind John. "And his wife. Mrs. Anderson, formerly Miss Sophia Preston. They met at his most recent position at Lord Widlake's."

It was far more information than any housekeeper needed give her employer. Captain Attree raised his eyebrows. "Him who is in the broad sheets the last few days?"

"The one and the same," Sophia affirmed. Lord Widlake had indeed been in the news: the Bank of England was using all their influence with the press to pillory him with caricatures and scathing articles. As far as the country was concerned, a peer of the realm had been producing bad notes as a political statement against paper currency.

For the moment, Lord Widlake was the laughingstock of the nation. Though John had a feeling many of the common folk were laughing with him at the Bank, and not the other way around.

"Well, never say that life is boring." Captain Attree ventured further into the room and held out his hand to John. "A right honor to meet you, sir. Have you tried the tea cakes yet?"

It wasn't what John expected. The man practically crushed his hand as they shook. Attree smiled, too, then deposited himself in the frailest looking chair in the room. It creaked beneath his weight but otherwise held up. "Your mother found those tea cakes, even though I've been here for years and so has that shop down the corner. They're delicious, they are. Can't get through a day without them, now that I've found them."

Sophia lifted one from the plate. "I know exactly the feeling you describe, Captain Attree, only I happen to feel it about Mr. Anderson."

Amma grinned. John blushed. Sophia winked at him; she teased, and he would make her pay penance soon enough.

"I am not surprised that you are pleased with my mother's service," John said, "as she is a diligent and talented person in everything she does. Unfortunately, I must inform you I am here to invite her to join my household, instead."

Having said it, John braced himself for a reaction. He knew Amma would have preferred a private conversation first, but Captain Attree had provided the opening, and there was no point dilly dallying.

He expected the man to bluster about the contract. Or, having gotten a sense of his character, John hoped the captain might acquiesce to the wisdom of a mother in her son's household given that he could provide for her.

He didn't expect the man's face to crumple. He looked completely at sea—although, being a sea captain, perhaps the better term for

Attree was that he was on land. He turned to John's mother. "This is what you want?" Almost as an afterthought, he added, "Mrs. Ghosh?"

And John hadn't expected Amma's reaction, either: not a single spark of joy glowed in her eyes. She opened her mouth, closed it again, then turned to John. "We have not spoken of this, John Anderson."

"I should have waited until we had a moment alone," he allowed. "When Garrett first told me he had dismissed you, I was livid. Now, I am grateful to him, for it showed me how poorly I myself have looked after you. I am prepared to take care of you, Amma. You will live with me wherever I hang my hat, and your only care will be which tea to pour that day."

It was Sophia who added, "If that is what you want, of course."

He waited for his mother to break into another of her smiles. She would clap her hands together and declare he was the cleverest son she ever could have, and in a matter of hours, they would be off as a new family.

Amma did smile. But it was one of those complex expressions that creased her whole face into something resembling a frown. "I am happier here."

John paused, trying to make sense of her words. "I'm sure you are. Captain Attree seems much more agreeable than my cousin." It was true: here, Amma had only the one person for whom to care, and Captain Attree didn't seem to begrudge her the comforts of the house, including allowing her to serve her visitors his precious almond tea cakes. Still, it was a far cry from living as an unburdened member of the household. "Amma, with me, you will have no care in the world. I will provide for your every need."

She shook her head. "John, I am happiest here." And then, when all John could do was stare, Amma added, "I was not dismissed. When Garrett's wife arrived, I was delighted to give my notice so that I could come here. To Captain Attree."

With a great clearing of his throat, Captain Attree rose to his feet. "It is my fault, Mr. Anderson, and I must beg your forgiveness in the same moment I seek your blessing. You see, Mrs. Ghosh and I first met at the fish market, when I attempted to do my shopping on my own. Ever since, I...well, I am a man in love. I have a modest living to offer, this house, and a small income. I will take care of her better even than I see to my own heart. That much I can promise you."

John waited. Blood rushed his ears, so he wasn't entirely sure he could believe what he was hearing, but Captain Attree matched his words with a certain shining eagerness that John knew too well from his own feelings for Sophia.

For her part, Amma beamed, her eyelashes dropping girlishly, as if to hear the words aloud embarrassed and delighted her at the same time.

When Captain Attree didn't say anything more, John finally said, "Am I to understand a wedding is forthcoming, sir?"

"Ah." The man cleared his throat again.

John's stomach sank. And his outrage leapt up again. The nerve of the man, to ask his blessing for making Amma his mistress. As if John would condone another man disrespecting his mother, just because his own father had been too much a coward to treat her with honor.

Amma stood. "It is my preference. You know how people will talk if they see me as Captain Attree's wife. Some hussy, they will think. A swindler. Aiming too high for herself. It will be nothing but vicious gossip. Unmarried, I am his housekeeper, and they needn't know anything more about it. No one has anything against a woman like me keeping his house, so long as I am paid to do it and am not his wife."

She used the tone that brooked no argument. John wanted to protest. Wanted to demand all the legal benefits of marriage on her behalf. His mother deserved every ounce of respect and honor that any other woman received.

Sophia squeezed John's fingers. "I can see your point, Mrs. Ghosh. Marriage is not always the answer."

Captain Attree said forcefully, "In my heart, your mother is my dear and beloved wife. I never set much store in the Church or society anyhow. More comfortable at sea, I was, and now I'm more comfortable as long as Nora is near to me."

John should have found it embarrassing for a grizzled man to make so earnest a confession. But, perhaps because he himself was so tenderly in love with Sophia, John found himself feeling a curious kinship to Captain Attree.

"I am happiest here," Amma repeated, stepping close enough to brush a comforting hand across John's hair. "You must trust me."

It was simple. John looked from his mother to his wife–Sophia, a woman who didn't have to choose him but did. To impose marriage upon his mother and Captain Attree would be the same as trying to capture Sophia in the role of wife. Putting a box over something so wild and powerful that the walls would only burst.

He pressed a kiss to his mother's cheek. "I trust you. I offer you my warmest felicitations." Then he shook Captain Attree's hand. This time, he returned the man's squeeze. "You must be very happy together."

And he meant it. Now that he knew the truth about Amma and Captain Attree, John felt a new kind of peace. There was his mother laughing as she fetched a bottle of wine to celebrate. There was Captain Attree, sliding an arm around her waist with a tenderness John had never witnessed between his two parents.

And there was Sophia at John's side. Pear perfume in his nose, soft hand on his arm, sparkling gaze never far from his. His wife, whatever that meant. There was much of their future still to unfold, and John knew he couldn't predict any of it except to predict it would always surprise him.

But here in this moment of celebration, John felt safe and cherished and hopeful. And he supposed that, in the end, that was all anyone could ask for.

SECOND EPILOGUE

Thirty Years Later

London, November, 1844

THE TOWNHOUSE LOOKED A little the worse for wear since she had last seen it two months before. Its white façade was decidedly gray from coal grime. One of the lamps at its entrance lit at half the strength it was meant to. And the brass plaque proclaiming MR. ANDERSON, MAN-MIDWIFE TO ALL needed a hearty polish to gleam through the city fog.

A good thing she was back, then. Sophia tried very hard to keep the smile off her lips so that the driver wouldn't wonder if it was for him as she collected her valise. He was a handsome man, to be sure. Nice enough to ogle from a removed distance.

But he had nothing on her husband.

Locking the door behind her, Sophia took a moment to breathe in the smell of home: lemon soap, wood polish, and the spices of Mrs. Kumar's cooking.

In a few weeks, it would feel familiar again. In a few months, it might make her feel the walls were closing in on her, as sometimes happened.

For now, it was as exciting and new as all the Egyptian ruins she had just toured.

Her satisfaction dampened a little at the dead quiet of the house. It was late enough that she expected–hoped, even–that Mrs. Kumar had retired to her lodgings for the night.

The silence threatened that John was gone, too. Off delivering a baby, most likely, or tending some other medical emergency. Doing whatever he did while Sophia followed the whim of the month.

She couldn't hold it against him, no matter how much she hoped he would be there to greet her with open arms.

"I have returned!" she called out, in case she was wrong. Then, removing her hat and gloves and jacket, she began wrestling her valise upstairs.

"Would you like assistance with that?"

He asked it from the second-floor landing. He stood with one leg crossed over the other, hands in his pockets, for all the world a rake in the ballroom waiting for the women to flock over like moths to a flame.

Every time they reunited, Sophia discovered something she had forgotten about him. Last time, it was the trick his lips played, stretching down like a frown just before twitching into the most wonderful smile in the world. This time it was the way his breath caught just before a kiss. As if in that instant, he tried to freeze time by stalling his lungs, so that the kiss would go on forever.

Well, the kiss did go on forever, right there on the stairs, at least until Sophia's neck stiffened and her hand cramped against the banister. "You had better take me to bed to greet me properly, Mr. Anderson."

"Whatever you desire, Mrs. Anderson."

She heard his stomach growl, though. And she saw the exhaustion around his eyes. Telltale signs she had learned over the years: "You've just returned from a birth."

"It was simple. Ten hours. I've plenty of energy to welcome you home."

"Ah, but I have big plans for you, and I need you properly fed if you are to execute them properly."

Sophia took his hand to end the dispute and led him down past her valise–forgotten on the landing–to the kitchen. Mrs. Kumar had left out a supper for the both of them: curried chicken, rice, and almond biscuits. Sophia fixed the plates while John opened a bottle of wine. Then they snuggled together on the bench, Sophia half in his lap, to eat.

"Your correspondence, madam." John presented her with a stack of letters to sort. Sophia flicked through them, noting the missive from her old charge Danielle Cosgrove Pitt. She put it aside to read later, when she could savor news of the Cosgrove family, who last she had heard had celebrated Lord and Lady Widlake's fiftieth wedding anniversary at Robin Abbey.

"How fare the Preston women? Did you and Ellen manage not to argue?" John asked.

"Of course not. It would be too strange to spend two months with Ellen and not argue." This last trip had been a sojourn with both her sisters and sisters-in-law to celebrate the last of the nieces and nephews being officially launched from their parents' houses. "I miss her already, though, and have started composing my next letter in my head."

John grinned through his food. "Then tell me about all that has happened since you last wrote me."

Over the last thirty years, they had perfected the art of time away. They wrote each other regular letters, some detailed, some as short as *I miss you*. Sophia gathered up stories—the more outlandish the better—so that John could imagine himself beside her as she encountered new places and ideas and things. He told her about the little things that frustrated him every day, or about the births that presented the greatest challenges, or about being invited to a society wedding.

As she told him about the last leg of her journey—a train from Marseilles, a boat to Dover, and another train—Sophia drank in the sight of him. This man, her husband, who had empowered her entire life for more years than she dared to count. She considered him even more handsome than when they had met at Robin Abbey: where her hair was a dull, ratty gray, his shone like spun silver. His eyebrows were as yet untouched. He had always been handsome, but at this age, he commanded attention. When he walked into a room, heads didn't turn because of her anymore. It was John everyone admired. And Sophia rather liked it that way.

"Now tell me what has happened since your last letter," she said as she finished her stories. She nestled a little closer, so that his hand dipped lower from her waist down to her hip.

"Three births, and not much else. Except I did manage to find the time to get you a present."

He presented her with a jar. Its glass was green and opaque; Sophia had to unscrew its lid to discover it was filled with little scraps of paper.

"To commemorate our thirty years together," John explained as he watched her open it. "Some of my favorite memories."

She pulled out a few of the scraps:

Skating on the River Kennet

Kissing in the bell tower

That picnic at Northfield Hall

Sophia narrowed her eyes at this last one. "This is one of your favorite memories with me? The time Benjamin made me so angry I hit him?"

John grinned. "I refer to what came after that. When I pulled you away and we went for that walk and..."

Sophia remembered now: she had shown him a particular spot in the woods where they could spread out on their cloaks and have a little romp without anyone being the wiser. "Ah yes, that was a particularly spectacular trick you did with your tongue there."

He raised one of his fantastic brows. "I refer to the talk we had. You told me stories from your childhood I'd never heard before. How close I felt to you that afternoon."

That, too, Sophia remembered. They had walked hand in hand through the fields. She had let herself fall backwards in time, leaning into that sunny feeling of a childhood protected from fear and cushioned in love. And she remembered how John had clung to every word. Asked for more, whenever she neared the end of a story. Kissed her wrist when she remembered twisting it falling from a tree and unpinned her braid when she reminisced how wonderful it had been to ride her first mare with her hair let loose.

She pulled out another batch of papers:

Eating pasta al fresco in Rome

Opening night of William Tell

Every time you come home.

"I know what you are about. You are trying to make me cry." Sophia batted away the tears stinging her eyes. "It won't work. I am far too unfeeling for such tricks."

"Then let me try another tactic." Reaching into the jar, John reviewed a few of the papers. He pressed two into her palms.

Making you cry out in ecstasy under the summer stars

When you rode me to exhaustion on the carriage ride to Edinburgh

"You think these will make me weep?"

He smirked. "I was hoping for a different reaction. You see, Sophia, I can't decide: which of those was the better fuck?"

Sophia remembered them both: the first from early on in their marriage, when they were still full of optimism and plans and doubt. The second had been earlier that very year, when John was hired to deliver a guest lecture on his methods for keeping mothers calm during labor.

Both remarkable experiences. Impossible to compare, given their different circumstances. "The only fair way to judge is to try them both again, one after the other."

"My thought exactly."

They had eaten enough food. They had been civilized long enough. Sophia straddled John right there on the bench. "Let's begin with the carriage ride."

AUTHOR'S NOTE

THANKS SO MUCH FOR reading *The Governess Without Guilt*! Each novel I write demands its own unique process. In the case of Sophia and John, it was almost always enjoyable as I drifted deeper and deeper into each of their psyches, so I hope you were equally enchanted as a reader.

This novel is supported by a fair amount of historical research on a variety of topics. I share deep dives into my research every month with my newsletter subscribers. If you're interested in learning more about accoucheurs, governesses, Cistercian nuns, counterfeiting, or even the Corn Laws, be sure to subscribe to unlock my research archive!

That said, I can point you to a selected bibliography, including:

A Governess in the Age of Jane Austen: The Journals and letters of Agnes Porter edited by Joanna Martin

In the Family Way: Childbearing in the British Aristocracy, 1760-1860 by Judith Schneid Lewis

The Making of Man-midwifery: Childbirth in England, 1660-1770 by Adrian Wilson

"They Are Exactly as Banknotes Are": Perceptions and Technologies of Bank Note Forgery During the Bank Restriction Period, 1797-1821 by Jack Mockford.

A big thank you to everyone who helped me create this novel, including but not limited to: Abigail Strom at Victory Editing, Georgina Kamsika, Sara Israel at Thimble Editorial, Julia Gerbach, Asya Blue, Allison Manley of Novel Soap Co for being so swell, my sister Sarah, and my amazing husband Michael. His sneezes–and love–continue to inspire the Prestons.

BOOK CLUB QUESTIONS FROM ROAMING ROMANCE BOUTIQUE BOOKSHOP

GATHER YOUR FRIENDS FOR a rousing book club discussion of *The Governess Without Guilt*! I partnered with Roaming Romance Boutique Bookshop, a pop-up romance bookstore based in Long Island, NY, to offer some questions to get you started.

1. **Sophia considers herself a selfish person. Do you think she was selfish? Can she be selfish and still be a good partner to John?**

2. **John and Sophia look to other characters for examples of love, including Sophia's parents, Ellen and Max,**

Lord and Lady Widlake, and Amma and Captain Attree. Which relationships looked most like healthy love to you?

3. Do you think a formal marriage is necessary for a happily-ever-after? What do you think about Amma's choice not to marry Captain Attree?

4. John is offended that Sophia can't list everything she loves about him. How do you think people can prove their love to each other?

5. Sophia refuses to take the offer of clemency in exchange for a confession. Do you think she was right to insist on her innocence, even though she couldn't prove it?

Want me to join your book club discussion? Email me at katherine@katherinegrantromance.com to find out my availability!

Excerpt from The Charmer Without a Cause

Everyone knows a happy marriage begins with a lot of money and one good lie...

London 1817

In the sludgy spring of 1817, ten thousand pounds changed Benjamin Preston's life.

He knew, of course, from the moment he learned about his uncle's bequest that with ten thousand pounds, he would be a different man. A freer man, one who was no longer reliant upon his father and Northfield Hall for money. A more powerful man, one who could take those ten thousand pounds and wield them like a sword against the onslaught of injustices in the world.

He hadn't reckoned that his experience of a musicale in the middle of March would be any different. At the age of twenty-five, he had been attending musicales for seven London seasons already. Sometimes, he attended alone; others, he accompanied one of his sisters or Papa, as he did now.

Never before had the entire room hushed at his entrance.

Never had he walked through a crush and heard whispers from behind ladies' fans that were about him.

What a difference ten thousand pounds made.

He and Papa had barely removed their cloaks before their hostess, the famous actress Mrs. Atwood, rushed over to greet them. "How glad I am you could join my little soiree. Lady Howson was just wondering if she would have the opportunity to be introduced to you this evening."

She whisked them across the room to where a matron in swaths of silk waited with two debutantes, and before Benjamin could even realize what was happening, he was introduced to both young ladies and begged to give his opinion on the music they anticipated that evening.

It was not that no hostess had made an introduction for him before. But Benjamin wasn't sure it had ever been done so eagerly, and certainly not to a marchioness such as Lady Howson, whose husband often publicly called Papa a nuisance.

Ten thousand pounds, apparently, was enough to smooth over political differences.

"I must offer you my deepest condolences on the death of your uncle," the young Miss Kirby said, pressing close enough that the peacock feather in her hair bobbed against his forehead. "I hope you are not too overcome with grief."

Benjamin didn't quite know how to respond. *I am not* would be the truth, but it would not be fair. He could not be overcome with grief. It was only ten years ago, when Benjamin's mother died, that he had even met his uncle, the earl. The countess was Mama's sister, estranged until Mama was so ill from her wasting disease that it was time for final farewells. The earl and Aunt Charlotte had arrived at Northfield Hall in outfits of imported silk and rings encrusted with Indian jewels, a chest of tea tucked in their carriage to keep them comfortable during their stay.

They were kind people, but not principled. Not the way Benjamin and his family were. They did not mind spending more money than a man's yearly wages on a piece of art or keeping shares of the East India Company. Still, after Mama died, they let the Prestons stay at their townhouse when necessary. Aunt Charlotte hosted parties to introduce them to likeminded people in London. She told stories of Mama as a girl and always had a coin purse with her to hand money to urchins on the street.

And now the earl had bequeathed Benjamin ten thousand pounds. Without a single string attached.

He replied to Miss Kirby with a different version of the truth: "I wish I'd had more time with him."

Her companion, Lady Philippa, huddled in. "Do tell us if there is anything we can do to comfort you."

"Now, now," their chaperone admonished, but with such a twinkle in her eye that Benjamin half expected her to rush them off for a private romp in the garden. "Do not overwhelm Mr. Preston with your womanly care, young ladies."

Benjamin wasn't about to complain. Miss Kirby seemed lovely, compassion written across her every expression. Lady Philippa, too, was beautiful, if a little young. Benjamin didn't feel the familiar, exciting flutter of new love for either of them, but still. If these young ladies wanted to cozy up to him—even if all they saw were his ten thousand pounds, and not him—Benjamin didn't mind at all.

Beside him, Papa cleared his throat. "It is lovely to make your acquaintances, but you must excuse us. I promised the Duke of Berkwell we would pay him our regards, and I see him across the room."

As they moved through the crowd, Papa warned, "Don't get carried away by all the excitement. It worked for your mother and me, but it is better to know your spouse well before marrying them than to end up committed to a woman who can't accept the way we live."

As if he needed the warning. Benjamin had no intention of marrying for any reason other than love, and his father damn well knew it. "No one even whispered the word marriage. We were only getting acquainted."

"Caution is your best friend, even when only getting acquainted. Your heart is very large, after all."

Before Benjamin could defend himself, they reached Robert, the Duke of Berkwell. A man only ten years Benjamin's senior, he was both an ally to Papa in Parliament and a friend to Benjamin when in town. He was also wealthy and unmarried; as usual, a dozen women hovered nearby, waiting for his notice.

Benjamin fancied that, for the first time, a few of those women perked up at his arrival, too.

"Ah, my favorite radicals," Robert greeted them. "Good to see you back in the thick of it."

"If you can call a Mayfair musicale 'the thick of it.'" Papa shook the duke's hand.

Robert grinned at Benjamin. "Spent all that money yet, Preston?"

"I still have a few shillings left."

In reality, Benjamin had it in an account at the Bank of England, and he woke up nightly in sweats of dread, afraid of what to do with it. The Prestons were a titled family, but they were not wealthy, particularly not since Papa had divested from colonial and slave imports thirty years ago. Everything they consumed came from their country seat, Northfield Hall, and any profit they earned from their surplus was split among the family, the household, and the laborers.

Benjamin had never imagined possessing ten thousand pounds of his own. Ten thousand pounds was enough to break off into his own household. It was enough to buy private carriages and a whole stable of horses and still have remaining funds. It could pay for a run to win a seat in the House of Commons. It could feed ten thousand children for half a year. It could fund a hundred volunteers to round up signatures for a petition to set a minimum wage for weavers, or for a lecture campaign to gain energy around abolishing slavery, or to establish schools in London for orphans and urchins.

In short, it was more money than Benjamin knew what to do with.

"You'll be getting an invitation from me in the next few days for an afternoon review of my investments" Robert said. "I thought you might be interested in sharing some of that money with one or two of the causes closest to my heart."

"Ah. Thank you."

A footman paused, offering up a tray of drinks. Benjamin followed Robert's lead, accepting a cut-crystal glass of ratafia.

Papa declined anything. Even though he didn't comment, Benjamin could hear the critique: *There is rum in that punch, and you know how rum is manufactured, don't you?*

Benjamin believed in avoiding slave imports as much as the next Preston, but if the punch had already been made and the alternative required some poor maid to go in search of a glass of milk especially for him, then he considered ratafia a perfectly fine choice.

"You'll be particularly interested in the plight of the chimney sweeps," Robert continued. "Have you ever considered how a chimney is cleaned?"

Benjamin had, in fact, and he knew all about the chimney sweeps. He opened his mouth to reply when his attention was stolen: there, in the far corner, the most arresting woman he had ever seen. So tall that her hair, styled high atop her head, nearly brushed the door lintel. Her dress offered the impression of a long torso and even longer legs. She waited on the threshold between the parlor and the corridor, even as two lords passed through. When he first noticed her, she was looking far off in the distance, at something Benjamin felt sure didn't exist in reality. As he watched, she blinked, turned her chin, and disappeared into the corridor.

Benjamin couldn't say what it was about her exactly that caught his attention. The confidence with which she carried her height. The impression that even among a crowd, she had carved herself a private moment. Whatever it was, Benjamin knew, even in that instant, that he needed to meet her.

Mrs. Atwood rang a chime to collect the crowd's attention, then invited everyone to take their seats for the performance. Benjamin followed Papa and Robert, but not before looking again for the woman. His eyes roamed the crowd, searching for her golden head rising above the rest. There: moving towards the seats on the far side of the room, neck bent in a slope as she conversed with a man who barely rose to her shoulder. Benjamin watched long enough that her gaze rose and collided with his.

He looked away first, but not before he recorded the shape of her face in his memory: eyes set close together; a small, solemn nose; lips the color of pink summer roses.

The music began. They were treated to a chamber ensemble of violins, viola, and cello playing a selection of Bach, followed by a German flautist, and finally a furious solo by the first violinist. Benjamin tried to attach his attention to the instruments, or at least to the thick brown eyebrows of the flautist, who swept deep glares across the audience at the start of every phrase.

Yet his mind wandered back six rows and over seven seats to the woman he had never met. The vision of her was already burned into his memory. He hadn't spotted a mother or sister or friends, but a young woman like her wouldn't come to a musicale alone. He wondered who she sat with, and whether they were her relations or friends or—God forbid—her husband.

Benjamin turned his head, just an inch, to see if he could glimpse her over his shoulder.

She was beyond his field of vision. He saw instead the elderly Lady Leighster, a few rows behind, pointing her fan at him as she murmured something to her neighbor. And a whisper from someone else carried over the decrescendo of the flute: "He's still a Preston. Ten thousand pounds doesn't change one's blood overnight."

Benjamin straightened, joining in the applause for the flautist. Papa and Robert both leaned in to murmur advice in his ears:

"I wish *I* were a Preston," said the duke.

"The only opinion that matters is your own," said Papa.

Hearing them together, it came into Benjamin's head as something like, "The only opinion that matters is a Preston's."

The violinist began his solo before Benjamin could deliver a rebuke. He didn't care about gossips; he had walked into the musicale expecting that, as always, people would spurn him because he was a Preston. He had known for years now what he hunted for: a woman who could love both him *and* what his family stood for. A partner who would cherish him as much as she shouldered his burdens with him. A soulmate who cared for the parts of him no one else could know.

Whoever that was would not care about the direction of Lady Leighster's fan or the content of the whispers about him.

He wished his father could understand that, instead of always assuming Benjamin would fall in love at the drop of an elegant hat. He yearned for Robert to know it, too, to stop acting like he was some fragile lamb who needed protection from circling wolves. Giving his heart easily did not make him weak. Being vulnerable did not mean he could not shield himself from blows.

If he were ever going to marry, he must first fall in love. Perhaps this time, he would fall in love with a woman who would marry him.

The music ended, to another burst of applause. Benjamin followed the cues of the crowd: standing, turning to each other to comment on the music, waiting for the ladies before filing out of his row. The whole time, he cautioned himself not to look towards the back. He didn't want to signal his interest too early, not when all eyes in the room seemed to be tracking his movements. He wanted to learn her name before she saw him through the veil of ten thousand pounds.

But when finally he filed into the parlor where refreshments awaited the crowd, he couldn't spot the woman anywhere. Her golden hair didn't extend above the heads of any men; her slender arms didn't fold against any chairs; her rosebud lips didn't purse against any punch cups.

She might be in the courtyard for a breath of fresh air. She might be in the retiring room, seeing to a personal need. She might even have left.

Papa touched his arm. "Time for our farewells. Oliver will be waiting at the coaching inn."

Oliver Chow, just arriving from Northfield Hall for his first trip to London. Oliver, who was practically his brother.

Oliver, Benjamin repeated to himself, tearing his attention away from the crowd. Oliver deserved his focus more than some nameless woman who might or might not care that Benjamin Preston existed.

And yet he looked behind him once more, before taking leave of Mrs. Atwood. And he knew himself well enough to predict he would be looking still, in every theater, in every assembly hall, in every alleyway, until he found once more the woman he didn't know.

Keep reading The Charmer Without a Cause from your favorite bookstore or library!

ABOUT THE AUTHOR

K ATHERINE GRANT WRITES AWARD-WINNING Regency Romance novels for the modern reader. Her writing has been recognized by Foreword INDIES Book of the Year Awards, the Next Generation Indie Book Awards, the National Indie Excellence Awards, the Romance Slam Jam Emma Awards, and the Shelf Unbound Indie Book Awards. If you love ballgowns, secret kisses, and social commentary, a book hangover is coming your way.

Her ideal day includes a cup of tea, a good book, and a board game with her husband. Find out more at www.katherinegrantromance.com

Connect with Katherine on your favorite social media platforms:

instagram.com/katherine_grant_romance/

tiktok.com/@katherinegrantromance

facebook.com/groups/katherinegrant

bookbub.com/authors/katherine-grant

goodreads.com/author/show/19872840.Katherine_Grant